THE FUNERAL LADIES OF ELLERIE COUNTY

Also by Claire Swinarski

What Happened to Rachel Riley
The Kate In Between
What Happens Next

THE FUNERAL LADIES OF ELLERIE COUNTY

A Novel

CLAIRE SWINARSKI

AVON

An Imprint of HarperCollinsPublishers

THE FUNERAL LADIES OF ELLERIE COUNTY. Copyright © 2024 by Claire Swinarski. All rights reserved. Printed in the United States of America. No part of this book may be used or reproduced in any manner whatsoever without written permission except in the case of brief quotations embodied in critical articles and reviews. For information, address HarperCollins Publishers, 195 Broadway, New York, NY 10007.

HarperCollins books may be purchased for educational, business, or sales promotional use. For information, please email the Special Markets Department at SPsales@harpercollins.com.

FIRST EDITION

Designed by Diahann Sturge

Pie illustration © Nata_Alhontess/Shutterstock

Library of Congress Cataloging-in-Publication Data has been applied for.

ISBN 978-0-06-331988-2 (paperback)
ISBN 978-0-06-331987-5 (hardcover library edition)

24 25 26 27 28 LBC 5 4 3 2 1

In memory of my grandmother Louise Uselman
and her grandmother Mary Kraemer
and her grandmother Margarethe Wutz
and on, and on, and on

Deep roots are not reached by the frost.

—J. R. R. TOLKIEN

One

$\mathcal{E}$sther Larson knew the only good way to make a piecrust was with your own two hands.

Sure, the recipe books may have said to use forks. A knife, perhaps. One of those pastry cutters Katharine Rose had, or even a food processor, which Esther's eldest granddaughter, Olivia, had insisted on registering for at her wedding two years back.

"Grandma, that just doesn't seem . . . hygienic," she had pointed out last week, watching Esther make this exact same piecrust. The same cups of flour, the same sprinkles of water, the same pinches of salt, the same scoop of lard, sifted through with her own fingers.

"I washed my hands," Esther responded confidently.

"But if people knew that was how you make it . . ."

"Olivia, this is how everyone who makes a quality piecrust makes their piecrust. I've been making this same crust for years. We didn't have food processors then."

"Well, you also didn't have statins then," Olivia's mother, Mary Frances, had butted in.

Heart attack medicine! It was a low blow. Her daughter always felt the need to bring up Esther's age. As if Esther's impending death was on her mind constantly, as if she walked into her house and fidgeted about, wondering which granddaughter was going to get the porcelain rabbit on the mantel and the wall clock from 1900 and her ancient old cookbooks, weathered and stained. No, she shouldn't think like that—Fran was a good kid. Esther was lucky; her daughter had turned out mostly okay.

But still. The death thing. The checking in, the reminding her to spend less time on her feet—it was exhausting, trying to always reassure her daughter that people like her were too determined to die. And she didn't need the reminder. She saw it every single time she looked in the mirror, every time she climbed up the stairs from the church basement.

She especially felt it today, as she leaned into the kitchen counter. These warm summer days could wear her out. They reminded her of all the things she used to be able to do that she couldn't anymore, like ski across the lake and dive off her dock. But no, she thought, digging back into her crust. She shouldn't think like that. She should be grateful for her years, however many of them she had left.

"Esther!"

She broke out of her reverie and turned to see Katharine Rose, shoving open her heavy front door and hobbling into the foyer. Her varicose veins must have been acting up. Katharine Rose had lived next door for the past fifty years, just across the patch of knee-high grass and wildflowers that separated the two homes.

Esther and Felix had bought their house in Ellerie County the year after he returned from Vietnam and they got married. It had been a steal—a four-bedroom house overlooking Musky Lake, with rickety stairs leading down to the dock and fresh pine beams. All it needed was a new roof, and Felix had four brothers to help with that. Katharine Rose had barged right in with a platter of cookies to welcome them. On the other side was Patricia, or, as she introduced herself, "Mrs. Thomas Murphy." Not even a name of her own, and she had had those long stick-on fingernails, too. She was a Lutheran, not that there was anything wrong with that. Esther was very open-minded. But still, they didn't spend much time with her.

Back then, Esther and Katharine Rose had been new wives together, and they'd spent the past fifty years helping each other
through pregnancies and always-working husbands, sharing recipes
and beers and tips for how to keep the dock spiders away. Esther's
daughter and Katharine Rose's three boys had spent ages out on
the lake together, splashing around and pushing each other off the
piers. When Ed had left Katharine Rose for the tourist he met working as a fishing guide, Esther had cooked her dinner for a month,
and Felix mowed her lawn every week till the day he died.

"Hey there," said Esther.

Katharine Rose plopped down at her kitchen table. "Is that pie
for today?"

Whenever someone in Ellerie County died, their funeral was
held at St. Anne's if they were Catholic or Trinity Church if they
weren't. Esther and Katharine Rose were the longest-standing members of the funeral committee at St. Anne's. Every week, they provided luncheons for the bereaved in the church basement. Photos
were passed, stories were told, and casseroles were consumed. The
funeral ladies showed up with platters of peanut butter bars and
steaming bowls of shredded beef, knowing they couldn't fix broken
hearts but might as well feed them. The long, cafeteria-style tables
would fill with cousins and neighbors, all squirting ketchup into
buns and talking about old times. A funeral was basically a family
reunion, when you really thought about it, and family tensions are
always soothed with a decent meal. It was the funeral ladies' job
to make sure the mourners had enough to eat. The last thing you
needed to worry about after a funeral was where the nearest drive-
through was.

Esther always did a couple of sides, but she was typically in
charge of dessert, too. She preferred pie, which was consistently a
hit. Cookies tended to be left untouched. Who knew why? But a
crumbly pie, made with Door County cherries, was always gone by
the time the last mourner was starting their car. There was never

any left to scoop into Tupperware and send home with the widow or daughter-in-law.

"Sure is," she said.

"Well, that's why I came by. Do you know who today's funeral is *for*?" Katharine Rose asked.

"No," Esther replied. She usually didn't. It didn't matter, really; all families needed the same type of food when someone died. Heavy food—food that stuck to your gut and filled you up. Occasionally they'd get a request for a vegetarian meal, or something gluten-free, which she admittedly didn't excel at. Gluten-free flour just wasn't the same.

"Annabelle Welsh," Katharine Rose said, as if Esther should know exactly who that was. Esther just stared at her blankly, and Katharine Rose whacked the table. "Annabelle Welsh! Ivan Welsh's wife?"

Ivan Welsh. She racked her brain. Damn it, she hated getting older. *Hated* it, and was embarrassed by her hatred of it, too. You weren't allowed to forget anything when you were eighty-two. Olivia's husband, Kurt, never remembered to put out their garbage can on Thursdays, was always having to drive over to the dump on Friday morning with a pile of recycling in his truck bed, but nobody accused *him* of dementia. Esther could still recite her mother's recipe for pork roast at gunpoint. She could rattle off any number of novenas at the drop of a hat. But some of the names and faces were starting to quietly slip away. It felt like she was constantly groping around in a dark spice drawer, looking for the oregano.

"Ivan Welsh, from *Ivan Eats*?" Katharine Rose insisted. "On the Food Network!"

"Oh," Esther said, relieved. It wasn't an old neighbor. Esther didn't watch the Food Network. She didn't have cable anymore, since Fran had helped get her set up with YouTube TV. What did she want to watch a bunch of people on TV cook for, anyway? What these people called a profession, Esther just called something she did three times a day. "Here, chop an onion, will you? I've still got to make coleslaw later today." She handed Katharine Rose the vegetable and a cutting board.

"Apparently, she was from here," said Katharine Rose, reaching into the silverware drawer for a paring knife.

"What was her maiden name?" Esther asked.

"Robertson. Was she—wait, would her mother have been Agatha?"

"Alice," Esther said, a latchkey in her brain turning with a *click*. Alice Robertson, and Bill. They'd lived on the other side of the lake. They weren't real social people, but they came around to church most weeks. Alice had worn a chapel veil, which was an odd sight in Ellerie, but to each their own. They'd had enough of the Wisconsin winters about ten years back and moved down to Florida. If Esther thought real hard, she remembered their daughter: Annabelle, who would float across the lake in an inner tube on most warm days. She'd been in Fran's grade at school, but they'd never been close. Annabelle Robertson, dead. She'd have to call Fran.

"Well, that's a shame," Esther said. Funerals for younger people were always heavier. When the elderly died—well, it was sad, to be sure. But it was the way of things. It was how the world was designed, really, that you would have children and a career and grow up and die, heading off to heaven with all those years tucked under your arm. When it was a middle-aged person, or worse, a child, the luncheon was softer, more muted. There was much less food consumed. Less chatter, too. More just sitting in grief and the knowledge that this wasn't the way things were supposed to go. The quietest luncheon Esther had ever cooked for was when four-year-old Luke Fischer had drowned in the lake. That was probably the worst funeral of her life, besides her own husband's five years ago. But Felix had been seventy-eight years old—not ancient, by any means, but a whole life lived, with a beautiful daughter, two loving grandchildren, and a long career at the insurance company. And the lung cancer had been quick.

At her age, Esther had attended plenty of funerals. But she preferred to be on this side of the kitchen. She liked having something to do when people were grieving. There was no amount of words that would make a daughter feel better when she'd never see her mother again. But she needed to eat. A countertop needed to be wiped. A drink needed to be refilled.

"A car accident, I think," Katharine Rose said, even though Esther hadn't asked.

"Why would the funeral be here? Alice and Bill moved ages ago," Esther said.

"Who knows?"

Esther didn't need to ask where Katharine Rose had gotten all this information. She got it the same place she always did: the church hall. Probably from Barbara Whittig. That woman's nose for news could have given Dan Rather a run for his money.

"Anyway," Katharine Rose said, sliding the cutting board full of chopped onion back to Esther, "I should get back to check on the chicken."

"Oh, are you doing shredded in the Crock-Pot?"

"No, I'm on casserole duty. I have a few different ones planned."

Esther nodded, giving Katharine Rose a wave.

Ivan Eats, she'd said. When the door shut, Esther picked up her phone and headed to Google. People always acted as if women her age didn't know how to use the internet, but she'd taken a class at the library a few years ago, and besides, her granddaughter Iris was always willing to help her.

She clicked on the show's Wikipedia page. *Ivan Eats* had been airing on television for nine years. *Ivan Welsh is an American celebrity chef, author, and reality television personality.* There it was, under personal life—Annabelle was his second wife, and he had two children, Cooper and Cricket. What kinds of names were those?

So Annabelle Welsh had done pretty well for herself. A Hollywood husband! That was something. Esther still didn't understand why on earth the funeral would be at St. Anne's. But she supposed that wasn't her business to know. It was her business to cook the food that people could eat while they cried and told stories, and that was exactly what she was going to do.

ESTHER WAS THE first to get to St. Anne's, like always. She flicked the lights on, and with a low hum, the room lit up. It wasn't a spectacular room, but the high school confirmation candidates had given it a fresh coat of paint last year and that had brightened things up a bit. She pulled out the display easels that would soon host poster boards of photos of Annabelle Welsh and went to go preheat the oven and pull out the serving platters.

"Hello, Esther," a voice called down the stairs.

"Hi, Father," she called back. Father Sam was young, one of the Schumakers from over in Moose Junction. Some of the others at church didn't even refer to him as Father—he was simply Sam, even though he'd been ordained two years now. But she was raised to respect priests no matter their age. Although she supposed that unending loyalty was probably what had gotten the Church in the mess it had been in for the past few decades.

Esther had been going to St. Anne's for fifty years. She'd seen plenty of priests come and go. She knew every corner and broken cabinet of the place, as if it were her own house.

Her house—she winced just thinking about it. She *adored* her house. She'd cared for it meticulously, cleaning every inch of it until it shined, always making sure to keep the garden weeded and the porch rail stained. Her house was one of the most beautiful homes in Ellerie, and it wasn't prideful to say that—it was just the truth. But it'd been hard, since Felix died, to keep up with the property taxes. She was quite a few months behind in the payments. The bank had been sending her letters in the mail, and she'd just let them sit in her mailbox, afraid to open them. Esther wasn't some feeble, elderly charity case. She was still sharp as a tack, thank you very much. But those banks tried to make things confusing on purpose. She wasn't even sure quite how much she owed. Besides, she was expecting a payment any day now from her friend Hazel, whom she'd lent some money a few months back. It was quite a bit of money. She'd carry the check over to the bank herself, and maybe bring some cinnamon rolls to soothe any tensions. Bea's grandson was a teller there.

Besides, Esther wasn't one to sit about just worrying and waiting. She kept herself busy, what with the Legion of Mary and the funeral committee and keeping up the house and helping Katharine Rose after her hip surgery. She'd joined the funeral committee back when she was a young mother and had found herself desperate for adult conversation. Katharine Rose had invited her after tasting her devil's food cake. The key was making the water as hot as possible—scorching, preferably.

Back then, the group had been bursting at the seams, women arguing over who got to bring the brown sugar pie and who was stuck with the ham loaf. Now the funeral committee at St. Anne's was only Esther, Katharine Rose, and a handful of other women. All of them grandmothers, all of them complaining about hips and joints and arthritis. All of them standing in the kitchen, saying the Memorare and chopping salt pork for Irish stew.

When Esther was gone, when all these women had had funerals of their own, who would cook these meals? Who would load up the plates of the sons and daughters and brothers and sisters left behind? Who would plug in the Crock-Pots and set out the napkins? People needed a place to eat, after a funeral. They had a hole that needed filling, and it was best filled with piecrust made by the hands of a woman who'd been making it the exact same way for fifty years.

Two

Cooper Welsh considered himself a pretty positive person, but he hated three things: fireworks, Jeep Cherokees, and his father.

He hadn't known he hated fireworks until Memorial Day. He'd gone with a couple of buddies to watch the spread over Lake Michigan, with a cooler of beer and some chips from the gas station. They were meeting up with some girl Brian had been matched with on Tinder and her friends. But when the fireworks started going off—

Bang.

Pop.

Crack.

—he'd started shivering, even though it was 87 degrees. The heat that night had been thick and unforgiving; every inhale felt like sucking through a straw. But he shivered so hard, he'd dropped his beer.

"Party foul!" Brian had crowed, his arm slung around Tinder Girl, who had blue hair and looked bored. But Cooper couldn't hear him. All he could hear were the explosions.

"Dude, are you okay?" One of Tinder Girl's friends had reached over and touched his elbow.

"Too many Busch Lattes," Brian said.

"Cheap beer doesn't make you shake, asshole," the friend snapped. "He's really freaking out. Are you—"

There's blood and the taste of metal and a girl with her hand out—

Help—

Help me—

He leaned forward and vomited all over his shoes, and some of it splattered on the Birkenstocks of Tinder Girl.

Brian never got another text from her, and Cooper vowed never to go see fireworks again. This summer, he'd stayed home during the Fourth of July festivities. He'd put in his AirPods and listened to music as loud as humanly possible.

The second thing he hated? Jeep Cherokees. It was a malfunction in her Jeep Cherokee that had left Tiana Lopez suddenly slamming on her brakes as her vehicle's transmission stopped sending power to her front wheels and her car shut down in the middle of the highway. And when her car shut down in the middle of the highway, it was George Parker who had to dramatically swerve across several lanes so he wouldn't slam into her. And when George Parker dramatically swerved across several lanes, it was the Subaru belonging to Cooper's stepmother, Annabelle Welsh, that he T-boned, killing her instantly.

And that brought him to the third thing he hated: his father, Ivan Welsh, who was currently muttering under his breath as he tried to find the church.

"We're going to be late," Cricket said from the back seat of the Tesla.

Ivan glanced at her in the rearview mirror. "We're not going to be late." It was Cooper's car; a guilt gift from Ivan after the thing in North Harbor. Only Ivan would think buying someone a car was easier than calling to see how they were. He'd flown in from Los Angeles to the tiny Rhinelander airport, but he hated being in a car he wasn't driving, so Cooper had been kicked to the passenger seat.

"We were supposed to get there fifteen minutes early. I heard the priest guy say that yesterday," Cricket said.

"We're not going to be late," Ivan repeated.

Cooper stared out the window. It was impossible to know where you were in Ellerie County. For starters, all the roads looked the same—thin strips of rocky asphalt surrounded on either side by fat towering evergreens. As you drove, you could see splashes of lake between the tree branches, and occasionally a curve in the road would expose you to a pond named after a woodland creature. Instead of road signs, there were simply posts with wooden arrows pointing in different directions, with words like *Cubby Lodge* and *Tom's Fishing Hole* written on them. None of their phones got any service. Unless you knew the twists and turns of the road like the back of your hand, you'd wind up driving in circles around Musky Lake, looking for one particular cabin in a sea of cabins.

"Shit, what street was that?" Ivan said, squinting out his window.

"The church is on Main Street," Cricket said. "Two-two-one-seven Main Street."

Ivan turned the Tesla to follow a brown wooden arrow that read *Main Street* in small carved letters. "If this goddamn town would get some actual street signs . . ."

But they knew they were on Main Street when they found it. There wasn't much, but just past the library and Coontail Market was a small church. There was already a handful of cars parked in the lot out back.

Add a fourth thing Cooper hated: funerals. He was twenty-eight years old and this was only the third funeral he'd ever been to. It was also the one he'd hate the most.

"Your tie's kind of messed up," Cricket told him. He looked down. She was right—it was a few inches shorter than it should be.

"Thanks," he muttered. "Good to have a thirteen-year-old around for some fashion advice."

She rolled her eyes. His half sister was good at that. Cricket and Cooper had the same dark hair, the same love of fried cheese, and the same father. Cooper's mom lived out in Maui, teaching surfing lessons and posting Instagram poetry. Annabelle—well, she'd been everything a mom should be ever since Ivan had married her.

Annabelle didn't have a lot of family besides the three of them. Her parents had died just a few months apart about five years back. Cooper remembered their funerals, too; they'd flown down to Florida from Chicago and Annabelle had drunk an entire bottle of wine on the airplane. She didn't have any siblings. There was a solid number of people at the church, though—friends from her work at the ad agency, mostly. But some other people, too, who had her nose. They introduced themselves as Annabelle's aunt Lucy or her cousin Julia or her uncle Tucker, hugging an uncomfortable-looking Cricket and shaking Cooper's hand as if they weren't quite sure what to say to her almost-son.

But nobody looked more uncomfortable than Ivan. He kept glancing at his phone. Cooper wanted to throttle him. His god-damn *wife*. And sure, he traveled a ton. Didn't act much like a husband. About five years ago, he had gotten a girlfriend and stopped coming home altogether, and Annabelle had pretended she didn't know why, even though she clearly did. *Catholics don't get divorced,* she had told Cooper, and he had refrained from pointing out that he doubted the pope would approve of getting a girlfriend while you were still married, either. Annabelle and Cricket had moved to Chicago, where Annabelle had a cousin she was close with, and Cooper got a job as a paramedic in Milwaukee to bolster his eventual medical school résumé.

But you'd think Ivan could at least put down the phone. All week he'd been taking calls from his agent and publicist and producer, all giving condolences and muttering what a shame it was and half-heartedly inquiring about the service, and Cooper'd heard Ivan say over and over: *We appreciate it, but the funeral's all the way in bumfuck Wisconsin.* And look at him now, in his fancy suit. He'd shaved off his beard, too; he looked weird without it. The last time

Cooper had seen Ivan freshly shaved and in a suit had probably been at his wedding to Annabelle. Cooper had been thirteen years old and still looked like an awkward preteen, with ears too big for his head and acne sprinkled across his forehead. *People* had gotten the exclusive wedding photos, and he'd hated them. The one Annabelle had hung in her and Cricket's house wasn't one of those overly lit portraits; it was a simple one of her and Cooper and Ivan, their cheeks squished together. She'd left it hanging there, all these years, even after Ivan and that actress got their picture splashed across the news.

Annabelle. Annabelle! Shit, he was going to miss her, and he didn't want to cry at this thing because Cricket was there. If anyone got to cry, it was his sister. He wandered over to the easel holding up a poster board that read *In Loving Memory* in cutout letters. Who'd made it? He had no idea. But there were photos: Pictures of Annabelle as a teenager, wearing a bikini and laughing at something off camera. Her wedding photo with Ivan—whoever made it didn't really know her well, then, because she would've hated that it was there; she always complained about the dress Ivan's publicist had made her pick because it would look the best in *People*. Photos of Annabelle and Cricket, their arms thrown around each other on a beach and on a hotel bed and at Cricket's elementary school graduation. And there—one of Cooper, too. Annabelle was squeezing him and Cricket tight, and she looked so happy. It was from a thousand years ago. Well, ten. They were dropping Cooper off for his freshman year at Marquette, her alma mater; Cricket had started preschool that same year, back in California. Ivan couldn't make it. He'd been filming a special in Thailand.

There was a hand on his shoulder.

"Excuse me." Cooper turned and stood face-to-face with an elderly woman wearing an apron. "Are you the family?"

"Um." He cleared his throat. "Whose? Hers? Yeah, I'm her . . . I was her—she was my mom."

"I'm sorry," the woman said.

He nodded. "Thanks."

"We were just wondering if you'd be taking the food home afterwards or if you'd like someone to drop it off."

"Sorry?"

"The food," she said simply. "The leftovers. A crowd this size, and what we've got . . . you'll have plenty to take home afterward. You can either take it after the luncheon or someone can drop it off later today. Either is fine. But I'll grab your address if you'd prefer to have it delivered."

"Um—oh, gosh. I don't know." He couldn't even picture Ivan's face if someone handed him piles of Tupperware. Cooper and Cricket were planning on staying for a week; he'd taken a vacation from work and he thought Cricket could use some time to lie by the lake and read. Plus, Annabelle had a storage unit full of things they needed to go through. Then he and Cricket would be heading back to Chicago to pack Cricket's things, and she'd come to Milwaukee with him to share his two-bedroom apartment while he flipped pancakes at the diner downstairs for hungover Marquette and UWM students. Ivan, however, was leaving the very next morning.

"We really don't need food," he said, embarrassed. "I mean, any to take home."

"Everyone needs food," the woman said. "Especially someone whose mother has died. With all due respect. I know he's a big fancy chef, but you'll be thankful for something that can be microwaved at ten o'clock at night."

He looked around helplessly, hoping he could mentally signal Cricket to come save him. But she was in her own awkward conversation, getting her cheek pinched by someone with Annabelle's green eyes.

"I knew Annabelle," the woman said abruptly.

Cooper started a bit. "You did?" Well, of course she did. She looked about a billion years old, and this was Annabelle's hometown.

She nodded. "I did. Well, her parents . . . are Alice and Bill still down in Florida?"

Cooper shook his head. "They passed, actually. Alice had a heart attack and Bill had . . . some kind of bone cancer, I think."

She nodded. "Well. People our age . . . you know."

And what was he supposed to say to *that*? Where was Cricket when he needed her?

"Can I ask why the funeral was here, anyway? Far as I've gathered, most of the Robertsons are over in Waukegan now."

"She wanted it here," Cooper said simply. And that was the truth. Annabelle was always telling him and Cricket about Ellerie—the way you could hear the loons call in the middle of the night in the summer, and the way the lake was so frozen solid in the winter that trucks drove on it to go ice fishing. The way you could look up at the sky and see more stars than you could possibly count. The way you had to wear bright orange hats when going for a walk in the winter so a hunter wouldn't mistake you for a buck. The way it tasted like fried fish and marshmallows. The way it smelled like home.

"Bury me there," she'd always say dreamily, closing her eyes.

"Jesus, Mom. You're morbid," Cricket had said the last time, a couple of months earlier, as the three of them were eating tacos out of crinkly paper bags and watching some HGTV star help a couple find a house in the Northwoods. Cooper had come to visit them in Chicago and brought them dinner. Before he left, he'd helped Annabelle repaint the bathroom.

"Ellerie," she'd sighed. "My favorite place in the world."

But for all it was allegedly her favorite place, she hadn't gotten back there. They'd never even visited. The night after the accident, as they'd sat around her kitchen table, Ivan staring at his hands and Cooper staring at the ceiling, his father had tossed out the idea of having the funeral in Los Angeles.

"Mom hated it there," Cricket said. "She wanted to be buried in Ellerie."

"Cricket, we don't even know anyone there. And then her grave will be—"

"Ellerie," his sister said flatly. "She said to bury her in Ellerie."

Cooper snapped back to the present moment and the old lady in an apron staring at him curiously.

"I guess—I guess drop-off would be fine," he said.

"Where are you staying?"

"At a cabin we're renting. Calberg's Resort? We're cabin number thirteen, but we haven't even checked in yet."

"Hmm," she said. "Well, why don't I give you my phone number, just in case we need to coordinate something." She reached for a pen on the table next to her, but Ivan grabbed his elbow.

"Cooper. Someone for you to meet."

Cooper turned back to the lady in the apron, but another woman was pulling her back to the kitchen already. An older-looking man, someone about Ivan's age, stood next to Ivan looking way too cheerful for a funeral. He had dark hair and a tie that was a weird shade of purple.

"Cooper Welsh," the man said, clasping his hand on his shoulder. "The famous Cooper. Annabelle talked about you a lot. She was so proud . . . I had to meet you."

"Hi," Cooper said uncomfortably.

"Richard Gates. Your stepmom worked at my ad agency."

Richard Gates—also known as That Dick, according to Annabelle. The meanest thing she'd ever said about someone. She loved people, Annabelle, even the ones who were hard to love. Some people might have said it was one of her best qualities. Cooper considered it one of her worst.

"That was nice of you to come all this way," said Cooper.

"I've got a daughter over in Moose Junction. Anyhoo," Richard said, "Annabelle was always talking you up. Trying to find you a lady, maybe—ha! She'd talk about you to all the young interns. How she had a son who was a hero."

Damn it. Damn it, Annabelle! He didn't want to talk about this here, not with That Dick, not at her *funeral*. He smiled uncomfortably and saw the *Oh, shit* flicker across Ivan's eyes.

"That day . . . wow. Must have been something. You still a paramedic?"

"No," Cooper said. Richard stared at him, clearly waiting for him to offer up what he *was* doing. The answer was putting bacon on a griddle and adding extra cheddar to farmhouse scrambles, like a trailer-trash version of what his dad did, but he knew that wouldn't impress Mr. Big Shot, Mr. Owns-His-Own-Ad-Agency, Mr. Brings-Up-Things-Like-This-at-a-Funeral. He had half a mind to say he was a crack dealer.

Another elderly woman walked over to them and tapped Ivan on the shoulder. "Mr. Welsh? The service will be starting soon, if you'd like to make your way to the front pew."

"Well, I'll let you get seated," Richard said, smiling as if they were at a baseball game that was about to begin.

Cooper worked in a diner. But he'd still never seen so much food in one place.

There were four gigantic card tables filled with food. Shredded meats in Crock-Pots surrounded by pretzel buns and hamburger buns and Wonder Bread, every type of condiment imaginable lined up on the side. Huge Dutch ovens brimming with thick red pasta dishes, long silver spoons sticking out, waiting to be scooped. And potatoes—there was an entire table of just potatoes. Mashed, fried, french fried, baked. Potato casseroles, a big bowl of potato soup next to a stack of paper bowls, cheesy potatoes he remembered Annabelle making with frozen hash browns and shredded sharp cheddar. Even though Cricket was the youngest one there, there was an entire section of kid food, like homemade macaroni and cheese dotted with bread crumbs and a tray of dinosaur-shaped chicken nuggets. There was a make-your-own-sandwich station with lunch meats, and at least four trays piled high with brownies, cookies, and dessert bars. The bright plastic veggie trays were overflowing with raw cauliflower and halved cherry tomatoes, and there was enough fruit salad to feed every single person there three times over.

"Holy crap," said Cricket.

"Probably shouldn't say that in a church," Cooper muttered, glancing around.

"I was going to say 'holy shit,' but I stopped myself. Jesus and all."

He leaned over and flicked her temple before putting an arm around her and pulling her in tight. He loved his stupid sister. *Legal guardian*—those were big, thick, heavy words. But what else could he do? Let her live with Ivan? Have her spend eighth grade on airplanes or with some kind of nanny? She'd like Milwaukee.

The priest walked over. "My condolences," he said, holding out his hand. Cooper thought he looked a little younger than he was himself—twenty-five, twenty-six? How did someone their age become a *priest,* these days?

"Thanks, man," said Cooper, shaking his hand. "I mean . . . Father."

The priest chuckled. "It's cool. 'Man' works."

Cooper glanced over to see a couple of people whispering and looking at Ivan. Of course people would be looking at him—it was his wife's funeral. Estranged wife. Whatever. But this was a different kind of look. It was the *Ivan Welsh* look. The look people gave when they realized they were in the same room as someone who'd been on the cover of *Rolling Stone*.

Ivan had always been successful, ever since Cooper was born. His first restaurant, Papu, had been an upper-class establishment known for foie gras and smoked lake trout, and won California's Best New Restaurant of the Year before Cooper hit kindergarten. After his mom took off for the beach, tired of being the wife of someone who came home at 3 A.M. every night smelling like garlic, Ivan started spending his mornings typing on his laptop instead of sleeping in. His dad may have been a fancy chef, but Cooper had taught himself how to make Kraft macaroni and cheese at age seven so he'd have something to eat for breakfast. He still remembered the time he told the mailman he was home alone—he couldn't have been older than second grade—and the guy actually called the cops. Ivan would chain-smoke and write and chain-smoke and write and chain-smoke and write, and when *Confessions of a Cook* came out and hit the *New York Times* bestseller list, everything changed. Suddenly, there was a swarm of people in his house—agents and publicists and art directors. Then their house wasn't even their house anymore; he and Ivan moved into a massive brownstone farther away from Papu. And when he started his Food Network show and had episodes discussing the local cuisine of Florida and Maryland and Georgia, Cooper found himself constantly under the care of Daniela, a nanny/housekeeper Ivan's assistant had found who read him the Bible in Spanish and made sure he did his homework.

But when Ivan came home from filming an episode in Wisconsin, something was different. A girl—he'd met a girl, in Milwaukee, a girl who waitressed at a supper club.

Annabelle.

God, he was going to miss her. He really was. Annabelle had been so many things his own mom had never even tried to be. Annabelle had asked him how school was and told him to invite friends over and come to every stupid choir concert, where they all had to wear those matching white T-shirts. When he was a teenager and Annabelle had Cricket, she had never asked him to do annoying crap like changing a diaper or babysitting her. But he liked doing it anyway. Cricket had been so tiny and helpless, and Annabelle was always so happy, and there were a few good years there.

But *Ivan Eats* grew and grew, and another book came—*Dinner's at Eight: More Confessions of a Cook*—and Ivan was never home. Ever. Cooper went to college at Marquette, because it was Annabelle's alma mater and her photos of Milwaukee always looked so cool, and he was tired of the ocean and the palm trees. Then he was a paramedic, before it all went south, and he'd been bouncing around the coast of Lake Michigan ever since, doing odd jobs at diners that he mostly got by mentioning he was Ivan Welsh's son.

"Want me to damn them to hell?" the priest asked, nodding at a couple sneakily trying to take a photo of Ivan. Cooper startled, but the priest just laughed. "Dude, I'm joking. Relax."

He cracked a grin. "Too bad."

Too bad. Too bad, a lot of things. Too bad Cooper was stuck with such an asshole for a father. Too bad he was about to get handed a bunch of Tupperware containers full of fried potatoes. And too bad Tiana Lopez had driven a Jeep Cherokee.

Three

"*G*randma?" Iris stuck her head in the front door of Esther's house.

"In here," Esther called out. She was standing at her massive kitchen sink, scraping food off a plate.

"Sit down. I can do that." Iris kicked off her shoes.

"No, no. You sit. Get a water from the fridge first. I got that French kind you like."

Iris grabbed a LaCroix and a clean dish towel to dry with. "You have a funeral this morning?" There was something vaguely depressing about her grandmother spending every Saturday morning in a dark church basement, plugging in slow cookers and setting out ketchup bottles. Iris hadn't been to many funerals herself. But a couple of years ago, a friend from college's mom had died, and Iris had made the trip to Madison for the funeral. The entire event had been catered with fancy flatbreads and kale salads. She had thought of her grandmother, buying Lipton's onion soup mix in bulk at the Costco in Waukegan.

"Sure did," she said. "A young thing, too. Only in her fifties."

"That's too bad. What happened?"

"Car wreck."

"Someone from Ellerie?"

"No," said Esther, shaking her head. "Born here, but hadn't lived here in ages. Actually, you might find this interesting. It was the wife of one of those cooks on the Food Network."

"Really?" asked Iris, surprised. Not that she was an avid Food Network watcher. But still. That was about as famous as a person could get in Ellerie. "Who? The guy who hosts *Chopped*?"

"No. Ivan Welsh? Looks kind of like a thug."

"Grandma. What does that even mean?"

"These tattoos on his biceps, and he drives a motorcycle. I saw it on the show. I YouTubed it."

"You *YouTubed* it?"

"It wasn't on Netflix. It had Japanese subtitles."

Iris laughed. She wasn't quite of the generation that had grown up with a phone attached to her hand. Her mom was the kind that had practically locked her and her sister, Olivia, outside for hours. But by the time she was in high school, everyone she knew had a cell phone, and by the time she was in college, "social media manager" was a job title. She was constantly amazed at how quickly her grandma was able to pick things up. People thought the elderly didn't know how to use tech, but look at that—Esther could find bootleg Food Network episodes on YouTube.

Esther's phone rang, and Iris held it out, waiting for her to dry her hands on a tea towel with a faded Bible verse on it.

While her grandma talked on the phone, Iris looked out over Musky Lake. Her grandparents had always had the most beautiful home on the entire lake, most beautiful in the whole of Ellerie County, in Iris's opinion. The giant back window looked out over their rickety dock, where she and Olivia had spent hours as kids eating sour-cream-and-onion potato chips and getting grease marks on library books. There was Grandpa's old fishing boat, bobbing in the water. Next to it was the newer pontoon her mom had insisted they should buy, back when she and Olivia were teenagers. That thing never got driven, except when her parents were trying to show

off the house to friends with cocktail cruises. Iris and her sister preferred the speed of Grandpa's fishing boat. It could pull their giant
inner tube, Big Mabel, around the lake, and Grandpa would try to
take sharp turns and throw them off, which Iris's mom always said
gave her heart palpitations. Grandpa had always told her he had
been a medic in Vietnam, and he could handle a grandkid's broken
bone. But nobody ever broke anything; not even a toe.

Iris wondered if Esther even got down to the dock anymore. Her
dad had been complaining about having to put the dock in the water this year; he said it was too much work for an old man and that
it was time to teach Olivia's husband, Kurt, how to do it. There
were still plenty of ideas about which gender performed which duty
clinging stubbornly to the Northwoods. Women hunted and fished
just as much as men, but nobody had ever asked Olivia or Iris to
put the dock in, and they probably never would.

"Iris?" her grandma called. "Honey?"

She turned back to the kitchen. "What's up?"

"That was Irma, down at the Fox and Hounds lodge. She said
the family of the woman whose funeral was today showed up looking for a room, but they're sold out."

"The TV chef guy and his kids?"

"Yes. They were supposed to stay in one of the Calbergs' cabins."

"Oh, geez." Iris rolled her eyes. The Calbergs were notorious for
double-booking, losing registrations, and trying to convince you
that you were losing your mind. She had never really been sure she
believed in gaslighting until she thought about it as related to the
Calbergs, who would look at the email confirmation you had shoved
in their face and just shrug their shoulders, suggesting maybe your
computer had been hacked.

"She wanted to know if your place is ready," Esther said. "She
thought maybe they could be the first guests at Redstone."

"Redstone?" Iris asked, panicky. "*My* Redstone?"

"Where else?" Esther asked simply.

Redstone had been a passion project of Iris's. All the best resorts and cabins in the Northwoods filled up months in advance. If you wanted a July or August vacation right on the lake, you'd better have it booked by the previous Halloween. She'd loved the idea of opening an Airbnb. *The side hustle economy is the future,* her old classmates from UW–La Crosse had all assured her. Even with their degrees, they all sold True U makeup in Facebook groups or made fifty bucks here or there writing listicles on "What Your Favorite Type of Potato Says About You." A cabin in the woods seemed like a better bet. It's not like there was much else to do in Ellerie, unless you wanted to work at one of the shops on the main drag or drive into Waukegan every day. Everything in Ellerie revolved around the tourists, not the people who actually lived there.

So she'd worked almost every night during college, pulling shifts at the student library while everyone else took shots of blueberry Stoli at Howie's. Graphic design had seemed like a safe path. When she'd told the advisor that her freshman year, the woman had nodded encouragingly. Iris had always been aesthetically minded; she got her ability to put together good colors from her mother and her entrepreneurial spirit from her father. And someone always needed a logo. But instead of joining some large ad firm after college, she'd simply come back to Ellerie, thrown up a website, and worked a few connections from school for her first few clients. She'd been back in Ellerie for two years, living in a ramshackle house and doing freelance graphic design and whatever else the internet would pay her for, money that was now going toward payments on the small cabin she'd bought earlier that year.

Her mother and grandmother would never have said so, but she knew they were thrown off. Larsons worked fifty-hour weeks. They put their backs into it. Better to be anything than lazy. She still remembered watching her grandfather work into his mid-seventies, heading off to the office with a briefcase long after they'd mostly fallen out of fashion. Her grandmother had spent years and years greeting people at the Full Moon Lodge in town, until she couldn't stay on her feet that long and reservations all went online anyway. Grandpa had complained endlessly about Iris's generation—the way they dressed, the way they ate, but above all else, their fear of hard work. The way they all hunted for side gigs and moved back in with their parents. He could get a little we-walked-to-school-five-miles-both-ways about it. Her parents were the same way. Her father owned a financial services company and her mother had helped tourists design their summer homes for as long as Iris could remember. They always came home at six fifteen, ate a quick dinner, and pounded out more work on their laptops until late into the night.

Iris wasn't afraid of hard work. She'd worked her ass off to get Redstone. But if she could find a way to avoid being a seventy-two-year-old with a briefcase, she would.

Redstone wasn't ready, though. She'd had plans to repaint one of the bedrooms and switch out the countertops from quartz to a more stylish butcher block. The microwave hadn't been delivered. She'd had plans for a grand opening later in August—autumn in the Northwoods would make her a killing. October in Ellerie was like a postcard.

"I don't know, Grandma," said Iris. "That was nice of you to try and help them but it's not really . . . ready . . ."

Esther patted her on the hand. "It's beautiful. What's more to get ready? They're just happy to have beds to sleep in, I'm sure."

Iris looked back out over the lake. Esther was from an age where loving your neighbor meant loving your actual neighbor, not just adding an emoji to your Twitter name in times of crisis. She helped people just because they were standing in front of her. Iris tried to be that way, but it didn't come naturally to her. Maybe it would, in fifty-six more years.

"Fine," she sighed.

"That's my girl."

"Tell Irma to let them know I need an hour or two, though, okay?"

"She can send them to Northern Latte's for a coffee. They'll be fine," Esther promised.

On the way to Redstone, Iris called her mom, which she did approximately four times a day.

"And now I've got a freaking movie star staying in my unfinished Airbnb. He's probably going to take a photo of that ugly gray bedroom and put it on Instagram."

"His wife's dead, Iris," her mom said, sounding distracted. "I'm sure he has bigger problems."

"What are you doing?" Iris asked, kind of annoyed. It was unfair of her to expect her mother to just be sitting around, ready and waiting to hear about Iris's life problems at any moment. But that didn't stop her from expecting just that.

"Flipping these damn rocks," Fran said.

"The ones out front? God, Mom, who cares. They're *rocks*."

"Yes, and they're dirty, and they make the landscaping look trashy."

"Nobody is looking at your rocks."

"You're lucky," Fran retorted. "Your sister said I should call and make you come help me."

Iris rolled her eyes. Olivia was pregnant with her first and acted as if it made her incapable of lifting a dirty cup into the dishwasher. She was always insisting Iris go help Fran, or go help Esther, because Iris wasn't married or gestating and worked her own hours. Well, sue her for designing her life the way she wanted it. She loved her stupid sister, but Olivia could drive her nuts.

"Come on by for dinner after you get your guests settled," her mom said. "I've got some brats for the grill. I told Grandma to come. Olivia said she'll swing by if she feels up to it."

"Will do."

Iris pulled up to Redstone and got out, thanking God there was a Best Buy box propped against the door. That'd be the microwave, hopefully. She typed in the entrance code to the padlock and shoved the heavy front door open.

It was a beautiful house. Not as gorgeous as her grandma's, but nobody's was. She'd made a good decision, she thought. She'd make more with this Airbnb than Katie Beekwood from statistics class had made hawking eyeliner over Instagram Live, that was for sure.

She hurried to do all the things she'd planned on doing before her first guests arrived. A vase of flowers she'd picked up at Coontail's for the kitchen table. A case of sparkling water and a six-pack of Spotted Cow for the fridge. She'd wanted some Wisconsin cheese, too, but she didn't have time to go all the way into Washport for the good stuff. She opened the doors, letting the breeze float in off the lake to cool the place down. Fresh linens were put onto beds, towels were put into bathrooms. The downstairs living room needed a solid vacuuming; somehow a bunch of flies had found their way in and decided their time was up.

But now it looked just about perfect. She still had time. Maybe one more wipe-down of the counters, to make sure they sparkled. She took her phone and started playing an Olivia Rodrigo song on Spotify, cranking the volume up. She loved that song. A rag and some granite cleaner and some elbow grease—that counter would look perfect.

"Hello?" a voice called out.

Iris jumped about a foot in the air. "Hi. Oh my gosh." She hurried to turn down the music. She'd been dancing, hadn't she? Damn that Olivia Rodrigo! A teenager singing about heartbreak, what did Iris know about that? Her only boyfriend had been Jake Sweeney, who always tasted like the cheap cigarettes he smoked. That had lasted about two weeks of junior year, and *she'd* dumped *him*. Still, Olivia Rodrigo made her want to move. "I didn't . . . I didn't see you come in."

There were three *you*s: a teenage girl, a guy about Iris's age who was trying to hide a smile, and—oh, wow. There he was. She recognized him now. Ivan Welsh. He was shorter in person, and his hair looked grayer, too. And no beard like he always had on TV.

"Thank you so much for this," Ivan said, running a hand through his hair nervously. "I don't know what happened to the other cabin. My assistant probably fucked something up."

Iris just smiled. She'd be happy to throw the Calbergs under the bus like an old can of beer, but she could feel Esther reminding her to be nice.

"Here's the Wi-Fi password," she said, handing over an index card where she'd hastily scribbled it twenty minutes prior. "There's a sheet on the fridge with the padlock code, and some basic instructions for the Apple TV."

"We'll be out of your hair tomorrow afternoon," Ivan said.

"No problem at all," Iris assured him. "You guys have dinner plans? Or do you need a recommendation?" Then she felt like an idiot. Ivan Welsh: He could cook them up a gourmet meal himself. And if he wanted to go to the type of restaurant he was used to, she'd have to send them all the way to Waukegan. Not even—Milwaukee, probably. She couldn't exactly send them to Vernon's for a Reuben made with bottled Thousand Island dressing. A green salad that was just some iceberg lettuce and baby carrots Vernon had probably picked up at the Kwik Trip.

"Apparently, we have more food coming," Ivan said, glancing at the guy, who just rolled his eyes in response.

"What was I supposed to say? Besides, it was good food."

"Right," said Iris, realizing. "The funeral ladies will bring by the leftovers. That should keep you fed for the next twenty years or so." She wondered if Esther had any shame about feeding a world-renowned chef her sauerkraut casserole. But then she felt a surge of defensiveness for her grandmother: Esther could cook, and she did it well, and she'd done it for thousands of people. Iris loved that sauerkraut casserole, with its layers of sausage and shredded cabbage and noodles and canned cream of mushroom. It was the type of food you could inhale. The type of food that just made you happy. Screw the Food Network.

"You have my number if you need anything," Iris said. "Enjoy your stay."

"Thank you so much," said Ivan.

"And nice moves," the younger guy said as she was almost to the door. She winced. Okay. She had definitely been dancing.

Iris waved and headed back out to her Camry. She had just stepped onto the driveway, clicking unlock on her car keys, when Ivan called out to her.

"There is one thing."

"Sure."

"You think I could get the recipe for that pie?" he asked. "Your grandmother made it, right?"

Iris nodded.

"That crust . . . ," he said.

"I'll get it for you before you leave," she said. It wasn't until she was backing down the driveway that she realized how much she wished she could rattle off her grandmother's pie recipe by heart. And it wasn't until she was pulling into her parents' driveway that she'd realized a James Beard Award–winning chef had just asked for a recipe from an eighty-two-year-old woman in the Northwoods who spent her Saturdays making pies for funerals.

Four

*E*sther swung by St. Anne's that afternoon, waving to Father Sam in the parking lot. She wanted to say a Rosary for Hazel, and she always felt better saying it in front of the blessed sacrament. Mary was everywhere, sure, but why not hedge her bets? As nervous as she was about the pile of envelopes in her mailbox, she was just as nervous for Hazel. Esther was beginning to feel like something terrible had happened. She'd just seen an article about rising maternal mortality rates in the US, as if they were back in the frontier days. With her own uterus problems—well, it gave her the shivers.

Afterward, she drove up to Fran's house. Mary Frances was her only daughter, and she was always so helpful, inviting Esther over for dinner and driving her into town for doctor's appointments. Fran's eldest girl, Olivia, didn't quite catch the helpful-daughter bug. She was married and pregnant, with one of those careers that required her to always be on her phone. She was texting on Thanksgiving last year, and Esther had had half a mind to bat the thing out of her hand. But she had to admit that Olivia was impressive. She was one of those girls who saw what she wanted and went after it. *She* wasn't spending her days bringing guests at a lodge their towels, like Esther had done for so many years. Olivia always gave such nice gifts, too. She'd gotten Esther headphones last year so she could listen to Hank Williams while she washed dishes, and they didn't even need to be plugged into her phone.

But Olivia paid people to do the sort of things Esther had always thought a woman could do on her own. If she'd hired a cleaning service, Felix would have just about keeled over and died, and he was considered modern for their day, too, being so helpful with Fran when she was born. Olivia must have been handing most of her paycheck over to the parade of people who kept her house clean and her lawn mowed and her dog walked.

It wasn't Olivia walking up to Fran's front door when Esther pulled into the driveway, but Iris, holding a bag of chips.

"Grandma!" said Iris. "I could have swung by and picked you up."

"Oh, I can drive just fine," said Esther, smiling tightly. She knew they worried about the curves in the road as it looped around the lake, but for God's sake, she'd driven that road a thousand and one times, including after a cocktail or two, and never so much as hit a deer.

"Well, your big movie star arrived," Iris said. "With his kids. I got them all settled. They seemed relieved."

"Oh, good," said Esther. "We can't have him going off on TV and talking about how the hick towns in the Northwoods don't take care of their guests."

"What do us hicks do?" Fran called out as the two of them walked in. "Oh, are those chips for us? Thanks, honey."

Iris shook the bag at Olivia, who was standing there scrolling on her phone. "Best Daughter Alert."

"You won that award years ago. I'm growing a *human,*" Olivia said, without even looking up.

Esther resisted the urge to roll her eyes. She'd had a toddler by the time she was Olivia's age, and she'd found time to join the Legion of Mary, the local knitting club, and the funeral ladies besides. She would never have shown up at her mother's for dinner without bringing something.

Esther had been on the funeral committee ever since she and Felix had moved to Ellerie. She knew most people still didn't view them as true Ellerians: They were both from the suburbs of Milwaukee, small towns right next door to each other. She'd been serving waffles and coffee at the Pink Mocha and contemplating going for a teaching degree when he'd walked in and ordered hash browns. Night after night, this young man with the dark hair and kind eyes had sat in the corner booth, always ordering hash browns with an over-easy egg, and night after night, she had lingered at his table, asking if he needed more coffee or ketchup. Finally, he'd stopped her one night, a hand on her arm, and asked if she wanted to go to the movies the next weekend.

It had been a whirlwind, but back then, you didn't need to know each other so well to get married. Not like these days—Olivia and her husband, Kurt, had dated for three years before he'd gotten down on one knee. Felix was kind, and intelligent, and *oh,* he had made her laugh. A week before he died, he'd muted the newscasters on TV and mimicked their voices. The two of them had howled over that one in bed.

Esther and Felix had gotten married at St. Mary's in Elm Grove, and Esther was sure they'd live in the same town till they died.

But Felix had had a bit of difficulty after the war. The VA was getting better at handling these kinds of things, or so they said. At the time, though, it was hard to understand why he jumped at loud noises, or why a car backfiring would send him shaking. He had wanted to go up north, where there was more space and they could have a boat. They'd stumbled upon the house in Ellerie because Esther's uncle Jim had a friend from medical school who'd just passed away, and his widow was looking to sell the house quickly.

"It's a lot of upkeep," the woman had said nervously, twisting her ring around her finger. "It needs to go to someone who's ready to handle it."

Oh, they'd been ready. They'd poured heart and soul into that house. Esther didn't like to brag, but every fall her mums put everyone else's to shame.

The house. Just thinking about it, and that pile of envelopes—well, it could give an old lady heart trouble.

"Mom, you okay? You're looking kind of pale," Fran said.

"I'm not quite on death's doorstep just yet," she snapped.

"Okay, okay!" Fran threw her hands up. "Did you bring the—"

"Right here." Esther reached into her purse and pulled out a Tupperware full of homemade Mounds bars.

"Iris, put those in the fridge for your grandmother, would you? And grab yourself a beer. Mom, you need something?"

"Oh, a Lite's fine, if you've got it."

This was how Esther Larson was happiest: surrounded by her family, on Fran's back porch, drinking a beer and looking at a campfire. She may have lost Felix, but she was the furthest thing from alone.

"And then," Fran was saying, "she said she wants more of a *Great Gatsby* vibe. What does that even mean? We're in the woods, not New York City."

"Stick a green flashlight out on the end of the pier and call it a day," said Olivia.

"Maybe, like, gold accents? Metallics?" mused Iris. Esther had always wondered why Iris didn't just go work with her mother. The girl had an eye for design; the house she was renting out was beautiful. Then she could actually *live* in Redstone, maybe with a husband and a few great-grandchildren for Esther. Not that anyone had asked her opinion.

"Not a bad idea," said Fran. "It just doesn't really go with a summer lake house. Isn't that a book about an affair or something? I haven't read it since AP English."

"How many bedrooms?" asked Iris.

"Three. The master, the guest room, and one for her daughter. Who, by the way, is twenty-three years old. And still spending her summers lounging around at her parents' lake home?"

Esther bit her tongue. Her daughter forgot, apparently, that when Fran's husband, Aaron, had had his knee surgery a few years back, Felix had been over at their place at least three times a week to change lightbulbs or kill spiders, and Esther had brought over the Crock-Pot almost every night. Everyone needed a little help from time to time.

"You're making Grandma mad," Iris said, glancing her way.

"I'm not mad," said Esther.

"Mom, come on. Twenty-three years old and living at home?"

"I just—well. I won't say."

"Oh, don't do that thing," Fran said. "I hate when you do that thing!"

Esther held her hands up. "I'm just saying! You don't know *why*. You don't know their situation. We raised you to be a helper, didn't we? If Olivia or Iris needed help, and you had the means, you'd give it to them. We should help one another out." They did, didn't they? Aaron made plenty of money helping people figure out their finances, and they always treated when everyone got Culver's. It was what you did—supported your family and friends. Even Felix, with all his ideas about making your own way in the world, was a sucker when it came to his daughter and grandkids.

"It's kind of weird at our age," said Olivia.

"She's not '*our age*,'" Iris countered. "Only twenty-three. Younger than us. Maybe she has to pay off her student loans."

"Don't get started on the boomers-ruined-everything rant, please," said Fran, taking a long swig of her beer.

"My friend Hazel said that there's almost two trillion dollars owed in student loans," Esther said, proud to be able to contribute to the conversation. She hated them thinking of her as some small old lady with a bleeding heart. She *knew* things. Plenty of things.

"Two trillion," said Olivia with a whistle.

"Who's Hazel, Mom?" Fran asked as she got up to add another log to the fire. "I've never heard you mention her."

"You don't know everyone I know," said Esther, her chin in the air.

Oops. She'd gone and done it now. Fran wouldn't approve of her friendship with Hazel, surely. But why shouldn't she have a friend over the internet? That was how people did things these days. Katharine Rose's three sons had all met their wives on apps.

"Is she a new funeral lady?" Iris asked.

"No," said Esther flatly.

"Someone from church?" pestered Fran.

"She's just . . . a friend."

Felix used to tell Esther that when she was digging a hole, the first thing to do was stop digging. But it was too late. She was in a hole now. Damn it, why couldn't she just lie? It was the Catholic in her. The guilt clung to you like powdered sugar. You'd find the stuff in your hair days later. And the Larson women, they let nothing go. Fran and Olivia and Iris may have technically been Kellehers now, but Larson blood ran thick.

Aaron came out with a tray of summer sausage and Esther tried to stand to help him, but Fran put her arm out. "Mom, *who* is this mystery friend? I do too know everyone you know. Stop being weird."

"I met her online," said Esther. "Not in a lesbian way."

"Oh my God, Grandma," said Olivia, covering her face with her hands. "Talk about not wanting people to think we're from a hick town."

"You met her *online*?" Aaron laughed. "How?"

"Twitter," said Esther. "I like to read the pope's tweets, and that nun with the YouTube channel."

"You know he's not actually sending those, right?" asked Fran. "The pope, I mean."

"Of course I do," said Esther, annoyed, even though she was pretty sure he wrote at least *some* of them.

"How do you meet someone on *Twitter*?" said Iris.

"She direct messaged me. Sometimes I tweet out Bible verses and she said she found them very helpful!"

"I'm following you," said Olivia, gleefully pulling out her phone.

"Just be careful on there, Grandma," said Iris. "Nothing weird, right? She hasn't, like . . . sent you any weird pictures, or . . ."

"Of course not!" Esther insisted. She just—well, she *liked* Hazel. She was fun to talk to. She was only twenty-six years old, the same as Iris, but she didn't have a grandmother to look after her, to remind her to be kind and make the right choices in life. That was how she'd gotten into the trouble she was in.

"Why are there so many Esther Larsons?" asked Olivia, scrolling.

Sometimes, Esther just wanted someone to talk to. She had her daughter, of course—Fran was right here, always happy to come over for lunch. She had Olivia and Iris, her grandchildren, who she'd do anything for. She had Katharine Rose and the rest of the funeral ladies.

But they all *knew* her. They'd known her for years as sweet Esther, Esther with the good piecrust, Esther who could sew any button back on their blouses and drive the homework they forgot to school. Not Esther with a brain. Esther with desires. Esther who had thoughts about welfare and gun control and school shootings. Hazel *listened,* and she didn't pat Esther's hand and ask if she needed anything from the fridge. There was something so nice about talking to someone who wasn't going to see you run out of breath on a walk around Turtle Pond. Hazel told stories, too—funny ones, about her nights out with her friends. Until she got into trouble. Well, Esther should have warned Hazel. Or her mother should have. But nobody did. Esther owed it to her, really.

"Or asked you for money?" said Aaron, pointing a spatula at Esther.

Well.

Well.

She could lie. Surely she could! People did it all the time. Bishops, even. Bea from the funeral ladies, Lord in heaven, the stories that woman told. She'd tried to tell Katharine Rose that Sean Connery once took her out for Manhattans.

But when she opened her mouth, nothing came out. She just saw that pile of envelopes from the bank, asking where the mortgage was. Those dates, in angry red numbers. And then, she knew it.

She was busted.

"How could this have happened, Mom?"

They had moved into Fran's kitchen, and the mood had dropped off. Aaron was furiously googling, Olivia was barking at a lawyer on the phone, and Iris was just sitting next to her, holding her hand.

Fran, on the other hand, was interrogating her. As if Esther hadn't wiped her rump for two years, or taken her all the way to Milwaukee to go shopping after Scott McColsky stood her up at prom.

"She's a good person," Esther insisted. "She'll pay it back."

"Grandma. *She* is probably not even a *she,*" said Olivia gently.

"Thirty thousand dollars, Mom," Fran said through her hands. "I mean, *Jesus.*"

"Don't talk like that, Mary Frances."

"Thirty thousand dollars! To a perfect stranger—"

"She's not a stranger," Esther insisted. "We've been talking for months, and if you heard her story . . . a single mother. How could I not help her? I'm all she had." Hazel wasn't like Fran, who'd found a nice man and gotten a nice job and lived in a nice house. She wasn't like Olivia, with her career and her accolades. And she wasn't like Iris, with her pack of family around her and a home to rent out. She was alone. Except for Esther.

"Mom, she's not who she says she is. She's probably living in her mother's basement." Fran groaned.

Esther wanted to cry. What they were saying—it couldn't be true. Hazel was her friend.

And if they were right, it meant Hazel was never paying her

back. But she'd *promised*. She was a Catholic, too. And that thirty thousand dollars . . . Esther had to get it back. If she didn't—

If she didn't—

Her house, those envelopes—

"Stop it, you guys," Iris snapped. "You're scaring her."

"She should be scared. I mean, my God, Mom. You're a smart woman," said Fran, and Esther wanted to slap her. She really did. As if Fran even *knew* she was a smart woman, even knew she had opinions on things other than botanical gardens. What did Fran know about Esther?

She opened her mouth to bring up that idiot Scott McColsky when Aaron interrupted.

"It says we should locate our FBI field office," Aaron said. "Would that be in Washport? Milwaukee, maybe . . ."

"I could talk to Leah at church," Fran mused. She was the only police officer in Ellerie. It was the kind of place where you left your keys in your car in case your neighbor needed to borrow it.

"Isn't there something we can file?" Iris asked, looking at Olivia.

Olivia hung up her phone. "Doesn't really sound like it, since it was a wire transfer. But we'll try. I'll call again tomorrow morning."

"You don't have to do that," said Esther. "I don't want to make any trouble . . ."

"It's not trouble, Grandma," Olivia said. "I can help. We'll figure this out."

"With the baby—I mean, you don't need the extra stress." She felt bad for thinking a tad cruelly about Olivia earlier. Olivia didn't vacuum, but she helped in her own ways. Important ways.

"Her grandmother being out thirty thousand dollars is probably giving her plenty of stress, Mom," said Fran.

Thirty thousand dollars. She hadn't realized it. Hadn't quite added it up. But when Hazel had gotten pregnant, Esther had offered to add her to her Rosary list. And when she mentioned not having enough money for a bassinet—that she was going to let her baby sleep in a dresser drawer—what was Esther supposed to do? And those medical bills, well, they were *outrageous*. She knew all about that: The VA had barely thrown them a bone when Felix had all those back issues. And then the fees for day care. It just . . . added up so quickly. Hazel had said it was all a loan. She would be starting her new job six weeks after the baby was born, and her due date had been May 24.

But it was early August, and she hadn't heard from Hazel in weeks. Not even an update on how the birth had gone.

Esther's family was horrified. But she was certain Hazel would get back to her soon.

"She could have had a traumatic birth," Esther said. "Maybe she's still in the hospital."

"Grandma," said Iris, "it's not that we don't believe *you*, it's—"

"Grandma, this dude is probably in Tahiti," said Olivia.

"Drinking mai tais," said Fran.

"On a beach," added Aaron.

Esther shook her head. "I know Hazel. She wouldn't do that."

"Sometimes people on the internet pretend to be someone they're not," said Iris kindly.

"I know that," snapped Esther.

"If you know that, why did you give thirty thousand dollars to a perfect stranger?" said Fran angrily.

"Stop yelling at her, Fran. We'll figure this out," Aaron promised.

Fran put her head back in her hands. "How could I have let this happen?"

Esther was annoyed now. She wasn't some pet to be looked after. She was in charge of her own mistakes. This was exactly why she liked talking to Hazel in the first place.

"Esther, I'll go with you to the bank Monday, and we'll get this all sorted out," said Aaron. "I'm sure there's *some* kind of fraud protection they can do. They can't just let this happen. We'll get it all worked out in the morning."

Esther nodded, even though she wasn't sure her agreement was necessary. Her family could drive her so completely mad, but look at them—dropping everything for her. That's what the Larsons did. That was who they were. It was in their bones, buried deep, with all the novenas and chicken potpies. See? They were helpers, after all.

"Come on," said Olivia. "I'll drive you home, and Iris can follow us in your car."

Five

"I think it's the lard," Ivan said.

They were standing in the kitchen looking down at the last slice of pie, the chunks of cherry starting to dry out. There it sat, the last sliver they'd kept around for purely research purposes. Cooper squinted at it. It was like they were Holmes and Watson, trying to decipher how the dead body had gotten into the kitchen.

"The ratio? With the water?" he asked.

"No," Ivan said, shaking his head. "I'm wondering about the lard itself. If it's a special brand."

That pie—well, Cooper had eaten a lot of pies in his life. McDonald's ones from a paper sleeve, pumpkin ones with a congealed layer of canned jiggle on top, chocolate cream ones made in-house at the diner. But *this* pie was probably the best he'd ever eaten.

"It's late," said Ivan, glancing at the clock. It was almost one. Cricket had been asleep for hours. "I should call it."

"What time is your flight tomorrow?"

"Ten A.M."

The airport was all the way down in Rhinelander. Cooper and Cricket would drive Ivan tomorrow. Then they'd spend a few days packing up Annabelle's things from her storage unit before driving down to Milwaukee. Cricket would like it there, Cooper thought. They'd bring up all her things from Chicago and make it feel just like home. She was only going from one shore of Lake Michigan to another. Cooper had taken some time off—Frank had promised his job at the diner would be waiting for him in September, when all the Marquette students went back to class, and he was planning on spending the next couple of weeks just helping his sister get settled. Finding her a shrink, probably. Between the famous dad and the dead mom, she had to be kind of messed up.

"Going to bed soon?" Ivan asked.

"Yeah. Maybe gonna Netflix for a little bit."

Ivan nodded and disappeared into his room without so much as a *good night.*

Cooper didn't sleep very much. It was like he'd trained his body to exist on two to three hours. Annabelle used to give him shit about it constantly, sending him studies about the importance of getting eight hours a night. But if she'd seen what he'd seen, she'd understand. He hated lying in bed, turning from side to side, willing himself to be tired when he wasn't.

He grabbed a fork and took one last bite of the cherry pie before finding the Apple TV remote and turning on an episode of *The Office* he'd seen so many times, he could recite it. It was dark as hell outside, and he wasn't used to it. The lake sounded pissed off. It slammed against the shoreline, a steady *thump, thump, thump.*

Thump, thump, thump, thump—

Bang.

Goddamn it.

Bang. Bang.

It wasn't a gun. Obviously. If it were, it would probably be someone shooting a deer or something. He glanced out the window into that big, dark expanse. The lake felt like it could go on for miles.

Bang. Bang.

He took a deep breath. One, two, three, four—

Help me—

Please, help me—

"Jesus," he whispered. Not talking to the actual guy. But just—sometimes, it's all you can say.

"What's that noise?" A groggy Ivan stuck his head out of his room. "You still up?"

"I don't know," said Cooper. "Something's banging around down there."

"Something broken?"

"I have no clue."

"Should we text the girl?"

"It's three in the morning."

"But it's so loud. What if it's like . . . her dock coming loose?"

"*What?*"

"I don't know!" Ivan threw his hands in the air. "What if it's important? Something broken and important? Or, like, something about to crash down and kill us?" Cooper winced at the wording, and so did Ivan, because of Annabelle, and because of Cooper's own story.

"I'll text her," Cooper said, pulling out his phone.

> Hey. I'm so sorry to be texting you in the middle of the night. But there's a really loud banging noise and we just wanted to make sure everything was ok in the house.

> Oh, crap. I'm SO sorry. I know what it is. I'll be right there.

"She says she's coming," said Cooper.

"She's *what*? Now?"

"You're the one who told me to text her!" Cooper insisted. "Go to bed. I'll handle it."

Ivan went, and Cooper willed himself to not hear the noise. He grabbed his AirPods and turned the volume on the Lumineers up as high as it would possibly go.

As he sat and waited for the girl to come fix whatever it was that needed fixing, he thought about all he needed to do before he and Cricket returned to Milwaukee. First and foremost, he had to enroll Cricket in school. She couldn't go to Milwaukee public; Ivan would have to pay for her to go to Pius or Divine Savior.

It was weird, growing up and having an endless supply of nice things. They weren't *rich*-rich, with Kardashian-level wealth. Cooper had met enough wealthy people to know the difference between rich and wealthy. Ivan Welsh was rich. David van der Woule, who owned the network *Ivan Eats* was on, was wealthy.

But still, Cooper wasn't an idiot. He had no idea what it was like to not know where dinner was coming from. As a kid, if he wanted a new pair of shoes or to play in a sports league, he asked and the check was written. If he dropped his iPhone and the screen got cracked, a new one was simply handed to him. If he *did* ever decide to go to med school, it would be paid for in full. He knew most kids in the world didn't get a week at Disney World for their birthday, even though Ivan couldn't make it at the last minute and Cooper had spent the whole time riding Space Mountain with his nanny. He knew most twenty-eight-year-olds couldn't have a mental breakdown and abandon their career to float by on Dad's name.

Cooper hated using Ivan's name. But what was his alternative? He couldn't work as a paramedic anymore, and that was all he knew how to do. He'd been saying for ages that one day, he was going to go to medical school, but that was seeming less and less likely. Ivan hadn't been the mentor type, not by a long shot, but he'd passed on enough information about food and cooking that Cooper could keep up with the best of them at any mediocre restaurant. He liked diners in particular; they always needed help, and people were usually pretty relaxed as long as you kept the coffee flowing.

People always thought being a paramedic was this crazy, dramatic career. But it really wasn't. He'd been so exhausted from four years of undergrad, and his MCAT hadn't been good enough to get into the type of med school he'd wanted to go to. Plus, his advisor had told him he needed more experience; he hadn't worked as a certified nursing aide since high school. Ivan's name could help him get a job flipping pancakes, but not a job saving lives. So he'd gotten accredited as a paramedic through a program at UW and found himself in an ambulance.

Most days, the work wasn't that exciting. Chest pain, chest pain, anxiety attack, broken arm. It was crazy how often people just called an ambulance because they had a doctor's appointment and didn't have a ride—like, didn't they know how much cheaper Uber was? He learned the difference between an asthma attack and a pulmonary embolism. He could start an IV faster than any nurse. He liked his job. A problem with a quick fix, right in front of you: That was what he could handle. In and out, in and out, patients being picked up and patients being dropped off. He liked his coworkers, too. Eddie, who had six kids, and Lyla, who had a different hair color every week, and Shakti, who would sing to calm patients down. They didn't give him shit about his famous dad, if they even knew about it. It's not like Welsh wasn't a common last name. He'd mentioned once that he was from Los Angeles, and that was about as much as he'd chatted about Ivan.

Sometimes, as a medic, he had to do random stuff around the suburbs. North Harbor was a small Milwaukee suburb, the kind of place with ancient brick houses that overlooked the lake and where none of the mothers worked. It didn't have its own police station; it certainly didn't have its own ambulances. He'd go into the public schools to help do presentations for elementary schoolers on the importance of memorizing their phone number, or how to stop, drop, and roll. He'd drive the ambulance in the Christmas parade and turn the lights on—the kids liked that.

The North Harbor Christmas Parade was always two weeks before Christmas. Think hot chocolate, think seeing your breath on every exhale, think the chief of police dressed up as Santa Claus.

The Boy Scouts literally roasted chestnuts on an open fire, and marshmallows, too. North Harbor was tiny, but the parade was always a hit, and it brought in people from other suburbs—Hartland, Merton, Pewaukee—grandmas with their folding chairs and little kids with matching Christmas jammies.

Cooper didn't really get why an ambulance was in a parade, but whatever, *the kids like the sirens*. He did what he was told. That was the kind of paramedic he was. He didn't like to cut corners. If he was told to be at the Christmas parade at 2 P.M., he'd be at the Christmas parade at 2 P.M. It was him and Eddie, who looked like he hadn't slept much. He had a new baby at home, and it wasn't like they got leave. Waking up all night with a two-week-old before returning to work sounded like hell. But the rest of his kids would be there, he told Cooper happily. His mom was bringing them. It's not like they got to come see Dad at work very often.

The parade started with a prayer. It was small-town Wisconsin; of course it did. And then the Corvette with the mayor and Little Miss Lake Country, a blond-haired, blue-eyed little girl who had on about ten pounds of makeup.

There were marching bands, dance troupes, vintage cars. The Lake Country Republican Party and the Lake Country Democratic Party, one right after the other. North Harbor's Little League, in blue-and-white baseball gear. And all the county vehicles: police cars, post office trucks, and, of course, the ambulance. Santa brought up the rear, handing out candy canes.

They had just started driving. The crowds were cheering. Eddie reached up and turned on the siren, and the kids on the sidelines squealed, reaching their hands out. Christmas music was blaring from all the speakers on Main Street.

Santa Baby, a '54 convertible, too—light blue
Pop.

"What the fuck was that?" Eddie asks. Cooper laughs. One of

these old cars backfiring. The Lake Country Classic Car Club is only a few groups ahead of them.

Pop.

Now there is a scream. *Multiple* screams, and—*pop.*

"Shit," says Eddie. Now Cooper freezes. Not a car. Nobody screams at a car.

Their scanner goes wild. *Shots fired, shots fired on Main. Multiple people down.*

Pop.

Shots fired! Corner of Bloom and Main, I see the shots coming from—

Pop.

Multiple people down! We need a bus!

Eddie slams on the horn as loud as he can and tries to swerve around the post office truck. They can barely move forward, though, everyone is running, screaming—it's pointless. Eddie is barking at people to move but it's a thick swirl of red-and-green chaos. Cooper jumps out of the ambulance while it's still creeping along at five miles an hour, clutching his supply bag. He runs, pushing his way through screaming families, moving like a sled dog against an avalanche of snow.

"I'm a medic!" he shouts. "Move, move, let me through!"

"Cooper!" he hears Eddie yelling, somehow, above the bedlam.

Pop.

Then he sees the blood. And the girl, with her hair matted to her forehead. Her shiny silver coat.

"Help," she groans. A teenager, maybe.

And hurry down the chimney tonight

He kneels by her side. "It's okay. You're going to be fine. I've got you." Those soothing platitudes that he's whispered over hundreds of people by now.

"Help me."

She's hit bad. Right in her stomach, the blood absolutely pouring out of her like a broken faucet. Cooper presses his hand over it, hard. He sticks gauze, all the bandages he has, as far into her gaping open wound as he can.

She coughs, and blood comes out of her mouth.

Pop-pop-pop-pop, and Cooper glances over. There he is. A crumpled pile of human flesh on the ground. Head-to-toe black, an automatic rifle six inches from his hand.

He looks back over to the girl.

"You're going to be fine," he says. "I've got—"

Her eyes are glazed over.

She is not fine. She's dead.

"Paramedic! We need help!" a man screams, and Cooper looks between the girl and another man, lying only ten feet away, blood seeping from his leg. The girl is gone to wherever dead things go, and he leaves her, running to the next wound, breathing in small, shallow puffs of air, air tainted by human evil and all its consequences.

A hand on his shoulder, and he's at that Christmas parade, and a gun, and blood, and—he *jumped.*

No, not a parade. An Airbnb. Wisconsin. The woods.

"Oh my God! I'm sorry! Are you okay?" The girl they were renting from stood there, and her eyes were terrified. Of *him.*

"*I'm* sorry," he said, yanking out his AirPods. "I—I didn't hear you."

"Yeah, that's why I came in . . . I'm really sorry. I fixed the door."

"The door?" He slid his earbuds back into their little case and clicked it shut.

She pointed. "Down there . . . there's an outhouse. It's from a million years ago, when this land was a resort. The door gets open and it bangs like hell. I need to get it torn down, but I haven't done it yet. This house wasn't even supposed to be open yet. I'm sorry."

He just nodded. He still saw that rifle.

"Do you need water or something?" she asked.

He shook his head. He hated that look in her eyes. Walking into a room and having everyone look at you like you're some kind of fragile trip wire was the worst, and that was the look she had right that second.

"Thanks for coming," he said. "I could have gone and shut it."

She shook her head. "You're my guests. Besides, I was awake."

"You were?" he asked, surprised. "It's, like, three A.M."

She smiled halfway. Her eyes looked defeated now. "Yeah. I had a weird night. This thing with my grandma . . . anyway."

"Your grandma? Pie lady?"

She nodded. "It's crazy. She—I don't even know why I'm telling you this. You probably want to go to bed."

He shook his head. He couldn't go to bed, not now. All he'd see when he closed his eyes was a gun. "Remind me of your name?" he asked.

"Iris. Iris Kelleher."

"Cooper Welsh. What happened to your grandma?"

She pressed her hands to her eyes, and that's when he realized it was serious.

"Is she sick? I'm sorry. I don't mean to pry," he said. "It's your business."

"No," she said. "It's . . . you're here for a funeral. I shouldn't be bothering you. My stupid outhouse already woke you up."

"I wasn't sleeping. I swear."

"My grandma is just the nicest lady in the world. The definition of salt of the earth. And some scammer somehow conned her out of thirty thousand dollars."

Cooper whistled. "Shit."

"Yeah. And now, apparently, there's an issue with her mortgage. I mean . . . thirty thousand dollars! And you just think, how could this have happened? How could I have let this happen?"

"Hey," said Cooper instantly, "it's not your fault."

"Isn't it, though? Kind of?" She twisted a ring around her finger. "I mean, we have to look out for our grandparents, don't we?"

"I wouldn't know," said Cooper bluntly. His mom's parents had died before he'd even been born, and Annabelle had never been that close with hers. Ivan's dad had ditched his mom before Ivan was even born, and Ivan's mom lived in Boston, where she smoked a lot of cigarettes and read about conspiracy theories on Reddit.

"Well, I do," said Iris. "People do, around here. And I just can't believe this is happening. That house means everything to our family."

"I'm sorry," he said. "That . . ." *Sucks*, he wanted to say. But how many times had people said that to him? *That must have sucked, being at the North Harbor shooting.* No shit, Sherlock. It really sucked. No need to point it out.

"Oh my God. Please don't leave me a crappy review, okay? I'm sorry. This is the worst trial run ever," Iris said. "God. Let me at least give you a full refund. That outhouse."

"It's *okay*," Cooper said. "I'm just . . . I'm really sorry about your grandma. What can we do?"

She looked surprised. "You? Nothing. I mean, unless you know who was impersonating Hazel Johnson on Twitter."

"I don't," he said. "But . . . I mean, we're going to be around for a week or so."

"You are?" Iris asked, surprised. "*Here?*"

"No! Don't look so terrified. We're supposed to check in to our other cabin tomorrow. There's a storage unit up here that belonged to Annabelle's parents, and then to her. We have no idea what's in it, but we've got to deal with it."

"Oh God. That sounds like a nightmare."

"It will be," said Cooper. "But I mean . . . if you need anything. If I can help with your grandma. She was so nice at the funeral. All that *food*, I mean . . . I owe her."

Iris smiled. "You're nice. You're a nice guy."

Oh God. Did she think he was hitting on her? Over her grand-mother's fortune being scammed away and his own dead step-mother? He was bad at this! Cooper had never dated much. Well, he'd—he wasn't a bad-looking guy, okay? And there were girls at Marquette, girls at diners, girls that helped him forget *The* Girl, The Girl at the Parade. But he didn't usually do much *talking* to them. He wasn't like his friend Brian from college, who would go into bars to just chat up the hottest girl he could find. That wasn't Cooper.

He just tried to be helpful.

But it always got him into trouble.

"Thanks," she said. "I don't think there's anything you can do. But thanks."

He nodded. "Well . . . would some coffee help?"

She glanced over at the coffeepot. "I think I'm just going to . . . go for a walk, or something."

Cooper raised his eyebrows. "It's the middle of the night."

"I know. But I'm all wired."

"I could come," he said. "If you want." Why, why, why had he said that? She didn't want company, she wanted space. But to Coo-per's surprise, she just shrugged.

"Sure," she said. "Grab a jacket."

He didn't realize until he was pulling on his North Face that he was wearing his pajama pants. They had *bears* on them, for Christ's sake.

As they reached the front door, she turned and grinned at him. "Want to see something kind of cool?"

"For sure."

"This way." She headed out, and he followed.

Together, they walked down the wide gravel road. It was weird, being outside in such black, black darkness, the only light coming from the smattering of stars and a sliver of moon. Cooper had never been somewhere with so little light in his entire life. It wasn't like Ivan had ever taken him camping. And man, why was it straight-up chilly? It was August.

He felt like he should start a conversation or something, but to be honest, it felt nice being in the dark quiet. It kind of felt like coming home after a loud, bright party, where people were screaming and lights were blinking, just to flip the switch off and lie in your bed in silence. He'd read an article once about how touching a tree could improve your mental health. *People must be really happy here,* he thought.

An owl hooted somewhere, far off, and then Cooper heard a long, high-pitched call.

"What was that?" he whispered.

"A loon."

"Like a duck?"

"No, like a loon! They're not ducks. They only go on land to lay their eggs."

Another owl, and some cicadas, too. Who knew where they were? Iris must have, because she was leading the way down a twisting road. One wrong turn, and you could get lost in a brutally dense forest like this, it felt like. The thick towers of evergreens on either side of them seemed to reach so high, they could graze the star-speckled sky.

"Stop," Iris whispered suddenly, holding out her arm. "Look."

She pointed to the end of a hollowed-out log, a few yards off the road into the woods. He saw a few pairs of eyes blinking at him in the moonlight.

"Baby coyotes," she whispered. "Where'd Mama go, huh, guys? Did she go get dinner?"

Cooper stilled. "Aren't coyotes, like, wolves?"

She chuckled quietly. "Nah. We have wolves here, but not too many. Coyotes are harmless. Unless you're a dog."

He stood in the small sliver of moonlight and just stared at those blinking eyes, that pile of fur. This felt like a holy place.

"I found them the other night," she said quietly. "I was driving back from Olivia's kind of late. My sister. Anyway, I almost hit their mom—I had to slam on the brakes. She couldn't have cared less. Coyotes don't give a shit about people up here. She was bringing them some kind of animal to eat."

They were so far from Milwaukee. What did he know about wildlife? Nothing, except for a bat he'd had in his attic that he'd had to pay Wally the Wildlife Controlman a fortune to catch. But he liked it—*loved* it—being here in the woods. Something about the dark, fresh air—it was so cool and crisp. The woods had a lush calmness to them. Cooper could practically feel his heart rate slowing down.

He had seen a lot of beautiful things. He was from California, a state known for its ocean views and perfect climate, and had spent a significant amount of time in Milwaukee, where you could look out on a ginormous lake dotted with sailboats and lighthouses. But the dark, deep woods of northern Wisconsin—and the girl standing next to him—were sights to behold.

"Thank you for showing me, Iris Kelleher," he said quietly.

"Thank *you* for coming, Cooper Welsh," she responded.

Six

Hazel, I know

Hazel, I was wondering if

Hazel, I hope you and your little one are doing well. I am so sorry to bother you about this while you are dealing with a newborn baby, but I was wondering if there was a possibility you could potentially give me an update as to when I can expect repayment on the loan I gave you. I really hate to bring this up, but my daughter is being dramatic (you'll see soon how hard it can be to deal with your children!) and insisting I get some kind of timeline. I told them that you are a trustworthy friend, but they really wanted me to send you a note, so I said that I would. If you are still unsure, that is totally fine. Just let me know. I am praying for you.

From, Esther

She stared at the message. It wasn't a *complete* lie, but Fran didn't want her to send Hazel a note. She'd pulled Esther aside after Mass that morning and suggested they report Hazel to the FBI. The *FBI*. As if they were on TV!

Of all the embarrassing old-person things to do, it seemed she'd done the very worst one, handing out money to someone she couldn't see face-to-face. Esther was born smack dab in the middle of the second world war and all it entailed. She grew up with Donna Reed telling her how to be a woman. Her family farmhouse looked nothing like Donna Reed's home. But her mother, after chain-smoking with the neighbors on the porch all day, still had dinner on the table for Esther and her father every single night. Some kind of meat, some kind of potato, some kind of vegetable, usually corn.

She'd always wanted a sister. Someone you could confide in in a way you just couldn't with anyone else. But that wasn't meant to be. Her mother had had some kind of health complication, and back then, they'd remove your entire womb without batting an eye. They stuck out among all the other Catholic families, whose fathers had sons to help with the farm and whose mothers had daughters to help with dinner. Their family had felt like a small, strange island of its own, and then when she'd gotten married, she'd had the same problems. They didn't do surgery, but they couldn't do anything to help, either, and she'd had the same lot in life as her mother: a single daughter. Not a day went by when she wasn't thankful that God saw fit to bless her with her two granddaughters, who would have each other for the rest of their lives.

If she had a sister, she'd tell her about everything. And she'd tell her about how ashamed she had felt, when Fran's husband, Aaron, had to open her bills, explain to her how much she owed. All that feminism that had been poured into her since the '60s, and she still needed a man to explain money to her. How it had felt to watch his face grow grimmer and grimmer. Fran, clutching her hands—why hadn't Esther *told* her, she kept asking.

Because she didn't want to see the look Fran had on her face that very moment.

Oh, she missed Felix in the hard times, and this was no exception. Felix, with his dark hair and kind eyes. She loved that man. She spoke with him every day, asking him to pray for her up there, hoping he'd run into all those saints he loved so much. Felix had kept a copy of Saint Augustine's *Confessions* in his nightstand, and sometimes he'd tell Esther about how Saint Augustine was so far from God. Just like Felix himself, he'd chuckle, even though he was one of the most faithful Catholics Esther knew.

But she also knew he'd done things he wasn't proud of overseas. Vietnam was a terrible war. Esther's father was a 4-F during World War II because of his bad ear, and his embarrassment over this had been unbearable, even years after the fact. Every other man was off fighting Hitler. He never got over the shame. But Vietnam— well, the soldiers who went there were treated like dirt when they returned. There were no noble heroics attached to the veterans. They were lucky if they got a discount on coffee at the Pink Mocha. And Felix had been a medic, always dealing with those bloody and battered men. It was no wonder he'd go through so many Hamm's in a night. He said it helped him sleep, made it so he didn't see his fellow soldiers all tangled and bloody when he shut his eyes. Esther couldn't imagine, she really couldn't. The bloodiest thing she'd ever been through was birth.

Felix wasn't a perfect parent. He'd get angry with Fran sometimes. He had quite the temper. He saw ghosts at night, sometimes. And selling insurance—well, that wasn't anyone's dream job. But he went to work every day so that they'd have food on the table. He could hold a job. And he never left her, unlike Katharine Rose's snake. He listened to her when she talked, and thought she had interesting things to say.

She wished he were there now, to grab her a beer and hold her hand and figure it out. Felix wasn't exceptionally charismatic. Nobody stopped and stared when he entered a room. But he was a problem fixer. He *handled* things, the way a husband should, and that was what Esther needed more than anything at that moment.

"Esther?"

She looked up from her hands. It was Katharine Rose, pulling a book from her purse. "I was just bringing this back," she said, holding it up. It was a historical fiction novel Esther had loaned her months ago. She loved that one. Anything that took place in Paris, she'd gobble up. She was surprised Katharine Rose had even wanted to borrow it. She usually only liked Amish romances. "Looks like Mrs. Thomas Murphy had quite the party last night," Katharine Rose added. "Her recycling bin is overflowing. You can just listen to the sound of her beer cans rolling down the street—it'll cue you in on the day without needing a calendar."

Esther laughed. "Katharine Rose. Be kind."

"You sound like my mother."

"Thanks for the book," Esther said. "Did you like it?"

"You know, I did. That main character was kind of a floozy, but . . ." Katharine Rose stopped. "What's wrong?"

"Nothing," Esther said instantly.

"Oh, stop it. What is it?"

Esther scowled at her. "None of your business."

Katharine Rose tossed the book onto the counter, and Esther winced as the back cover bent on the corner. "Esther Larson, I have got three library books to return and a chicken to marinate. My tomatoes need weeding. Keith and Clara are bringing the girls up this weekend and I haven't even washed the sheets. I have Adoration at three, the Legion of Mary after that, and I told Barbara I'd clean out the church dishwasher before the funeral next week. So if you think I have the time to sit here and be lied to by my oldest friend, you are a damn idiot."

Esther just stared at her, and Katharine Rose stared right back.

Then Esther opened her mouth and started talking.

"THIS IS AN outrage." Bea reached into Esther's fridge, helping herself to another Miller Lite. "I mean, she could be part of an international crime ring."

"Oh, for Pete's sake. Bea once thought her neighbor was wiretapping her," said Carlotta.

Esther stared at the women helplessly. "And were they?"

"Esther," said Katharine Rose flatly.

"We never found out," Bea insisted. "Are these twist-offs? I can never remember. Someone open this for me, my carpal tunnel's acting up."

Esther reached over and wordlessly opened the beer. Katharine Rose—well, it takes a certain kind of gumption to go on living after your husband leaves you, and she supposed it was the kind of gumption that could also cook food for one hundred and get the funeral ladies to Esther's house at a moment's notice. Marvin Gaye was singing over the little speaker Fran and Aaron had gotten her for Christmas last year, and the women were all helping themselves to drinks and pulling up chairs around the kitchen table. It was a battle station. A war room.

"Maria's always telling me not to talk to people on the internet," said Carlotta. "But isn't that what the internet's *for*?"

Katharine Rose shook her head at Carlotta. "Are you kidding me? It's full of perverts. I don't go near it." Esther wasn't sure the internet was actually chock-full of men hoping to take advantage of Katharine Rose, but she bit her tongue. Her friends were here to make her feel better, after all.

"I love to google people," said Bea. "It's my favorite thing to do after JP falls asleep. I just look up random people from high school. Some of them . . . the weight these women put on! Like they don't own mirrors or something."

Esther hated that she'd gotten herself into trouble, and even more, she hated that Katharine Rose felt the need to tell people. Esther knew everyone loved to talk about money these days, but that wasn't how she was raised. It all felt so gauche. Iris had showed her a website once where people shared how much money they made and how they spent it. Esther could feel her mother shuddering all the way up in heaven. Felix had handled all the financials for their whole marriage.

"You all don't have to worry about this. It isn't anyone's problem but my own," said Esther. But she knew that wasn't how this group worked. When Bea had gotten COVID, the funeral ladies had created an entire spreadsheet to be passed around church of who was going to mow her lawn and weed her vegetable beds and cook dinner for JP, who couldn't even fry an onion. She still had to drag around the oxygen tank.

"First things first: How do we hunt down this conniving little witch?" said Bea.

"Esther's insisting she's a young mother who's got herself in trouble, and not a delinquent with too much time on his hands," Katharine Rose said. "But either way, she's disappeared. Vanished without a trace!"

"She hasn't posted on Twitter, or responded to any of my messages in over a month," said Esther. She hadn't even liked any tweets. Olivia had showed her how to check that, and had turned on notifications for her phone so that if Hazel *did* say anything, it would pop right up.

"The real problem," said Katharine Rose, "is that we need the money to keep the bank off our asses."

"Can't Peter do something?" Carlotta asked Bea.

"Hand me a napkin, will you?" said Bea, motioning toward the neat pile of paper napkins Esther had put on the counter. "And no, he can't just get the bank to let Esther off thousands of dollars."

"We need to raise money," Katharine Rose said. "Not the whole thirty thousand. How much did Aaron say you absolutely, positively needed?"

Esther winced. Her son-in-law's sad face, almost in tears. Fran had found such a gem. Esther adored Aaron; she had ever since he came to pick Mary Frances up for their first date. He seemed capable, like Felix, and Felix had insisted Aaron had a great handshake. That was important.

Instantly, Aaron had talked about pulling money out of retirement, talked about selling the car. Esther had hushed him up immediately. But the ten thousand they had on hand that they could give—she'd take that, because pride was a sin and she loved this house that Felix had lived in. This house where she'd raised her daughter, this house where her grandchildren had learned to walk. She hated this. And, for an unchristian moment, hated Hazel, too. But there was no shame in honesty. The Lord knew your secrets, anyway. And Aaron and Fran were the most generous people she knew.

Aaron had actually called Peter, and it was kind of him to answer, considering Sunday was his day off. But there wasn't much they could do. Esther had sent the money willingly. File a police report, maybe. The best they could do was give her more time.

"Twenty," she said. "By the end of the year." *You're lucky,* Peter had told Aaron. *Wisconsin has some of the most forgiving foreclosure laws in the country.*

"And Hazel's ass on a platter," said Carlotta.

"Her name isn't Hazel. It's probably Frank. Or *Butch,* maybe," Bea piped in.

Oh, her friends. Her friends! The people who knew her. Esther was about to get kicked out of the home she'd lived in for fifty years and probably be homeless, but these people, they loved her so well.

"We'll raise it," said Katharine Rose. "That's all there is to it."

"*Raise* it?" said Esther. "It's not a barn. Or a child. It's twenty grand."

"A lemonade stand," chortled Carlotta.

Bea started telling some story about a nun who needed a hundred grand to keep her convent, and how the hundred grand showed up from an anonymous donor the next day. Bea: She was full of those stories, stories of good old-fashioned hope tangled with miracles. Saints who walked down the right street on the right day; wine turning into blood in a priest's hands.

A loon sang out on Musky Lake, and the four of them sat and listened. You did that, in a place like Ellerie. You honored the loon and you honored the land. Soon enough, the loons would go away, and the long, dark months of winter would creep in, sinking their teeth into the Northwoods. Esther hadn't gotten down to the dock much this summer; the stairs were too steep.

A memory, then, or a montage of them: the hours and hours and hours she'd spent out on that dock with Felix, his hand in hers as they ignored the mosquitos and listened to the loons. Then Fran and her friends, smothering themselves with baby oil and carrying stacks of library books. Eventually, Olivia and Iris, running and leaping off the dock, creating a splash so large and cold that the adults would holler at them. The dock was where they sat, where they lounged, where they gossiped, where they listened to the radio from an ancient boom box. Dinner was chunks of cheddar cheese cut with Felix's pocketknife, cold grapes still wet from the sink, and sour-cream-and-onion chips eaten straight from the bag. They sat on that dock in their own little paradise, shielded from the rest of the world by thick pine trees and no Wi-Fi, the breeze off the lake shooing the mosquitoes away while they consumed entire coolers of beer. The kids would roll frosty Miller Lite cans across their foreheads to stay cool. One adult would be on kid watch, and they'd suddenly, mid-conversation, stand up and shield their eyes from the sun with their hand. They'd yell for the kids to sound off, and the kids would throw their hands in the air, kicking to avoid seaweed. Say what you will about the number of beers consumed on the dock on an average summer day, but nobody had ever drowned at the Larson home. At least one child would be on the dock with their feet propped up on Felix's or Aaron's lap, dripping cold lake water all over his legs as he slowly removed a splinter from the pad of their big toe. They'd raise a hand to wave at any boat or jet-skier that came by, fewer and fewer of which they knew personally as the years passed. And as the sun set and the crickets started to sing, the sweatshirts would come out, the beer would change to cocktails, and the kids would race upstairs to beat one another to the showers. They'd sit around a fire, whoever happened to be there—friends, friends of friends, cousins, just the family. S'mores and pudgy pies and popcorn, all eaten while Felix told ghost stories that Esther always insisted were too frightening for the children. She had to remind them as she tucked them into bed to say their guardian angel prayers when they got scared. And she'd glance out, just before she went to bed, at her strong, sensitive husband, carefully placing the cover on the firepit so they wouldn't all burn to a crisp. That house: That was the song of the Northwoods, the backdrop to their entire family story.

And these women, with their oxygen tanks and novenas, were here to save the day. They filled her heart with an aching hope that she didn't know she still had. Hazel—how could she compare to the flesh-and-blood women standing before her? Carlotta reached over and turned up the speaker, letting Marvin serenade them a little longer. Esther would whip them up some dinner while they were here in her kitchen. Nobody went hungry at Esther's, that was for sure. She grabbed a pot and filled it with water, and Katharine Rose, without being asked, reached over and grabbed the noodles from the pantry.

If there was one thing the funeral ladies understood, it was the power of a goddamn casserole to lift your spirits.

Seven

"We have to *do* something."

Olivia kept saying that, and it was really starting to tick Iris off. Once again, she was full of the understanding that a solution was needed, but unwilling to provide the solution herself. Olivia poured herself LaCroix after LaCroix while Iris sipped wine. Her mom was already on her third Bloody Mary. She kept dunking cheese curds in them. The three of them had stress eaten almost an entire bag from Willoughby Cheese Mart.

"She should have known better," said Fran.

"Mom, quit it," Iris said. "What's done is done. What we need to do now is problem-solve."

"She's not a goddamn feeble old lady. The woman has a brain in her head," snapped Fran.

"Thirty thousand dollars," said Olivia, for the ninety-seventh time. "We have to do something."

"Will you shut up?" snapped Iris.

"Well, we do!" Olivia snapped right back.

"Girls. Stop," said Fran. "Focus. We *are* doing something. We gave her a check for the property taxes, *plus* some. But it's not enough. She's living off Dad's old VA pension and Social Security."

Sitting around Fran's kitchen table, they felt completely hopeless. They weren't exactly the brain trust.

"I gotta go, anyway," said Iris, checking her phone. "I have a call with a client. I'll stop at Grandma's later, maybe. I called her earlier but she said the funeral ladies were coming over."

"Bring her this," Fran said, handing her a Tupperware container. "She brought it over last night with those Mounds bars."

ONE OF THE best parts of Iris's job was her ability to do it from her screened porch.

Was her actual house as nice as Redstone? No. Or as nice as her grandmother's? Not even close. But that didn't mean she didn't love it just the same. It wasn't on the lake, but she could still *hear* the lake on windy days like this one. The waves slapped against the rocks and splashed up onto paths, and she heard a gaggle of kids shriek with delight.

She stared hard at her laptop, trying to focus. But creating a beautifully designed welcome packet for seasonal employees at Mrs. Claus's Christmas Barn was a little hard to do on a 73-degree day.

Her phone buzzed, distracting her. A text from Olivia—some funny TikTok clip about telling a story when your mom is in the background, interrupting with questions. She laughed; Olivia always knew which memes would make her laugh. But since she'd opened her phone, she found her fingers drifting to Instagram, and before she knew it, she was judge-scrolling. Her least favorite hobby, but one she couldn't quite quit. She knew that all the books and podcasts and experts on TV said endlessly scrolling Instagram was sucking everyone's will to live, and that it was giving teenage girls anxiety and eating disorders. But she couldn't help herself. As she scrolled through old high school friends' profiles, she considered the mile-wide differences in their lives. Some were married, some were single, some were already on husband number two. Some had two children. Some ran companies. One was an Instagram influencer who was paid more than Esther owed the bank to snap a shot of her latest handbag. God, there were so many ways to be twenty-six.

Most people Iris knew who'd grown up in Ellerie had left and hadn't come back. Her friends from high school had scattered with the wind. Friendships that had seemed like they would last forever were now gray-edged memories. They ran away to Madison or Milwaukee or Eau Claire and never came back. Ironically, one of the only people Iris knew from growing up who'd returned was Father Sam—they weren't in the same friend group, but they'd had precalculus together, and she'd always seen him at football games on Friday nights. But Iris, too, had returned to the Northwoods. Four years at La Crosse, and she missed the lake. She liked Ellerie, with its waves and sharp edges. It was a place for people who weren't full of shit. Esther was the purest, kindest, most hardworking soul she knew—if Ellerie was good enough for her, then it was good enough for Iris.

Besides, what was she supposed to do? Go get a job somewhere, wear a pencil skirt, date Chad in finance? She'd miss her family. She'd spent almost every single Saturday of her life surrounded by her sister and her mother, and usually her dad and Kurt, too. Chad didn't have those people, probably.

Iris hated doing this. The constant comparisons she felt like she had to make. To make sure she was doing it right, setting herself up for the rest of her life. When was she just going to feel . . . settled? It was marriage, but it wasn't, too. Her grandmother and her mother had already had kids by Iris's age, but those were generations past; she had tons of friends who were still single. They at least seemed like they had *plans,* though. Plans for their future—a map to adulthood that Iris felt she'd never gotten. Plans that were bigger than pushing pixels, which wasn't her passion and never had been. How could these people just move away and live lives separate from their family? What was wrong with Iris that she couldn't? Was she really any better than that twenty-three-year-old daughter of her mom's client? And why was she silently judging people whose stories she didn't know, anyway? Esther would never do something like that.

She put her phone down, turning back to Mrs. Claus and her instructions on company attire. She had a business, whether or not Gen X understood it. Two houses. A sister who loved her; a grandmother who cherished her. Two parents who would do anything for her. She should stop being so ungrateful, really. She should stop always concerning herself with what was around the corner.

Eight

"I understand that, Matthew. But what would you like me to do? Charter a plane?" snapped Ivan.

Cooper glanced up from his coffee. Ivan's flight had been canceled. He was trying to rebook, but apparently there was some kind of issue with a shoot in Abu Dhabi the next day.

"This is what I get for trusting some backwoods airport," Ivan muttered, slamming his phone down on the table. "Production's going to be pushed back. I can't get a connection in New York for two more days. Gabi's useless."

"Really?" asked Cooper. "That sucks." He meant it, too. Sucked for Ivan. Sucked for him, since he was now stuck with Ivan.

This was probably the most time Cooper had spent with his father in years. And already, he was remembering why. The phone that was permanently glued to his ear, the *tap-tap-tap* sound as he typed emails, the way he'd stop and glance at his reflection in every mirrored surface. He'd checked it in the *fridge* last night. He hadn't asked about Cricket's plans—about finding a school for her, a therapist, a dentist. He hadn't offered to help clean out Annabelle's storage unit, either. He hadn't done much of anything besides show up and play the part of Sad Husband, even though they had been divorced in all but name when Annabelle's car crashed. That was Ivan: always playing a part, whether he was chatting with Vietnamese locals at a food truck or attempting to surf in Melbourne. A thousand different masks, each soon to be replaced by the next. The role of "dad" or "husband" simply wasn't interesting enough to keep his attention. It didn't get you the cover of *Time*.

Ivan reached over and grabbed a blueberry muffin from the platter Cooper had thrown together out of funeral leftovers. Esther was right—he was thankful for microwavable things this morning. Reheated chili had made a nice breakfast. "These muffins are good."

"Those old ladies know how to cook," muttered Cooper.

"Of course they do. They were doing it before it was a hobby, or a blogging avenue," said Ivan, taking a bite.

You'd think Ivan Welsh would be a food snob. After all, he'd eaten twelve-course world-class tasting menus; he'd eaten every delicacy from ortolan in France to shark fin soup in Taiwan. And when he cooked, his food wasn't just good—it was legendary. He could elevate something as simple as scrambled eggs to a heavenly experience. (He told Cooper it was the chives, and the importance of shaking the pan the entire time the eggs cooked.) But Ivan abhorred food snobbery. He liked diners and potlucks.

Cricket walked into the kitchen, her eyes sleepy and her hair in her face. Her striped pajama pants were too long, and they dragged on the floor, getting ratty at the bottom. "Coffee."

"You don't drink coffee," said Cooper. "You're thirteen."

Cricket ignored him and grabbed a mug. "No talking. Too early."

"It's nine A.M., kid," said Ivan. "Time to greet the day."

Annabelle had let Cricket drink coffee? Apparently so, since she was expertly pouring milk into the mug and adding a spoonful of sugar, stirring it to the perfect shade of beige. Cooper thought you weren't supposed to give kids coffee, were you? But if Annabelle had, it must have been fine. God, these were the questions he didn't know. It's not like he could text his mom, in Maui with her surfboards. Ivan would probably have given Cricket a tequila shot if she'd asked. And Annabelle was in the cemetery at St. Anne's, next to a statue of an angel. Was he going to have to join one of those Facebook groups for parents that he'd read about? Where you ask about finding your kid's secret Instagram accounts and which was the best brand of laundry detergent?

"When's your flight?" Cricket asked through a yawn.

"Never," Ivan bit out.

That woke her up a bit. "Huh?"

"Canceled," Cooper filled in. "It was canceled. The soonest he can get a new one is in two days."

"Tuesday? Shit," said Cricket.

"Yeah." Ivan rubbed his jaw.

"Want to come with us on our walk down memory lane?" asked Cricket.

Say no, say no, say no, Cooper willed. He didn't want to spend all day in awkward silence. He wanted to tell stories about Annabelle and laugh with his sister.

"I should get some work done," said Ivan. "Edits on the new book."

"Let's get going soon," Cooper told Cricket. "It's gonna take a while."

Cricket nodded. "We moving into the new cabin today?"

"I need to call and make sure it's ready," Cooper said.

Cricket sat down and took another long sip of coffee. "I'm going to FaceTime Sophie this morning, then I'll be ready. Okay?"

Cooper nodded. His own shrink, Dr. Hoss, had been helping him get ready to take on the role of Cricket's guardian. *Keep routines normal in any small ways possible,* he'd said. Cricket and her best friend were inseparable. She'd been going through data like crazy FaceTiming her. But it felt like an island of normalcy in a sea of rapid change.

Dr. Hoss. He should really text him. Cooper had been forced to go for work, initially, before he'd decided his medical leave was going to turn into a forever leave. He'd sat on the uncomfortable blue couch and explained, as patiently as he could, that he really just needed the therapist to sign a form saying Cooper wasn't going to go absolutely batshit while dealing with a patient. And then—it couldn't have been timed better—a friggin' car had backfired outside. Practically *right* outside the window. And of course he hit the ground, because it had only been a week. A *week*. The funerals were still happening and the hashtag was still trending and senators were still giving speeches, so of course Cooper was still a little messed up. He hit the floor, hard, and when he realized he was being an idiot, he looked up to see Dr. Hoss just regarding him calmly from behind his glasses. Not at all weirded out, or judgmental. Just calm.

And Cooper thought, maybe he wouldn't be messed up from this permanently, but it was nice to be around someone he could act like a total lunatic in front of and not feel like they thought he was an idiot. Plus, Ivan was paying for it. He liked the idea of Ivan having to spend his hard-earned cash on the mental health issues of the son whose upbringing he'd outsourced to an army of nannies.

It had been helpful to have Dr. Hoss around when he agreed to be Cricket's guardian. He felt like he had a parenting coach.

Remind her it's okay to feel her feelings, Dr. Hoss had said. So now, as they stood in front of the storage unit, staring at the giant garage-style door, he turned and looked at his sister.

"You gonna be okay?" he said. "It might be a lot. I don't know what's in here."

She rolled her eyes. "Please don't go all shrink on me."

Okay, then.

Cooper lifted the heavy door, and the two of them immediately coughed as they were hit with a wall of dust. Shit, nobody had been in there for *years,* he thought. If they made it through without finding a dead mouse, it would be a miracle.

Cricket kicked a cardboard box. "What's the plan here?"

"I brought these." Cooper opened the trunk of the Tesla and pulled out a few plastic bins. "Thought we could make some piles.

Some stuff we want to keep, some stuff we could donate or sell, some stuff that can go in the garbage."

Cricket leaned down and picked up a piece of paper from the box she'd kicked. "Like a library receipt from 1982?"

"Hey. We could sell that receipt. Someone could put it in an eighties museum," Cooper joked.

"Who do you think checked out *Story of a Soul*? Grandma Alice or Grandpa Bill?" asked Cricket, squinting at the receipt.

"Come on," said Cooper. "This is gonna take a while."

IT DID. HOURS and hours, and for northern Wisconsin, it was *hot*. Cooper needed to drive to Coontail's over in Moose Junction that night for a couple of box fans. He was sweating so bad, he'd stripped down to his shorts, and Cricket kept having to take a break to chug some of the bottled water they'd brought. The Robertsons should have been on *Storage Wars*. They definitely had a thing for paintings of western scenes and portraits of Jesus looking sad.

His sister held it together pretty well. He almost thought she needed to cry *more*. She seemed oddly detached, going through things from her mother's childhood. She saved a photograph here, a necklace there, but mostly she tossed things into the garbage bin or the donate pile. The most emotional she got was when they found a dress they assumed Annabelle must have worn to prom, a sequined sapphire-toned gown with a punch stain on the skirt. Cricket brought the dress to her face and breathed, and Cooper understood. She was looking for it. The scent of Annabelle.

Cricket and Cooper barely even noticed when a navy-blue minivan pulled up. Ivan hopped out, carrying a giant Jimmy John's bag. "Lunch delivery," he said. "Thought you might be getting hungry. Do you know how long it took to get an Uber? What else do they have to do up here?"

"I'm starving," said Cricket, carefully folding the dress and placing it in the keep pile. "Did you bring mayo?"

"Extra," Ivan replied.

"You didn't have to," Cooper said. "We could have ordered something."

Ivan shrugged and handed over the bag. He had a drink carrier, too, with three sweating sodas. "Find anything interesting?" He waved at the Uber driver, who sped out of the parking lot.

"Mostly old art, a bunch of files . . . nothing much," said Cooper.

Ivan riffled through a newspaper article about Annabelle playing soccer in high school and a few framed photos of her with her parents. "You think you'd be able to hire someone to come do this," he said, glancing around.

Cooper glared at him. He didn't *want* to hire someone to dig through Annabelle's stuff. He wanted to hold it in his own two hands. He wanted to hold pieces of her and remember the chapters of her life, one by one. Typical Ivan. Storage units, sons: If you throw enough money out the door, someone else will handle them.

The three of them leaned against the Tesla and wolfed down their subs. Cooper thought Ivan would hightail it out of there after eating, but he must have been bored, because he kept standing there, watching as Cricket and Cooper dragged out boxes and opened them up.

"What do you think are the odds this china set is actually worth two million dollars?" said Cricket, holding up a teacup with a rose pattern on it.

Two million dollars—it reminded him suddenly of Iris, whose Airbnb they had crashed at. The nice funeral lady with the pies, Esther, who was in financial trouble.

Marquette, where he'd gone to undergrad, was in the heart of downtown Milwaukee. He'd seen poverty there for the first time in his life, not just through a TV screen, as his dad walked through war-torn streets in Libya wearing two-hundred-dollar sneakers.

The Jesuits who ran Marquette had purposely put it in an area where they could stand in solidarity with the poor. Every day as Cooper walked to class, he found himself walking past homeless encampments and panhandlers. He'd throw some change in their cardboard boxes if he had any on hand, but he usually didn't.

That look of fear in Iris's eyes for her grandmother—it was a feeling he didn't know. He almost wanted to ask Ivan to cut the woman a check. And Ivan probably would. Say what you wanted to about his father—and oh, the things you could say—but he'd always had an open wallet.

Cooper opened another box and found a pile of books. A Bible, a few novels . . . and a small leather-bound book.

The Legion of Mary Cookbook: Recipes from the Women of St. Anne's

He opened it and coughed at the dust that puffed out. The pages were paper-thin and the binding was barely holding together. It was covered in tape, as if it had been carefully put back together time and time again. There were mystery stains on the back cover. This book had been used, he thought—no, this book had been *loved*.

"What is that?" asked Cricket, glancing up.

"A cookbook, I think," said Cooper. "Some kind of cookbook." He turned the pages as carefully as he could. Page after page of recipes, each with a woman's name under it:

Roast Chicken: Dorothy Gay
Baked Ziti: Nancy Cucia
Fried Green Tomatoes: Mildred Robertson

Robertson. A family member of Annabelle's?

"How old is that thing?" asked Cricket.

"I don't know," said Cooper. "Old." There were notes written after many of the recipes, temperatures crossed off and corrected, faded pencil adding how many biscuits or sweet-and-sour pickles a recipe made. Dates scrawled, too—across the top of the recipe for Hunter's Dream Stew, *Apr. 4, 1941—Fr. Patrick for dinner.* Above the ginger drop cookies, *Jul. 17, 1950—Alice born.*

"Alice," said Cooper. Annabelle's mother. "So, definitely owned by someone related to Annabelle. Probably her grandmother."

Cricket looked at it with the disdain of a thirteen-year-old who could find any recipe she wanted on Pinterest. But Ivan walked over and carefully took the book.

"It's a community cookbook," he said.

"What?" asked Cooper.

"Wow. This is something," Ivan muttered, carefully handling the pages. "This is how a lot of churches used to fundraise. The ladies of the town would all test out recipes and bring their best ones to use in a community cookbook. Then they'd get some local sponsors and sell it."

"So it's like . . . a group project," said Cooper.

"Exactly. A scrapbook. A time capsule, even. Of what life was like in 1939. Hell of a long time ago. Pearl Harbor hadn't been bombed."

"Chuck it?" asked Cricket, pointing to the plastic bin full of random scraps of paper and receipts from doctor's appointments decades ago.

"No," said Cooper instantly. Iris's face flittered into his mind, although he wasn't exactly sure why. "You kidding me? This is, like, a family heirloom."

Cricket leaned over and glanced at the book. "I'm not planning on making salmon loaf anytime soon."

"I had salmon loaf in Seattle once," Ivan mused. "With thyme. And dill . . ."

Cooper looked at the book in his hands. He had absolutely no reason to keep this cookbook, but he was going to. That was decided. There are moments when you don't know why something is important, just that it is. Fate could be like that.

"HELLO?" COOPER STUCK his head awkwardly into the entrance of the church. The foyer? He wasn't sure what the big room outside the main church-y room was called. Annabelle had been the churchgoer. Ivan only prayed when he needed to find a parking spot, and Cooper had adopted that philosophy. Sometimes in college, he'd seen the Jesuits walking to chapel between classes, and he'd wonder why they had decided on the career path they had.

Morning Mass was long over. It was completely silent except for the muffled sound of Cooper's feet walking across the red carpet. And creepy as hell. The statue of Mary in the corner seemed like it was glaring at him.

"Hello?"

He jumped about a foot in the air. There was the priest, the one his age, coming out of a small office.

"Hey," the priest said, sounding surprised. "We've met."

Cooper nodded. "Cooper, yeah. The funeral . . ."

"Right. Father Sam. Can I help you? You need something?"

"Um . . . kind of," he said. "I'm looking for the lady that made the pie for my mom's funeral." He'd tried to call the number on the Airbnb sheet that Iris had left, but it had just rung and rung before informing him the voice mail was full. Those idiot Calbergs still didn't have their cabin ready, so they were going to need to stay another night. He was hoping she'd just let them stay till they left next week. No point in moving all their stuff over for just a few nights.

But he'd also wanted to get a hold of her grandmother. He'd googled Mildred Robertson, but there were 5,100,000 results—it was too common a last name. He knew Annabelle's mom was Alice, but that was it. He had a feeling that Esther the Pie Lady would be able to tell him who, exactly, Mildred was. Then, when Cricket handed the cookbook down to her kid or whatever, she'd know whose it was. Or maybe he'd keep it. A small Annabelle souvenir all his own. Cricket had wanted to put it in the trash, after all. And Cricket had gotten so much of Annabelle. She'd gotten Mother's Day parties in kindergarten and a mom in the audience at her ballet recitals and someone to eat dinner with every single night of her entire damn life, so maybe she could give Cooper this one stupid thing.

"Esther?" said Father Sam. "Yeah, that's a legendary pie. Guessing you have your own family recipes, though, huh?" He grinned, but Cooper didn't return it.

"She around?" he said. "She work here or something?"

"Work here?" asked Father Sam. "No. She's a volunteer. Those ladies make food for every funeral. We aren't the kind of church with, like, a staff. I wish. This isn't even my only parish—I've got two more across the lake."

"Well, do you have her number or something?" Cooper asked. "Or, hey—you know anything about this?" He held up the cookbook.

Father Sam looked at it, confused. "St. Anne's? I mean, that's us. But I've never seen that before. Looks super old. I've been a priest for like, two years."

"I think it's a community cookbook, and I'm just trying to find out whose it was," he said. "Mildred Robertson. I think she may have been related to Annabelle . . . I thought maybe Esther could help me."

Father Sam nodded. "Wouldn't be a bad place to start. Esther's been around this church for ages. I mean, not as long as that book, by the looks of it, but she may know something."

"So . . . her number?"

"Sure." He opened the text. "Give me yours, and I'll send it to you."

Cooper opened the message from Father Sam and added the shared ESTHER LARSON contact. "Thanks."

"Hey . . . you okay? I mean—that's dumb. Your mom, and all. But I heard you were going to be your sister's new guardian. That's a lot. You ever need to talk . . ."

Cooper nodded. "Yeah, sure." Why was everyone constantly trying to get him to talk about shit? "We're heading out, Cricket and I. Early next week. Back to Milwaukee."

"Oh, sweet," Father Sam said. "Well, you got my number. Just let me know if you need anything else these next few days."

"Will do. Thanks for the phone number."

Nine

As Iris pulled up to her grandmother's house, she wasn't surprised to see a couple of cars in the driveway. She recognized Carlotta's battered pickup and Bea's Honda with the bumper sticker that read *Sweet Old Lady? Try Battle-Tested Warrior Queen*. But she hadn't expected to see Cooper walking out Esther's front door, holding a book and a brownie.

"You again," she said.

"*You* again."

"What are you doing here?"

"I had to ask your grandma something. I'm sorry. Hey, by the way—I tried to call . . ."

"Calbergs," she said with an eye roll. "Redstone is yours for as long as you want it."

"We'll pay whatever the rate is. Double. You should overcharge Ivan. He's an idiot," Cooper said.

That made Iris laugh, but of course he wasn't an idiot. You couldn't work your way up to the kind of brand Ivan had by being an idiot. He was surely filthy rich, though, and she had no problem exploiting his desperation for extra cash. *His wife died,* the good angel that sat on her shoulder reminded her. *La-la-la.* It was getting easier and easier to ignore that thing.

"He leaves today, yeah? Or, left?" she asked.

Cooper shook his head. "Canceled flight. He's stuck here two more days."

"Got it."

"Stuck here . . . that sounded dumb. That's not what I meant."

"Oh, believe you me, I get it. Been stuck here my whole life, except when I was at UW," she lied. It felt lame, admitting that parts of her heart lived in the lake, floating among the lily pads that outlined a path for boats every spring. She wasn't stuck. She could go wherever she wanted.

"Did you go to school in Madison?"

"La Crosse," she said. "What'd you have to ask my grandma about? The pie?"

Cooper laughed. And look, all she'd say was this: she wouldn't mind if he laughed again. He was . . . she had *eyes,* was all. She liked his laugh. She liked that she made him laugh. She liked his dark hair and the way his forearms looked, crossed in front of him. She liked—

This was what happened when you lived in a town the size of a sneeze. A male even remotely close to her own age crossed the city line, and it was like she couldn't contain herself. Well, except Father Sam—the collar was a good reminder that he wasn't exactly available.

"No," he said. "I should, though. Damn good pie. Sell it to Ivan, ha. I found this book, in my mom's stuff." He held up a faded leather book.

"Oh, cool." It *did* look cool, and old, too. He carried it like it was important, as if someone might race by and snatch it from him at any minute.

"Yeah, it's—they called it a community cookbook. I was hoping Esther could tell me a little more about it."

"Was she helpful?"

"Super," said Cooper excitedly. "So . . . let me show you." He carefully opened the book and flipped to a page where a recipe was labeled *Mildred Robertson.* "That was Annabelle's grandma. Esther actually knew her from church. Her daughter was Alice, and *her* daughter was Annabelle."

"Your mom."

"Yeah," he said. "Cricket thought this thing was totally stupid. But I feel like one day, she'll be glad we kept something of her great-grandmother's."

"For sure," said Iris. "You don't always notice that stuff when you're a kid. My dad's mom used to write for the *Lakeland Times,* and he saved all of these old newspapers. I used to be like, 'Why? Recycle bin's right there.' But now . . ."

"You want your history," said Cooper.

"*Exactly,*" she said. They grinned at each other. "So . . . a bunch of women got together and made a cookbook?"

"Yeah," responded Cooper. "Esther said it was actually before her time. It was made in 1939. But they did it to raise money for a new parish hall."

Iris laughed. "These days, we'd make a GoFundMe. Or just find the richest dude at church and name the hall after him."

"Right? Anyway. Just thought it was cool. She has a couple of friends over and they told me a little about Mildred. It was nice."

"The funeral ladies . . . they can be a handful."

He laughed. "They were nice. But I think 'handful' is a good word for it. What are you doing here? Just being world's best granddaughter?"

Iris opened her mouth. She should lie, surely she should lie. She should—

"Iris Frances Kelleher, what the hell are we going to do with that grandmother of yours?"

Katharine Rose was hurrying over from next door. *Oh, crap. Oh—*

Katharine Rose let out a whistle. One high note, one low note— the international sign of attractive men and embarrassing the youth. Iris's religion was a mix of Catholicism and begging God to get her out of holes she'd dug her way into, so she hoped he was listening as she mentally demanded he suck her into a different space-time continuum.

"I don't know who's better looking, you or the movie star," Katharine Rose said cheerfully to Cooper. "I recognize you from the funeral. What are you still doing in town, now that your sweet mama's been laid to rest?"

"Um." Cooper glanced between her and Iris.

"Katharine Rose, Cooper," said Iris, nodding at them. "Cooper, this is Esther's neighbor and henchwoman, Katharine Rose."

"Hi," said Cooper. "Nice to meet—"

Katharine Rose turned on Iris. "And what, exactly, do you think we're going to do about your grandma's conundrum?"

Iris glanced at Cooper. She wanted him to leave. She wanted him to laugh again. She wanted to find Hazel and wring his or her damn neck.

He was frozen in place. Katharine Rose could do that to you. There was a reason Esther was the one who usually talked to the families at funerals.

"Well, I'm not sure," Iris said. "But we'll figure something out."

"Something I can do to help?" asked Cooper.

"No," said Iris. "Just—the stuff I told you about the other night. That's all."

"The other night?" asked Katharine Rose, her eyes sparkling.

"Nothing!" Iris insisted. "I had to go fix the outhouse door for him at Redstone."

"Speaking of that . . . thanks for letting us stay," he said, nodding at Iris. "You just—you let me know how you want to settle the bill. We really appreciate it. Take care."

Iris gave him a nod. She watched as he got into his car and started it up, peering carefully over his shoulder as he backed out of Esther's curvy driveway. Her heart panicked for a moment, because— what if this was the last time she ever saw him? She didn't know why that seemed like such a horribly big deal, but it did. And then he was gone.

She followed Katharine Rose into Esther's. Carlotta and Bea were already there, sipping old-fashioneds. God, these women could put away the liquor. It wasn't even 3 P.M.

"Iris, get over here and let me look at you," shouted Bea. She'd always been a little deaf.

"Is that my long-lost granddaughter?" Esther said. "My golly, it's been years."

"Not even forty-eight hours," said Iris. She leaned over to give Esther a hard kiss on the cheek. "You girls behaving?"

"We're brainstorming," said Carlotta. "And praying for the souls of our grandchildren."

"Don't you have a direct line to the heavenly Father by now?" said Iris.

Carlotta waved her hand. "If I did, Riley would still be going to Mass instead of tending bar and marrying a Southern Baptist."

"A Southern Baptist?" said Katharine Rose, helping herself to a cocktail. "Aren't they the dry ones?"

"She has a *spiritual life coach* now," said Carlotta. "Told her to just follow her heart, and she said her heart led her to Wallace Wilber the third in Birmingham. I swear. Don't let your grandchildren out of your sight."

"More like it led her to marry an anesthesiologist so she can spend the rest of her days doing *pie-lattes,*" said Katharine Rose.

"That's my grandbaby you're talking about, ma'am," said Carlotta. "Watch the mouth."

Katharine Rose zipped her lips with an imaginary zipper and toasted the other women with her amber glass.

"Well, I came to check on you, but I see it's been covered," said Iris.

"You're the second hot young visitor we've had," said Bea.

Carlotta rolled her eyes. "They'll put you in prison, talking like that. He's a baby. Younger than some of your grandchildren, probably."

"Hubba-hubba," sang Bea, shimmying.

Katharine Rose pointed at Iris. "He was laughing with this one outside."

All at once, four eagle-eyed old ladies turned to look at her. Her nonexistent love life was one of this group's favorite conversations. She'd once gone on a Bumble date just because the guy looked ridiculous and she thought he'd make a good story for the funeral ladies.

"We *weren't*—he was asking about the Airbnb. He's crashing at that new cabin I bought," said Iris. "A Calbergs incident. Grandma here took pity on him."

"Let's kidnap him and extort Ivan Welsh for twenty grand. That could work," said Katharine Rose.

"Katharine Rose, you're a Christian woman," gasped Esther.

"Iris can be the bait," Carlotta cackled. She and Katharine Rose high-fived, laughing as they missed on their first try.

"I extorted a man once. In Cuba, back when that was allowed," said Bea.

"Cuban tourism, or extortion?" asked Iris.

"Iris, my girl," said Esther, "don't worry about your grandmother. I don't need you checking up on me. Did Fran send you?"

"We're *concerned*, Grandma," said Iris. "That's all."

Carlotta leaned over and turned up the radio, where Kenny Chesney was singing about a sexy tractor. "He was asking about his great-grandmother. That woman—she ran that church, believe that. Mildred Robertson. Like we could forget her!"

"She taught our catechism class," said Katharine Rose. "Let's just say she wasn't a nun, but she had the knuckle-rapping thing down."

Esther handed Iris a beer, and she took it.

"You know . . . that book has me thinking," said Iris. "What about a fundraiser?"

"A *fundraiser*?" Esther said. She acted as if Iris had said "walrus." Or "checkerboard." Or "tae kwan do."

"You know! To raise money! Grandma, we can't lose this house. This house, it's . . ."

"One of a kind," said Carlotta.

"The essence of *Esther Larson*," said Bea.

"At least three college educations," said Katharine Rose.

"Exactly," said Iris. "And more than that . . . it's *home*."

Esther shook her head. "Ask for money? That's ridiculous."

Iris knew this wasn't how things were done in the Northwoods. You simply handled your business. People would tell you what size deer they shot and how many DUIs they had before they'd mention they were maybe having a bit of money trouble.

Well, when business couldn't be handled, sometimes you had to call in backup.

"We should help one another out," Iris said.

"What?" asked Esther. She pulled out a bag of Ruffles and began to pour them into a bowl. Why she had to get a bowl dirty when people could just stick their hands in the bag, Iris wasn't quite sure.

"That's what you said, the other night at Mom's," Iris reminded her. "That we're helpers. We have to help each other out."

"I didn't say that," said Esther.

"*Sounds* like you," said Bea. "You got any of that French onion dip?"

"In the fridge."

"You did, too," insisted Iris. "When Mom was talking about her client, remember?"

"Great," said Esther. "So I'm the grown woman who can't pay her own bills?"

"No. You're the grown woman who is loved," said Iris.

"We've been telling her this," said Katharine Rose. "And she's not listening. We told her earlier we had to raise the money. That's the only option."

"And what, exactly, do you think we could do that would raise twenty thousand dollars?" asked Esther. "I believe a lemonade stand was mentioned."

Iris wasn't one of those people who saw the Virgin Mary in lattes. Esther or her mom could see a rainbow in the sky and insist it was a wink from God. Her high school math teacher used to say that Jesus sent him messages over Facebook (he wound up institutionalized, the poor guy). That wasn't her.

But she knew a sign when she saw one.

"A cookbook," she said.

"Now *that's* an idea," said Bea, slapping the counter and wincing at the pain.

Carlotta scooped some of the French onion dip into a ceramic bowl Olivia had made Esther in grade school. *I love you, Grandma* was written on it in lumpy purple paint. "Very vintage. I like that."

A cookbook made by the women in this very room. Decades of experience making meals for people in moments of grief and moments of joy. Appetizers, salads, desserts—all of it. Everyone in town knew Esther, and everyone had eaten her pie while mourning some second cousin. They owed her this, in a way; all she'd ever done was cook for other people, and it was time she got paid for it. Iris's brain started to whir. The Gen Z in her coughed, shook out its tired limbs. They would need some publicity. An Instagram account, maybe. Definitely a Pinterest. A friend of hers from college was interning with Anderson Cooper. Another was a production assistant on *The Great British Baking Show*. They could—

"Problem," said Bea. "We don't write our recipes down. I make my Jell-O salad by heart. That's the way I've done it for seventy-five years."

"First of all, nice try—you aren't seventy-five. Second of all, there's a first time for everything," said Katharine Rose. "We can test them, even. Like on TV."

"Get some sponsors in town," mused Iris. "Everyone will pitch in, I bet. If we got some advertisers, that could cover our printing costs."

"It'll be huge!" said Carlotta. "Bigger than the movie star in Iris's Airbnb, even. Riley got me his newest cookbook for Christmas last year. Like I need some Hollywood idiot telling me how to make mashed potatoes."

"I saw that at Barnes and Noble. There's an entire chapter about eating *organic,*" said Katharine Rose, giving the word a weird accent that was probably meant to sound Italian. Iris snickered. The funeral ladies grouped organic devotees in with PETA activists, war criminals, and people who bought designer shoes. One time Iris's dad had accidentally brought plant-based queso to a cookout at Esther's, and they'd acted as if he'd murdered an entire village.

"I cannot just let everyone around me bail me out of a jail I put myself in," said Esther.

"Too late," said Katharine Rose. "Now, pour me another old-fashioned, Iris. We have work to do."

Ten

"Saving the grease?"

Cooper jumped. Ivan was behind him, walking into the kitchen.

"Uh. Yeah." Cooper shook his head. "I don't know why. Not like I'm going to drive it back to Milwaukee."

"Because bacon grease is the world's most underrated ingredient," said Ivan, with a half smile.

Cooper hated doing things Ivan had taught him to do. But it was in him, as simple as breathing or blinking. Make bacon—save the grease. There were no better pancakes than ones fried in bacon grease.

He finished siphoning the grease into a small Tupperware container that had previously held deviled eggs. They were officially out of funeral food. He and Cricket were planning on heading to the storage unit, packing up the last few boxes, and taking off. They'd drop Ivan off at the airport on their way.

"You seen Cricket?" asked Cooper.

Ivan reached over and grabbed a piece of bacon, crunching down on it. "It's a little crispy."

"I like it that way," said Cooper testily.

"If you're going to crisp it up more evenly, you really want a higher tempe—"

"Ivan, Jesus Christ. Have you seen Cricket?"

"She's on the porch," he said, nodding toward the back door.

Cooper pulled on a hoodie that was hanging on the back of the couch and ducked outside, away from the smoky bacon smell.

"Hey," he said when he found Cricket. "What are you doing out here?"

She didn't answer, just kept staring forward.

"Hey, Crick?"

His sister turned to him, and then he noticed her eyes. Wet and teary.

"Oh, bug."

She let out a little sob, and he immediately threw his arm around her and pulled her in. "This sucks. This is just so awful, isn't it." A loon on the lake sang out, and they sat there for a few minutes, just listening to Cricket's sniffles and the waves splashing onto the shore.

She mumbled something into his sweatshirt. He pulled back a bit. "What?"

"I don't want to leave."

"I know," he said.

"It feels like a bubble here. I just want to . . . stay here."

He nodded. "I get that. But—"

"Can we stay? Please, Cooper. For a few more weeks?"

He raised his eyebrows. "Cricket, I gotta get to work . . ."

"No, you don't," she said bluntly. Well, she wasn't wrong. The $18.25 an hour he made at the diner was basically hobby money. Ivan's bank automatically sent his landlord a check every month. He was probably supposed to feel embarrassed about that, but if Ivan wanted to buy away his bad-dad guilt every month, Cooper would collect.

"We can't avoid the real world forever," he said. "Your friends, Sophie . . ."

"Not forever. Just not yet. Please."

He sighed. Dr. Hoss would probably say this was the wrong decision. Normalcy: That was supposed to be the goal. They'd have to join the world again eventually.

But as he looked out over Musky Lake, he thought, *Shit*. Why *did* they have to go back? They didn't, not really. He technically didn't have to be back to work until September. He could find Cricket a therapist who would do Zoom calls. All this fresh air had to be good for grief. If Ivan would hurry up and leave, it would be peaceful, even. He'd have to see if they could stay at the cabin.

"Let me see about the cabin," he said. "For a couple more weeks. Maybe go back Labor Day. School probably starts that Tuesday . . ."

She nodded, wiping her eyes. "Sorry to—you know. Bawl at you."

"Don't be an idiot. Let me talk to Ivan."

She nodded, and he escaped back inside. Ivan was standing there, calmly eating more bacon.

"Thought it was too crunchy," Cooper said.

"It's fine." He cleared his throat. "I—I have to tell you something."

"Give me a sec. I gotta make a call." Multiple calls. First, to Iris. They couldn't stay if they didn't have a roof over their heads. She'd already been so generous.

"Cooper. Listen—I heard your sister, and . . . I'm going to stay, too."

Cooper just stared at him. He looked old. He *was* old, but he looked even older, somehow, especially without the famous beard. Frail, almost.

"Ivan," he said slowly, "you can't stay."

"Why not?"

"Um, your *job*? Aren't you supposed to be in Istanbul tomorrow?"

"Abu Dhabi. I canceled it."

"You—"

"Well, pushed it back. We're just pausing production for a bit."

"That's not how these things work," said Cooper, his voice just on the edge of frustration. He knew this, of course, because Ivan had missed every significant event of Cooper's entire life in order to make a production schedule. *That's not how these things work*—wasn't that the exact phrase Ivan had used when he told Cooper he couldn't make his high school graduation because he had to be in Zimbabwe? *That's not how these things work*—surely he couldn't redo his schedule so that Saturday mornings were free for Cooper's soccer games.

Ivan didn't answer at first. He looked down at his bacon. "I'm staying," he said. "Not for long. Just a few weeks."

"*Why?*" A few more weeks in Wisconsin with his sister sounded calming. A few more weeks in Wisconsin with his father sounded like hell.

"To be with you and Cricket."

Cooper just stared at him.

"Is this, like, a midlife crisis?" Cooper asked. "A guilt thing?"

Ivan just shrugged.

"Because, listen—Cricket needs stability right now. Her mom's *dead*."

"Yes, Cooper, I'm aware my wife died."

"Your wife? Your *wife*?" Cooper laughed. "When was the last time you saw her?"

"I've made a lot of mistakes. I've done shitty things. Nobody's giving me Family Man of the Year awards. That what you're waiting for me to say?" Ivan was getting angry, his thinning eyebrows bunching in the middle.

Cooper barked out a laugh and shook his head, walking over to the sink. He had to clean that bacon pan or it would get gross. "Whatever. Do what you want."

"Thanks for the permission."

Cooper wished Annabelle were here. Another person who could just be on his side, calm the tension. Even though she always forgave Ivan—*always*. She was way too forgiving. She'd welcome him back, again and again, even though he'd been God knows where doing God knows what, even though the paparazzi had published pictures of him and that actress in Sicily. What would she say about this? Maybe that was why Ivan was doing it: dead wife, crisis of conscience. Ivan brought out the worst in people, but Annabelle brought out the best. Too little, too late. Cooper wanted him gone.

He went back out front and pulled out his phone to call Iris.

COOPER HAD—WELL, he'd always had luck with girls. That's all he was saying.

It could be narrowed down to his looks. Guys who know they're good-looking can be real dicks about it, but Cooper never was. At least, he tried not to be. But he knew that his dad wasn't famous just because of his broiling technique, and he knew he wasn't voted prom king in high school just because of the way he held doors open for people.

The famous-dad thing didn't hurt, either.

There was Vanessa in high school, who'd written weird poetry on Mondays and taken tequila shots on Fridays. The volleyball player in college—how terrible was it that he couldn't even remember her name? A series of quick girlfriends just after graduation, all shrugged off with the honest truth that he wasn't *looking for anything serious*. Meghan and Mia and Morgan, one after the other.

Since the—the incident—the shooting—he never knew what to call it. Since *North Harbor,* he'd avoided anything that even remotely looked like a date. That didn't mean he'd avoided everything—he was a *guy,* after all. But.

Sitting there at some rinky-dink Northwoods coffee shop across from Iris, he could almost be convinced that *falling in love* existed. Because if that wasn't what he was feeling, what was it, exactly? He'd seen plenty of attractive girls. Plenty of confident ones, too. But this one felt different. And he shouldn't be thinking that, probably, since he barely knew her. But even the way she sipped her coffee seemed beautiful. She took it black, which impressed Cooper. Her grandmother had taught her to drink her coffee black, she'd explained. Esther thought fancy coffee made someone "difficult." That seemed like a major no-no up here, doing anything that might inconvenience anyone else. It was so different from Los Angeles, where everyone walked around as if they might bestow upon you the honor of doing them a favor. Different from Milwaukee, too. Once you crossed Highway K, some magical fend-for-yourself fairy must whack people on the head. These people still believed in pulling yourself up by your bootstraps, that was for damn sure. He had the feeling mentioning white privilege might get him shot, considering everyone also had a gun.

"It's insane," she was saying. Cooper nodded.

"If she loses that house . . . I mean, that house means so much to my family," she said. "*So* much, and . . . sorry. I'm sorry! I'm talking your ear off."

"*I* invited *you* here," he reminded her. "I don't mind my ear being talked off. It's the least I can do, after you said we can still crash at your place."

"I'm charging your dad through the roof," she said. "That bill alone is going to pay for the screened porch I wanted to add. Or a month of my grandma's mortgage."

"Good," Cooper said.

"But I guess I owe you. I mean, you're the one who gave us the cookbook idea," said Iris.

A little bell rang—someone new walking in. The elderly woman came over and kissed Iris on the head, hard, and she laughed.

"Another friend of my grandma's," she muttered as the woman went up to the counter to order. "Esther knows everyone, I'm telling you."

"You should sell a lot of cookbooks, then," he said, raising his eyebrows.

"I mean, here's hoping."

"We'll buy some. For sure. And I can probably convince Ivan to

Instagram about it. He has like, a billion followers." Cooper took a long sip of his coffee. It wasn't enough. Of course it wasn't enough. Ivan had three houses. But Iris just smiled at him.

"That would be amazing. Let me ask her about it. I don't usually . . . I'm not the kind of person who asks for favors. But my grandma is literally a saint on earth."

"I don't think you can literally be a saint on earth. Isn't the definition of saint to be in heaven?"

Iris laughed. "Okay. I use 'literally' like the Gen Z-er I am. You get what I mean."

Someone dropped a coffee cup.

Someone dropped a coffee cup, and a waiter rushed over, with a towel, and—

Someone dropped a coffee cup, and it was fine, it was fine, it was fine—

Someone dropped a coffee cup, and—

Help—

Help me—

Damn it damn it damn it damn it damn it—

"Are you—are you feeling okay?" Iris asked. She was ten million miles away.

And suddenly, he was there, in North Harbor, on Main Street, smelling coffee and cold air, and there was the girl, reaching for him, and she's bleeding, and—

"Cooper? Are you going to throw up? Do you need some water?" Iris said quietly. "You're . . ."

Help—

Help me—

He should text Dr. Hoss. That was for sure.

Inhale, exhale, and he was back. See? He had a handle on things. He was in Northern Latte's, a coffee shop in Ellerie. And sitting in front of him was Iris Kelleher, a girl renting him an Airbnb. There were flickers of The Girl—he didn't say her name, didn't even like to think it—but she was gone, and now it was Iris, and he was fine. He had this.

But Iris was looking at him in a way that—well. Didn't feel great. Like he was some kind of crazy person who just disappears. And he needed a minute to catch his breath.

"Sorry. I just had . . . my head hurt for a second," he said. He didn't need to call Dr. Hoss. He was fine. It took him a second, but he was fine.

"Okay. You freaked me out," she said. "Do you need an aspirin? I might have some . . ."

"No," he said quickly. "No, I'm good. I have some crap to do, though . . . a few more boxes of Annabelle's to go through. So I should take off."

"Okay," she said, nodding. "I'm going to stay here and do some client work. But seriously, you guys can be in the house as long as you need."

Outside, he took deep breaths as he walked back to the Tesla, gulping down the crisp Northwoods air. It smelled like pine, and tasted like lake water. He felt it fill up his lungs and clear them out, pushing away memories of anything but how pretty Iris looked when she laughed.

Eleven

"Thanks, Kit," Iris told the hardware store owner, reaching over to shake his hand. "We appreciate your business."

He grunted. Kit was a man of few words. But Iris had said ". . . to help Esther," and he'd purchased a full-page ad in a cookbook that was being distributed in a town with exactly one hardware store. Esther, he'd explained, had made a giant pot of barbecue when his daughter got sick a few years back, and three pies besides. Plus, she always saved him the jelly-filled doughnuts after Sunday Mass, tucking one into a napkin for him. She was *good people*.

Iris had been hitting the pavement all day, trying to drum up support for the cookbook. She couldn't exactly contribute ribs or rice pilaf, but she had a mind for business—at least, she liked to think so. She didn't share about the house hanging in the balance; Esther would have died from embarrassment, and that was her business. But she did imply that Esther's project was important, and that they really needed the support. And all day, she'd been hearing story after story about her grandmother. She'd learned that when Jinger at Northern Latte's had broken her leg and couldn't work for a few weeks, Esther had made all the bakery items for the coffee shop without being paid a cent. She'd learned that when Crosby at Lakeside Laundromat had first showed up in town, he'd eaten fries from Vernon's for dinner every night until Esther showed up with a trunk full of groceries and told him she was teaching him how to work a grill for himself. She'd learned that when Vernon's wife had that heart attack when Iris was in college, Esther had organized meals for a month from the entire town.

It was the kind of thing you'd read about in a Twitter thread, or some viral reel you'd see on TikTok. But it had all just been happening, quietly—Esther, feeding her town and her people. It made Iris feel completely useless. When friends from high school had babies, she just texted them DoorDash gift cards.

It was something that seemed so strange, this day and age—to have a group of friends, a *community,* who loved you so much, they'd do this for you. Iris thought of her college friends. They'd probably change their Instagram profile picture to a photo of Esther before they'd actually buy an advertisement or a cookbook. *Looking* like you cared was so much more important than actually caring.

But not to the funeral ladies. She remembered after her grandpa died, the way food kept showing up at not just Esther's house, but Fran's. They couldn't stop cooking. Feeding people was their Band-Aid, the thing they knew how to do. Bea's husband, JP, had come over and helped Iris's dad bring the dock in that fall, and Katharine Rose had slept on Esther's couch for two weeks, in case Esther needed something in the middle of the night.

She had one more stop on her list: the pottery store. Delilah—or as everyone in town called her, Grumpy Delilah—had scared the bejeezus out of Iris ever since she was a kid. Once, her elbow had grazed a vase while her grandmother picked out a new dinner set, and Delilah had acted as if she'd burned the place to the ground. Her son Joe, who used to work in her shop, had given Iris a sucker and a silent *sorry* with a wince. To this day, Delilah seemed to look at Iris and think: *Bad seed.* Delilah had always seemed impossibly old, older than was allowed, with deep wrinkles and hard, cold eyes. How she made such beautiful pots and bowls, Iris didn't know. It seemed impossible that someone could screech that loudly at a kid brushing against a vase and still create such colorful art.

Iris pushed open the door as gently as she could, trying to give off *mature-adult* vibes as the bell tinkled. Delilah stomped out of her back office and gave Iris a look that clearly said *You be careful.*

"Hi, Miss Delilah," said Iris nervously. "Um—you remember me, right? Esther Larson's granddaughter . . ."

Delilah nodded gruffly. "You need a gift, or what?"

"Um." Iris took a breath. *Confidence,* she reminded herself. *Calm, collected grace.* "I actually wanted to talk to you about something."

"Whatever you're selling, I ain't buying," she said with a wave of her hand.

Iris's carefully curated speech came out in a rush of words, a jumble and tangle of begging mixed with convincing. She couldn't help herself—more words came out of her mouth, words she hadn't told any of the other business owners. Words about the house, and Hazel, and the whole ugly story. Something about *cookbook* and *Esther* and *ad buy* and *people pitching in* and—

So much for calm, collected grace. More like hot mess.

Delilah held up a hand. "Stop," she said flatly.

Iris froze. They stood in silence for a minute. Should she apologize? Leave? Back away slowly, being careful not to nudge a vase?

"I'll do the biggest package you got," muttered Delilah. "The double-page thingamajig."

Iris swallowed hard. "You—you will?"

Delilah walked to the window of the shop and looked out. It didn't seem like she was looking at the thick tangle of trees in front of her store, or the weathered maroon *Delilah's Pottery* sign.

"Joe had some problems," she said quietly. "Not with the drugs, but with the . . ." She tapped her head. Iris had no idea what she was talking about. "Saw some things, after college. Don't ask me what. It's none of your business. But Felix—Felix always took care of him.

Took him to lunch. Helped him . . . do whatever it is men do, I guess. Said their novenas together and whatnot. Felix understood. Felix got it. Joe said if it wasn't for Felix—well. Let's not think about that."

Iris nodded slowly.

"You take cash?" Delilah asked.

That night, Iris went over her spreadsheet. They had more sponsors than they needed to pay for the printing. Their expenses would be zero.

All these people—this army of Ellerians, lined up to go to battle for Esther. It could make a girl's heart sing. Iris felt like she'd accomplished something more than a logo; like she'd been a *part* of something. Maybe this could be her future. Was there such a job as a professional old-lady helper?

And her grandpa, too. It felt like he was contributing. It felt like that little story from Grumpy Delilah wasn't small at all, but a treasure. A wink from her grandpa, and a piece of his story, too.

She was hungry. She'd forgotten to eat lunch, and now it was past dinnertime. She got out a box of cereal, then stared at it for a moment before putting it back in the pantry and grabbing the small metal recipe box Esther had given her a few Christmases ago instead. Something in her felt like cooking.

Twelve

"This official meeting of the funeral ladies has come to order," said Katharine Rose.

"Thank Padre nobody gave her a gavel," muttered Carlotta.

Esther chuckled. They were sitting around Carlotta's kitchen island, and Bea was mixing them drinks. Katharine Rose had her iPad in front of her. Esther had been forbidden from using technology, as if she were a child.

She couldn't believe what Hazel had done. It just seemed beyond cruel. She still wasn't as convinced as everyone else seemed to be that the girl was really a truck driver or a crime lord. But either way, to not write Esther back and explain why she hadn't paid her back was just rude. It wasn't as if she'd sent the girl ten dollars. It had been substantial. She still prayed for her and her baby every week after Mass, which she knew her girls wouldn't understand. But it was a difficult thing, to be a mother in this world. She knew that better than anybody.

"We can't just do our recipes. They remind people of death," said Carlotta.

Esther looked at the spreadsheet Katharine Rose had handed her. The goal was written across the top in bright red marker: *twenty thousand dollars*. What a number. Fran and Aaron had written her a check for the rest, and she would never get over her embarrassment. She felt like her 4-F father, shame clinging to his bones like dirt. Felix would never have accepted their money, but she thought of how he'd loved driving the girls around in the boat, and prayed he'd be all right with it.

The spreadsheet listed sections, just like a real cookbook—desserts, casseroles, meats . . .

"That's why I've been asking around town. Half of Ellerie owes me a favor," said Katharine Rose smugly. "And the other half owes Esther. I've made chicken cacciatore for every single person in this town's dead grandmother."

Katharine Rose had been the CEO of a Fortune 500 company in another life. Or at least, that's what Esther would have thought, if Catholics believed in such things. She'd taken charge of the cookbook with all the gusto of one of those women on the cover of business magazines. But really—wasn't running a household with three boys a requirement for organization and details? People these days thought women who worked on computers and bossed around boardrooms were the only ones with such skills. But Esther thought of her own mother, a farmer's wife. She hadn't had any brothers, so her mom had had to pitch in much more than the average woman. She'd milked and hauled and harvested, leaving her biceps thick and perfect for twirling Esther around.

Their old farm was now a subdivision with a giant *Jon Ebert Homes* sign in front of it. She hadn't been back in years. Every time she drove by, it made her sad. But those family farms were hard to keep up without piles of siblings to divvy up the labor.

As she looked around her kitchen table, she wondered if she hadn't just found a rowdy gang of sisters a bit later in life.

"We've also been invited to the Trinity Church women's luncheon this weekend," said Katharine Rose. "I watered Patty Clarkson's flowers that summer she went on the mission trip to Asia. We can ask them to contribute recipes."

"Any luck with the sponsors?" asked Carlotta.

"Iris is on it," said Katharine Rose.

"Iris?" asked Esther, surprised. "My Iris?"

"I called her last night. She was more than happy to ask around," said Katharine Rose. "She said she can design us a cover, too."

"Ask around?" said Esther. "Ask around *where*? Not here in town?"

"Yes, here in town," said Carlotta. "Where did you think she'd go, Mexico City?"

"And Father Sam said we could announce the book after Sunday Mass," said Katharine Rose.

"Sunday Mass? We can't sell things at church!" said Esther, horrified. They might as well have suggested she sell herself on a street corner.

"We most certainly can," disagreed Carlotta. "I think we need to aim for the Christmas Walk. Those FIBs—"

"Oh, don't call them that, Carlotta. It's so trashy," said Esther with a wince.

"It's what they are," said Bea, clinking the ice around in her glass. "One of them ran over my curb the other night and took out my rosebush."

"Those *Illinois* people, they'll be excited to bring home a real piece of the Northwoods," said Carlotta confidently. The Christmas Walk was the day after Thanksgiving, when all the stores on Main Street would stay open late and serve cookies and cocoa. Esther had loved the Christmas Walk when Fran was little, and then when Olivia and Iris came around, too. It was the kind of thing that made you feel lucky to live in a small town.

"That gives us a little over four months," said Katharine Rose.

Esther shook her head. She couldn't believe Katharine Rose had told Father Sam. The *betrayal*! Worrying a clergyman about her own silly mistakes. He had souls to save. He didn't need to be fretting about Esther and her house.

"I talked to Jerry over at FedEx in Washport," Katharine Rose said. "His wife just had twins! Anyway, if we want to make twenty thousand dollars, we'll need to sell a thousand copies at twenty dollars each. To get a thousand printed, they'll have to send the order out. So we'll need a draft over there a month before-hand."

"There aren't a thousand people in Ellerie," Carlotta pointed out.

"Tourist season! Gifts for others . . . we can do this, ladies," said Katharine Rose, using the same voice she'd used when she and Esther had had to spatchcock the Thanksgiving turkey the year before in order to fit it into the church's oven. As if determination could break a bird's spine and yank it out, even though all they'd had was a dull knife from the St. Anne's kitchen drawer.

Olivia had tried to convince her to just start a GoFundMe. It'd go viral, she insisted. A kind old lady who volunteered at a church? But the way she'd said it . . . it made Esther's skin crawl. *The kind old lady,* who was an idiot. *The kind old lady,* who needed a handout. Felix has been a conservative his entire life, up until the end, when he started believing every politician was full of baloney. Saying "handout" in these parts was akin to asking Stalin himself to show up on your door with a hammer-and-sickle T-shirt.

No, if they were going to *do* this, they'd have to provide a product. Something of value. And Esther didn't know much, but she knew her food fed people, not just in their stomachs, but in their souls. Why someone would buy a cookbook when they could just find recipes on Pinterest was a bit beyond Olivia, Esther could tell. But there was something about holding those papers in your hands, turning the pages, and deciding what to make for dinner, or a baptism, or a picnic. There was something about holding recipes in your hand that your grandmother had made, and her grandmother before her.

"Father Sam said he could contribute his mother's lasagna," said Katharine Rose.

But Esther didn't like this. She didn't like it at all.

THAT AFTERNOON, ESTHER went into town.

First, she stopped somewhere she hardly ever went: Trinity Church. Katharine Rose, Bea, and Carlotta met her in the parking lot.

"You ready for this?" asked Katharine Rose, flipping her sunglasses down.

Esther sighed. "You're going to do most of the talking, right?"

"She always does," said Carlotta, and Katharine Rose reached over and punched her in the arm with her flimsy fist. The four of them went in and followed the signs to the St. Luke Center, ignoring Katharine Rose's whisper that Saint Luke was a Catholic— *They must know that, right?*

There was Mrs. Thomas Murphy and her gaggle of friends, drinking lukewarm coffee.

"Our guests of honor," Patty Clarkson said. "You all know Esther, Katharine Rose, Bea, and Carlotta."

"Hello, ladies," said Katharine Rose. "We're here today to talk with you about an exciting new opportunity."

"Is this one of those multilevel marketing schemes? My grandson told me to stay away from anyone trying to sell weight loss shakes," one of the women said, pointing a long finger at them. Well, *she* looked like she needed a weight loss shake, Esther thought, then mentally apologized to the Lord. This was still his house, after all, even if it wasn't Catholic.

"*No*," said Bea. "This is a chance to contribute a recipe to a real-live cookbook. We're creating a community cookbook to capture what life is like in Ellerie County, Wisconsin, at this very moment in time."

Well, *that* got everyone talking.

Carlotta passed around a sign-up sheet, and Esther laughed as Patty told them about the cookbook they'd made when she was a girl.

"I still have a copy," Patty said proudly. "*The Trinity Church Cookbook*. Paid for the new parking lot. My mother and I were in charge of the breakfast section. Back then, we added a note about how if you get your eggs from the grocery store, you need to keep them in the icebox."

They'd gotten quite a few sign-ups. The funeral ladies congratulated themselves in the parking lot before going their separate ways. The rest of the girls drove back down M Road toward their homes, but Esther turned left toward Main Street. She needed a few groceries, and then planned to swing by Jana's nursery to grab some flowers for Felix's grave. It was looking a little lackluster. Bea's sister Mary had died of a heart attack last year, and her grave was always done up in fresh blooms. It made Esther want to keep up, even though she knew that was silly. Every time she went and planted flowers by Felix's grave, she saw her own headstone. The girls thought it was morbid. But if you didn't save your spot in the St. Anne's cemetery, you'd lose it. They'd run out of room eventually, and she knew she wanted to be next to Felix.

It was exactly the kind of beautiful summer day she used to spend with Felix in town. They'd grab coffees at Northern Latte's and pop into a few of the shops, say hello to women they'd known for years selling tea towels and specialty soaps. They'd go walk by the shore, maybe swing by St. Anne's for daily Mass. Felix would make her laugh, telling her stories of himself and his rowdy group of brothers growing up. They'd go home and she'd make a nice dinner while he watched the Brewers, thinking that this was finally their year, and they'd turn on the History Channel in bed while listening to the waves outside.

Oh, it hurt her heart to think of those days.

She parked at Zephyr's and went in, grabbing a shopping cart instead of a basket even though she didn't really need one; it helped her to be able to lean on it when she was on her feet for so long. Zephyr's had changed quite a bit in recent years. It used to be a place for staples: hot dog buns, milk, sugar. If you needed real groceries, or any meat besides a basic chicken breast, you'd have to go all the way to Pick N' Save in Washport. But these days, it had rows and rows of produce, and a full deli. There was even a gluten-free section, which Carlotta mocked, but Esther knew Barbara from church appreciated it, since she had a daughter-in-law with an allergy.

Ellerie in general simply felt bigger, busier. It had always been a tourist town, but summers felt more clogged than usual. There were more Illinois license plates than Wisconsin ones in the parking lot at Zephyr's. She knew a lot of people renting out homes, Iris included.

Aaron had even tossed the idea out to her a few times—of downsizing and renting out the house. She could make quite a bit on it, that she was sure of. But the thought of strangers sleeping in her bed and using her dishes? Strangers sitting on the porch where she'd rocked her daughter and grandchildren, staring out over Lake Ellerie and asking the Virgin for prayers?

Absolutely not.

"Excuse me," she heard someone say. She turned, but the man wasn't talking to her—he was addressing an employee, a high schooler with a stain on his forest-green polo. "You got fresh jalapeños anywhere?"

"Jalapeños are by the pickles," the kid muttered.

"No, not pickled jalapeños. A fresh one."

The kid stared at him, and that's when Esther realized why the man looked familiar. It was Ivan Welsh.

"Never mind," Ivan muttered, and the kid went back to stocking boxes of Apple Jacks.

"You need to go into town for fresh jalapeños," Esther told him. "Washport. They've got a Pick N' Save."

"Thanks," he said. "Appreciate the tip. Wait . . . the woman with the pie."

She smiled. She hadn't expected him to remember her name. It would have been nice if he had, but hey—this was a man with a television show. "Esther Larson."

"Esther Larson. Right. That pie, man . . . I've had a lot of pie. But that was a damn good pie."

"Thank you very much. I'll make you another. I heard you're in town a bit longer."

"Yeah. Spending some time with the kids," he said. "Trying to make tacos for dinner tonight. But the food-buying situation is a bit lacking."

Esther bristled. The people of Ellerie had been eating here just fine for decades, and that was *before* Zephyr's added on an international foods aisle.

But . . . he wasn't exactly wrong. And something about Ivan Welsh here all alone made her sad. These should have been his golden years, and his young wife was already dead. It could have broken her heart.

"One of the funeral ladies, Katharine Rose, grows tomatoes in her backyard. And they're the best in all of Ellerie. I can get you a few."

He nodded slowly. "Wow. Okay. Thanks."

"You just have to know what you're doing, around here," she said.

"I'm getting that impression. You know where I can find ground beef that doesn't come from a factory farm?"

She almost rolled her eyes, but remembered her manners. "You're in farm country. Drive down the road. Brahm's Butcher over in Moose Junction does it the best. Most people in these parts just buy a cow every year and keep it in a deep freezer." Brahm's was a bit expensive, which was why she usually just grabbed whatever cut was on sale at Zephyr's. But someone with a Food Network show could afford it.

He smiled. "You've been extremely helpful, Mrs. Larson."

She waved a hand. "Esther. Don't mention it. I'll bring a pie over in the next few days."

"I appreciate that. You're very kind."

Kind. She tried to be, at least. She'd get some apples—the good ones, from the produce stand Hank Becker set up on weekends. Make an apple pie with extra cinnamon and her famous crust. Maybe drop it off with some ice cream.

Thirteen

"And then," said Cooper, dipping a paintbrush into the can, "she sent them back because the blueberries weren't evenly distributed."

Iris laughed, leaning back into the hammock she'd set up in front of Redstone only a few weeks earlier. "How did you not throw the plate at her?"

"I can be very Zen when I need to be," said Cooper.

Painting the garage door was one of the final things Iris needed to do before listing Redstone on Airbnb; the cracked, peeling paint wouldn't look very good in photos. But when she asked if Cooper minded if she did it that afternoon, he had insisted on helping her. His help had turned into him mostly doing it himself while she sipped a beer. She'd tried to at least do the edges, but painting a straight line on an uneven surface was harder than it looked. Cricket had hung out with them for a bit, but she'd disappeared into the house a while ago.

"I'm giving you guys three free nights for this," Iris said. "I swear."

He shook his head. "You've been so generous to us. Please let me do this. *I'm* the one who owes *you*."

"I'm charging your dad through the nose. Believe me, you owe me nothing. I would have hired someone to come paint the door, but getting someone to come all the way out here is a pain in the ass," said Iris. She'd tried to convince Kit at the hardware store, but he'd wanted two hundred bucks, which felt like a waste. She had to save her favors for the cookbook.

Besides, now she got to watch Cooper do it. And admire the way his tongue poked out the side of his mouth when he concentrated. And listen to his stories about working at half the diners in Milwaukee. And—well, *okay*. He could keep his shirt off, if it was Iris's permission he was looking for. That was just fine with her.

She sounded like Katharine Rose.

"Speaking of your dad, where is he?"

"He had to run into town for something," said Cooper. "Who the hell knows. That man spends more time on his phone than anyone I've ever met. I think they're pissed at him for ditching production. How's the cookbook coming?"

She stretched her legs and wiggled her toes. God, this sun felt good. Summer in Wisconsin should have been on a postcard. At night, the mosquitos were so bad you could barely sit on the deck without a gallon of Off, but during the day, it was hard to feel anything but grateful. "It's coming," she said. "I've found enough sponsors to pay for the printing. We're doing these ads for half the places in town. Which is hilarious, because, like—there's only one hardware store and one grocery store and one coffee shop. They don't exactly need to advertise."

"It's such a cool project," said Cooper. "Seriously."

Iris had actually been enjoying it quite a bit. She'd helped the funeral ladies set up a project management site where they could keep everything organized, although she didn't think any of them actually used it except to post selfies of themselves sticking their tongues out.

"I know. I wish we didn't have to do it, though. If that Twitter idiot was standing in front of me, I swear to God, I'd wring his neck," she said.

Cooper nodded. He set down the paintbrush, being careful not to drip any paint on the driveway, and leaned back on his hands.

"I don't know what kind of evil person could do that to an elderly woman."

"Someone with a special place in hell," muttered Iris.

Honk-honk. Esther's car pulled into the driveway. Iris shielded her eyes from the sun with her hand.

"Grandma?" she called out. "What are you doing here?"

Esther got out of the car clutching a tinfoil-wrapped pie plate. "Just dropping off some pie. I ran into Ivan at Zephyr's and told him I'd bring him one."

"Oh, wow! Thanks!" Cooper stood up, wiping his hands on his jeans.

Esther looked back and forth between Cooper and Iris. *Shit,* Iris thought. Now she'd get it from her mother.

"You should come over for dinner tonight," said Cooper. "I mean—both of you. Sorry, it's weird to invite you to your own house, isn't it? But Ivan's gonna cook something, and now we have dessert . . ."

"Oh, that's kind of you, but don't you worry about it," said Esther. "We'll let you have your family time."

"I insist," said Cooper. "Ivan's—well, he's . . . something. But he's a hell of a cook. Obviously."

Iris grinned at Esther. "You can tell the funeral ladies you had dinner cooked by a Food Network star."

"I've already got some pork chops thawing," said Esther.

"Drop them off at Olivia's. God knows she'll take any free food she can get," said Iris with an eye roll. She wanted to try Ivan Welsh's cooking. And, okay, fine. She wanted to sit next to Cooper. She wanted an excuse for him to see her with something nice on. She wanted to hear him laugh again.

Esther fidgeted. "Well . . ."

"Six o'clock," said Cooper.

"Well—all right. But what can I bring? Let me make a side."

"Grandma, you made the pie," laughed Iris.

"Speaking of . . . I'll stick this inside," said Cooper, heading up the porch steps and letting the front door bang shut behind him.

Esther turned to Iris and wiggled her eyebrows.

"Stop," Iris hissed.

"Nice boy. Likes pie."

"Get," said Iris, waving her hand at her grandmother. "I'll see you tonight. Don't you dare bring anything."

"WHAT DO YOU wear to a date with your grandmother, a Food Network star, and your date's little sister?" mused Olivia, tearing through Iris's closet.

"Stop," said Iris. "It's not a date."

"Grandma said he was, and I quote, 'a real looker.'"

"Grandma thought a stump was a baby bear the other day. She pulled over to take a picture and everything. She shouldn't even be driving."

"She also said he was painting your garage. Ooh la la. No better way to woo them than by asking them to do manual labor."

"Is that how you snagged Kurt?"

"Ha. Yeah. Kurt's idea of manual labor is lifting a really, really heavy stack of library books." Olivia pulled out a copper-colored dress. "What about this?"

"It's kind of short."

"Show some leg," said Olivia. "Let the pregnant among us live vicariously through you."

"Speaking of, how long until baby?"

"Seven weeks. Allegedly. And I hate everything." Olivia held the dress up to herself and looked in the mirror. "Why have you never let me borrow this?"

"I just got it at the beginning of the summer for Ruby's wedding. You think it works?"

Olivia tossed it onto her bed. "Yeah. Or you could do jeans and that sparkly white top you wore to that thing in June."

"I spilled a Bloody Mary on it. It's ruined."

Olivia glanced at her phone. "I've gotta go. I'm covering Mom's Adoration hour. She has one of her headaches."

"Look at you, being a do-gooder," said Iris. "Pray for my soul."

"I told her to ask you, but that was when Grandma informed us about your big dinner. Bow-chika-wow-wow."

"Yeah, we'll make out at the table right in front of Grandma and his family."

Olivia snorted. "You did skip over the whole rebellious-teenager phase. No time like the present."

"Jake Sweeney . . ."

"Sorry. You had a single dalliance over the entirety of your high school experience, before you went to college, lived at the library—"

"College is *for* studying, and news flash, I also had a job."

"I'm just saying!" Olivia held her hands up. "You deserve a fun night out with a hot guy."

"And my grandmother."

"Well. There are worse third wheels," she cracked.

"You think he's hot? Really?"

Olivia reached over and yanked on her sister's ponytail. "Don't ask a married woman such a thing. Goodbye, sister mine."

Iris and Olivia hadn't always been *close*-close, but one sister plus a thirty-minute bus ride to school meant a lot of time talking about books and boy bands. "The Kelleher twins," teachers had called them sometimes, even though they were two years apart. They even had photos in the matching swimsuits Fran had forced them into every summer to prove it. They'd had to share a room growing up, and Iris had counted down the days until Olivia left for college and gave her some space. But that first night alone, in the bedroom downstairs, without her sister's annoying snores and shelf full of swim team trophies, Iris had actually cried.

They'd both come back after college, even though so few others did. More of Olivia's friends than Iris's, but still. Iris couldn't believe

Olivia had convinced a man to move up here, where there was mainly woods and tourists and loons. But Olivia said Kurt liked the open space, and she didn't mind the commute to Waukegan for work.

As her sister waddled out of the house and to her car, Iris tugged on the dress and looked in the mirror. Okay, so she wanted to look nice. Was that a crime? It wasn't like she was chasing after the famous guy's kid. It wasn't like she'd spent most of the afternoon daydreaming about kissing his face off. It wasn't like she'd practically doodled his name in her binder à la seventh grade.

She was so screwed.

Whatever. He'd be gone in a few weeks. She'd be back to saving up money to do . . . something. Maybe finally leave Ellerie. Go on a trip around Europe. Buy more Airbnbs. Figure that out, whatever it was. Her future: a bright, shining thing people had been talking about her entire life. Ever since she won the spelling bee in third grade, it felt like people had dreamed Big Dreams and envisioned Big Plans for her. Well, her future was here. And she wasn't sure what the hell she was supposed to do with it. Olivia had a ninety-minute commute and a sweet husband. Iris had a couple of side hustles and a celebrity staying in her rental property.

She drove over to Redstone and felt weird, walking up to the door and knocking instead of just going in. Esther's car wasn't in the driveway yet.

Cricket answered. "Hey," she said.

"Hi," Iris told her. "Wow, I like your earrings."

Cricket touched her ears, where a pair of dangling moons hung. "Thanks," she said. "They were my mom's."

"Oh," said Iris, not sure what to say. "Well, they're . . . pretty."

Cricket held the door open and Iris stepped in, and, yup, there he was—Ivan Welsh. Stirring something on the stove and whistling.

"Thank you so much for having us," said Iris as Cricket closed the door behind her. "I know my grandma was really excited."

Ivan smiled. "Thanks for coming! You're our guests of honor."

Cooper walked out of his room in a denim shirt with the sleeves rolled up. Even his forearms were hot. She really was turning into Katharine Rose.

"Hey," he said. He seemed happy to see her. *Stop it, Iris.*

"Hey, back," she said.

"Can I grab you a glass of wine? Or—you're more beer, right?"

"I'm anything," Iris assured him.

There was Esther's soft, gentle knock at the door. Cooper turned to answer it.

"Oh, wow! You didn't need to bring anything," Iris heard him say. Esther was clutching a bottle of wine, one of the fancy kinds with a metallic gold label.

"Is that from Otto's?" Iris asked, surprised. That was the touristy liquor store on Main Street.

"Hello to you, too, granddaughter. And yes, it is."

"You don't even drink wine."

"Otto helped me," said Esther defiantly. She'd ignored Iris's insistence on not bringing anything, of course. Esther would sooner show up naked than empty-handed. Iris felt weird showing up without anything to share, but Ivan seemed like the type of guy who wanted to be in control of the kitchen.

Before Iris knew it, they were all seated around the table, drinks full, candles lit. The sun started to disappear behind the lake ever so slightly. It was only mid-August, but when autumn came, it would come quickly.

"This is making me feel like I need a bigger table for this place," said Iris.

"Nah. It's perfect. Cozy," said Cooper.

Ivan was spooning pasta with sauce and garlic and butter onto plates, and man, it smelled good.

"This is such a treat. I don't get cooked for very often," said Esther. "Especially not by a professional."

Ivan smiled. "Well, we're very grateful for Iris letting us stay so unexpectedly. And for the kindness you showed us at the funeral, and afterward."

Esther nodded. "It must have been very difficult for you, losing your wife."

Iris saw Cooper and Cricket exchange a glance.

"It was," said Ivan. "Cracked pepper?"

There were happy eating sounds of forks scraping across plates and people passing garlic bread. Dimmed lights, happiness brimming, wineglasses clinking against one another. Maybe Cooper was right—the table was the perfect size, cozy.

"This is delicious, Ivan," said Iris. He nodded his thanks.

"Is there rosemary in these potatoes?" asked Esther.

"And thyme," Ivan said.

"Well, they are just excellent," hummed Esther happily. "My Felix loved Italian food."

"When did he pass?" Ivan asked kindly.

"Five years ago, now," said Esther. "His lungs gave out."

"I'm sorry to hear that," said Ivan.

"Esther, Iris said the cookbook's going well," said Cooper. Esther looked embarrassed suddenly, and Cooper looked as if he realized his mistake.

"Cookbook?" asked Ivan. "Are you a writer?"

"No," said Esther quickly. "Absolutely not."

"We're creating a community cookbook," said Iris. "Kind of like . . . a vintage thing."

Ivan looked at Cooper. "Like we found in the storage unit?"

"Exactly," said Iris. "Actually . . . Cooper helped me think of it. He gave us the idea, in a way."

"It's just a little project," said Esther. "Nothing fancy."

"Wow. That's very cool," said Ivan. "A community cookbook. Raising money for anything in particular?"

The table was quiet. Iris waited for Esther to deny it, but her grandmother was completely incapable of lying. She just looked around anxiously, waiting for someone to swoop in and save the day.

"No," said Iris. She had no qualms about lying, personally. Especially not for her grandmother. "Just a thing some women from church are doing. It won't be done for a while yet. We're aiming for the Christmas Walk. It's the big holiday celebration in town the day after Thanksgiving."

"Do people still use cookbooks?" said Cricket. "*Ow.*" She glared at Cooper.

"According to my publisher, they do," said Ivan, shrugging. "They just asked when the next one's coming."

Iris could see Esther blushing, and she could read her mind: Ivan was a *real* author. A real cook. Well, says who? Who had cooked more meals for more people over the course of their lifetime? Who had sautéed more green beans and shredded more chicken? Iris's money was on her grandmother.

"Yes," insisted Iris. "They're kind of coming back! Like . . . record players, or something." It was kind of weird, how most of their generation's new, exciting things were just things they'd dragged out of years past and put a little spit shine on.

"So how long are you folks planning on staying?" asked Esther, eager to change the subject.

Cooper helped himself to more scalloped potatoes. "What do you think, Crick? Another week or two? I got you signed up at Divine Savior. School starts the Tuesday after Labor Day, but I'd like to get us back before then."

"I keep telling you," she said, "I can do school online."

"And I keep telling *you*," said Ivan, "you're going to regret that. You need to make friends."

"And I keep telling *both* of you," said Cooper flatly, "that it's up to me, and I'm still thinking about it."

"What about you, Ivan?" asked Iris.

"Oh, we'll see," he said lightly.

"That must be nice, to have so much freedom over your schedule," said Esther. "Cooper, what do you do for work?"

"He's a cook," said Ivan, at the exact same time Cooper said, "I work in a diner."

"A cook! So it runs in the family," said Esther.

"Not really. I'm more like a glorified pancake flipper," muttered Cooper.

"Did you go to culinary school?" asked Esther. "Or just learn from your father?"

"He went to Marquette," said Iris.

"Oh, Marquette's a wonderful school. That chapel—they brought it over from France and rebuilt it piece by piece," said Esther excitedly. "I didn't know they had a cooking program!"

"They don't," said Cooper. "I was a chem major."

"He was going to go to medical school," said Ivan. The air felt heavy. They'd tiptoed into territory they shouldn't be in, Iris could feel it. But she was surprised to hear this. She couldn't picture Cooper in a lab coat, measuring things in beakers.

"You were?" she said. "What happened?"

"I was a paramedic for a few years. Wanted to take a break before med school," he said. "Who needs more wine? Esther?"

"Thank you, young man, but I'll switch to a cocktail, if you'd be so kind." Esther had choked down a glass of red, but Iris had sat through enough of her wine-is-for-sissies talks to know she was looking for the brandy.

"Now *that* I can do."

"Bar's stocked," said Iris. "Left of the—"

"Pantry," finished Cooper. "We've been helping ourselves. Hope that's okay."

"That's what it's there for," Iris assured him.

"Brandy old-fashioned, if you please. So, how did you go from being a paramedic to working at a diner?" Esther asked. "My Felix was a medic in Vietnam. That's a tough job."

Cooper opened his mouth, closed it. He walked into the kitchen and grabbed a cocktail glass wordlessly.

"Wasn't so bad," he said finally. "I wasn't in Vietnam, that's for sure."

"He got freaked out," said Cricket.

"Cricket," said Ivan quietly.

"What? It's true." Cricket turned to Iris. "He was at that shooting in North Harbor last year. The parade?"

"Oh my God," said Iris. *Everyone* knew about that shooting. It had been in the news for weeks. Eight people dead, including the shooter. It'd kicked off a Day Against Gun Violence on campuses across the country. The front page of the *State Journal* had shown all the empty lawn chairs, just abandoned there, in front of the shiny town Christmas tree. It was all anyone had talked about for months, before, like always, it faded into the background of Just Another Shooting. "I—I'm so sorry," she said to Cooper.

He shrugged. "Yeah. I guess after that, I just didn't want to do it anymore. So I got a new job."

Esther shuddered. "That must have been horrible for you."

"It was fine," he said quietly. They all sat in the awkwardness of the moment as Cooper poured Esther her drink. The lighthearted evening had now been smacked with two awkward conversations in a row; two moments discussed that the subjects didn't want to talk about. Iris took a big bite of pasta and let the warm butter slide down her throat, coating over the clumsiness of the evening with calories.

"So," said Cricket, "can I have some pie?"

ESTHER DIDN'T STAY long after the final bite of pie had been eaten. She insisted on helping to clean up, and even when Ivan waved her off, she soaked a dishrag in steaming-hot water and wiped down the counter of every last crumb. Iris helped her walk to her car, down the rickety front porch steps.

"I'll see you tomorrow at Mass?" asked Esther.

Iris nodded. "I'll try to get there."

"All right, sweet pea. You have a good night." She lowered her voice to a whisper. "That boy likes you."

"Grandma." Iris blushed.

"I have eyes! I've seen things, girl. I know it when I see it. There's a lot of fire in this furnace, just some snow on the rooftop." She pointed to her puff of white hair, which she had done in town once a month.

"Good *night*, Grandma," she said. Esther drove off into the night as Iris stood watching her go.

"You again."

She turned to see Cooper on the front porch, leaning against the stair rail.

"*You* again," she said with a grin. Their thing. They had a *thing*!

"Thanks for coming. It was . . . fun."

"Sorry about the third degree."

"Sorry for bringing up the cookbook."

Iris knew she should just get into her car and go. But there he stood, smiling at her, and his eyes were laughing. She felt like she'd learned something big about him, too. A piece of his history. There was so much to know about Cooper Welsh. And she wanted to know it all.

"So," she said, "I should be going."

He looked out over the lake. "*Or* you could stay and have one more drink with me."

She laughed. "I thought we finished up all of your dad's fancy wine, and my grandma's not-fancy wine."

He grinned. "We did. But we didn't touch the cheap beer I bought from the gas station."

They sat on the dock, down by the water, where they'd sat the first night. They clinked their bottles together before taking long sips. Iris was going to have a headache in the morning, combining wine and beer like this. She let her feet dangle down, almost touching the water. She would have sat there all night. She would have sat there five years. She'd never felt like this, not in her entire life.

"It gets so dark here," said Cooper. "I'm not used to it."

"There's no stars tonight. When they're out, you can see all the way across Lake Ellerie," said Iris.

"I remember from the night with the baby coyotes. Have you checked in on them lately?"

"They're gone," said Iris wistfully. "They must have found a new nest, now that they're getting bigger."

"You really going to Mass with your grandma tomorrow?" he asked.

She nodded. "Yeah."

He laughed before he saw that she wasn't kidding. "Sorry. I'm not much of a churchgoer," he told her. They just looked at each other for a minute. He chuckled. "Got something to say?"

She smiled and looked back out over the water. "Didn't you meet my grandmother in a church?"

"For a *funeral*," he said.

"You only believe in God during funerals?"

"I don't believe in God during funerals, either. I just go to them when they're for my mom."

She winced. "Sorry. I'm being a jerk."

He shook his head. "No, you're not. Fair question. You really . . . you believe in all that stuff?"

Iris leaned back and put her hands behind her head, staring up at the sky. It was as black as velvet. She heard the flapping mutter of a loon's wings as it took flight somewhere on the lake.

Catholicism—it was in her veins. Once you were baptized Catholic, her mother had once told her, you can't become un-Catholic.

There's literally nothing you can do. Sure, you can be excommunicated, but you're still technically in the family, a member of the tribe. Like a tattoo. Like a stain.

Iris was Catholic, but it was more than that. Her religion was an odd blend of Catholicism and Esther's wisdom; of her mother's scoldings and her father's whistling. All slow-cooked under the Wisconsin summer heat. Your people formed you. Her people went to Mass and prayed Rosaries. She remembered one of her great-aunts coming to her First Communion; her grandpa's sister with the glass eye, telling her she should be thankful to be part of the *one true religion*. How itchy that little white dress was.

"I wish I didn't," she said.

"What do you mean? Seems like it'd be so much easier. To know when you die you're not just . . ." He waved his hand.

"Easier? No. It's easier to do whatever you want. It's easier to just . . . go with the flow. It's harder to feel like your choices matter."

"Annabelle was Catholic," said Cooper. "It just . . . I always felt like it would be easier if she and Ivan could have just gotten a divorce. Ivan was such an asshole! And it's not like they were really married. He didn't *live* there. He had a different girlfriend every week. But the Catholic thing. It felt unfair. Like a trap."

"Speaking of Ivan, how long do you think you'll stay?" Iris asked.

Cooper glanced at her. "Why? Do you need to kick us out?"

She shook her head, wincing as it scraped against the wooden dock. "With what your dad's paying me? Hell no."

Cooper looked back up to the sky. "We'll be here Saturday night."

"Saturday night, huh?" she asked.

OLIVIA HADN'T BEEN wrong. Iris wasn't the girl who got asked out much in high school. In fact, it seemed as if every boy at Waukegan County High had been in love with the same girl: Samantha Bauer. Samantha Bauer had long, smooth, shiny brown hair that she'd brush between every single class. After math and woodshop and English, there she was, brushing her hair, pulling it up into the perfect high ponytail. She was small, too—the kind of girl who could be picked up and thrown over your shoulder. Guys would do that in the hallway, and she'd squeal and pound their back with her fists, and everyone would laugh. She didn't mind it, even though she pretended she did. When it was time for the winter ball or the homecoming dance, Samantha was on the dance floor every single song, her hips being gripped by any number of boys. Iris and her small gaggle of casual friends would mainly hang out by the punch, sipping and observing. She'd always wondered what it was about Samantha Bauer. She was pretty, yeah. Great hair, from all the brushing. But more than her looks, it was almost like there was a magnetic spark in her, where boys' desires couldn't help but be drawn.

Iris wasn't like that.

She liked to consider herself a confident person, and she was, when it came to things like designing brochures and decorating Redstone. But she was so anxious sitting next to Cooper on the back porch of Vernon's that her hands were shaking.

"Tell me about living here," Cooper said. "It seems like . . . a different world."

Iris nodded. She got that a lot. For someone like Cooper, who grew up in LA and went to school in Milwaukee, the Northwoods probably *did* feel like another galaxy.

First, they'd gone to Agnelli's over in Waukegan. Cooper had picked her up and she'd checked her lipstick three times before wiping it off because it looked ridiculous. She didn't know the first thing about lipstick. Her idea of makeup was a swipe of Carmex on her lips. But Agnelli's was the kind of place with dim lights and menus without prices. The kind of place people like him, sons of celebrities, went all the time. Iris had been there exactly once, for her high school National Honor Society induction.

And the food was *good*. Different from anything she was used to. If her mother had known she was eating truffle goat cheese crostini, she would've laughed her ass off. Iris had wine, too. Not beer, but wine, like the night when she and Esther had gone to Redstone for dinner. Someone had ordered wine once at Vernon's, and she still remembered the entire bar bursting into laughter. Vern had handed the embarrassed patron one of those tiny plastic bottles you get at bachelorette parties and asked if he wanted to taste it first, or do that swish-it-around-in-a-circle thing.

God, this town could make fun of you. It would rip you to shreds. It would throw hands for you in a parking lot—loyalty here was valued higher than any dollar. But they'd make you feel like shit while doing it. Vernon's could be cattier than a high school bathroom.

Sitting at Agnelli's felt a bit like pretending. She wasn't the kind of girl who usually ordered things with Italian names. And that fancy dessert—her dad would have had a field day with that one. It couldn't have been more than three bites of chocolate! He was always going on about how expensive restaurants always give you tiny plates. Cooper told her stories about his diner patrons and made her laugh. He didn't talk about his father at all. Not that she wanted the dirt on Ivan Welsh.

As they walked to the car, he was the one who suggested a drink somewhere. Yes, God, yes. Anything to be with him for a few more minutes. She was ridiculous. She was in love.

She thought for a minute about where they could go, but every time she opened her mouth, she closed it again. Agnelli's was the only fancy place she knew.

Cooper laughed. "Where do you usually go?" he asked.

"Usually?"

"Yeah. When you're out with your friends, or your sister."

"I can't take you there," she said immediately. *Oh shit. Shit, shit, shit,* because now it was a challenge.

"Why not?" he asked.

"Cooper . . ."

"Why? I'm not cool enough to hang with your friends? Somebody might see me?"

"Oh, people will see you," she assured him. "Half the town probably knows we're on a date right now. Ivan coming to Ellerie is the biggest thing that's happened here since the old barista at Northern Latte's got put in prison for racketeering."

"So what?" he said. "You embarrassed by my good hair?"

She laughed. She wanted to run her fingers through that hair, such a dark black that it was practically blue. "No. It's just . . . it's not your kind of place."

"I want your kind of place to be my kind of place," he insisted.

"It's not my kind of place, either! It's just *a place*. It's the only bar on Musky Lake."

"Then we have to go," he said. "And you don't even have to tell me where it is, because I can just drive around the lake until I find it."

And that's what he did. She stuck her feet out the window, not really caring if she looked like a country hick after three glasses of wine. Hell, why shouldn't they go to Vernon's? She was surprised that she already felt slightly light-headed. She was a Kelleher by name but a Larson by blood; she could put away a six-pack by herself and still drive home.

Vernon's was packed with tourists—it was the height of the season. But there were familiar faces, too. Bella from high school, who had moved back to Ellerie after getting fired from her fancy New York fashion job for stealing clothes, if you believed Olivia. Her mom's old friend Pat, who was complaining about the jukebox being too loud, same as every other night. Iris waved to them both and flagged down Vernon.

"Jack and ginger," she said, "and . . ." She glanced back at Cooper. This felt like a defining moment.

Please don't order wine, she thought.

"Same," he yelled over the noise.

Vern nodded gruffly and whipped up their drinks while arguing with some other guy at the bar about the Chicago Bears.

"Let's go outside," she yelled to Cooper, nodding toward the jukebox and handing him a red Solo cup.

"Definitely."

And so here they were, on the back porch. Legs dangling, sipping Jack and gingers, which Cooper had admitted he'd never had before.

"Did most of your friends from growing up stick around?" Cooper asked.

"No. Not really. I went to high school all the way in Waukegan County. There's only a handful of people my age around here. Father Sam, the priest? He did. But I mostly hang out with my family, to be honest. And work."

Cooper sipped his drink. "Your family seems so close."

"We are." That wasn't a lie. There was nobody she'd rather murder than Olivia on any given day, but Olivia had also egged Kourtnee Kleaver's house sophomore year because she'd started a rumor that Iris had made out with Thomas Becker under the bleachers. You didn't forget things like that.

"What about your family?" she asked. "I mean, growing up with Ivan Welsh. You must have so many stories."

Cooper smiled, but it was one of those I'm-not-going-there smiles. "I was really close with Annabelle, actually. Even though she wasn't technically my mom."

"She wasn't?" Iris hoped she was giving a good poker face. It was hard to pretend as if she hadn't googled every inch of him.

"Nah. My mom lives in Hawaii, doing . . . whatever. Living off Ivan's alimony and selling essential oils." He didn't sound bitter— just like he was stating facts. "Annabelle was more of a mom to me. And Cricket . . . I mean, I'd do anything for that kid."

"She's great," said Iris.

Cooper grinned at her. "*This* is great. I can't believe you thought I wouldn't fit in here."

"California boy!"

"I went to college in Milwaukee."

"Milwaukee's not the Northwoods."

"No," he admitted.

She stood up and stretched. The wine and the Jack Daniel's were mingling in her head, making her toes tingle. She wanted nothing more, suddenly, than to jump in the lake.

"Man, it's hot. I could jump in that water," said Cooper.

So she did.

Why not? It was deep there. She'd swam in this lake a thousand times, splashing with Olivia while the grown-ups sipped beers on the deck.

The lake was colder than hell, and her makeup would smear off her face, and the entire stupid town would talk. Her hair would hang in thick ropes down her back, and maybe she'd look like a crazy drunk.

But just then, she felt someone else next to her. A warm hand, around her arm. Warm lips, on hers.

You don't know, do you? You don't know you were empty until you're suddenly full.

They could talk all they wanted.

Fourteen

"Oh, we've been *over* this."

Carlotta thought they'd been over it, and so did Bea. But Katharine Rose was standing firm, and Esther was getting a headache.

"Noodles in chili makes it goulash," Katharine Rose insisted.

Bea slapped the table with her palm. "I've been putting noodles in my chili since my grandmother and I first made it."

"I don't care if you've been doing it since Jesus walked the road to Emmaus, you weren't making chili."

It wasn't that Esther didn't care about such an important debate. It was that if they were going to get the cookbook printed by their deadline, they had to finalize their recipes.

The appetizer section was done, and in good shape, more or less. Esther wasn't sure about Millie's crab canapés, but Katharine Rose said she'd had them at Earl's retirement party a few years back and they'd been decent. The soups were done, too, and the meat section. Even Mrs. Thomas Murphy had offered up her recipe for a cheesy taco bake. But the casserole section was too long—things needed to be cut. And they couldn't finish the pasta section until they settled this goulash debacle.

"What about desserts?" said Carlotta. "I hate to say it, but Ethel submitted her bread pudding, and that's what gave half the town food poisoning after the Christmas Walk last year."

"How can you get food poisoning from bread pudding?" asked Bea.

"The egg, maybe. I don't know."

Esther sighed. "The problem isn't the recipes. The recipes are terrific. The problem is the price. Who's going to pay for a cookbook of recipes from people they've known their whole lives?"

"Talk about things we've been *over*," said Bea. "People in this town want to help."

There it was again—the fury, rising up in her. Just the day before, she'd been at the grocery store with a full cart. The stupid handicap button on the door hadn't been working. She'd reached over with one arm and tried to open the door, maneuvering her cart with the other, and then she heard it—some tourist in a Cabela's hat. *Help that poor woman,* he'd hissed to his teenage son.

That poor woman. Poor Esther.

"It's a numbers thing," said Iris, who was furiously typing on a keyboard. "That's the issue. If we sell the book for twenty dollars, like we were planning, we need to sell a thousand copies. I'm just not sure if that's going to happen, even with the Christmas Walk. I think we need to get serious about the promotional aspect."

"Saint Rita. Patron saint of desperate causes," said Carlotta.

"There aren't even a thousand people who *go* to the Christmas Walk," said Katharine Rose.

"Exactly," said Iris. "So . . . we need to think about publicity."

Esther held a hand up. "Absolutely not."

"We need to go viral!" said Katharine Rose, pumping her fist in the air.

"'Viral'? What do you know about viral? Besides your sinus infections," chortled Carlotta.

"Katharine Rose is right. And I hate to say it, but so was Olivia. A GoFundMe might be the way to go," said Iris.

Esther hated when they teamed up like this. Her best friend and granddaughter grinned at each other, and she glared at them both.

"Well, one of us is dating Mr. Hollywood's son," sang out Bea. That gossip queen.

Iris turned red. Ha! Well, how'd she like that? Esther was happy to see her granddaughter dating. He seemed like such a nice boy. A real gentleman. And his face didn't hurt, either.

"If Big-Shot Food Network Man could share about it on Instagram . . . a poor old lady, about to lose her house . . . ," mused Katharine Rose.

"Call me that again and see who's still standing," snapped Esther.

"Work what you've got. When we were young, we worked our faces. Now that we're old, we gotta work our wrinkles," said Katharine Rose.

"Truth," said Carlotta, lifting her margarita.

Iris sighed. "I could do it. I could ask. Cooper already sort of offered."

"Iris, honey, no," insisted Esther. "This is all too much. All of the work we've all put in, and asking for all of this help . . . it's despicable. You're trying to get that boy to give you a ring, you can't be asking for favors like this. He'll feel like you're using him!"

"Grandma, *God*. Who said anything about a ring? We've been dating a *summer*."

Esther rolled her eyes. All these kids today thought you needed so much time. Time, time, time! As if another year would show you the kind of father a person would be, or how nightmares about battlefields in Vietnam would keep him up at night, or how many times you'd be yelling about refilling the toilet paper roll. No, those things were only learned by commitment. They all thought you had to be in love to commit. They didn't realize it was the other way around: that love *came* from commitment. Nobody ever tells you when you get married how many days you'll wake up in the morning and want to strangle the other person. No, to them it was all Pinterest boards and buttercream flowers.

"I've already lost my pride," said Esther. "It's gone. It flew out the door, right alongside my dignity. I do not want you asking Ivan Welsh for help. And I mean it. Do you hear me?"

"But, Grandma—"

"I said *no*!" She hit the countertop, hard. A look of hurt flittered across Iris's eyes. Well, good. Sometimes you had to scare people a little bit.

"Calm down, tiger," said Katharine Rose. "It isn't time for the circus."

"At least let me ask my friend if she has any ideas," Iris argued. "Grace, from college. She was in my Comms 101 class, and she works in food TV . . . that British show on Netflix I showed you."

"Fine," Esther sighed. "But that's it. Not a single other soul."

"I've got to boogie," said Bea, putting her glass in the sink. "JP's taking me for a drive to go see the Amish down in Dalton."

Iris groaned. "You still do that?"

"You used to love to see the Amish!" Bea insisted. "Esther and Felix would take you. They make the best doughnuts in town." It was true. Felix loved their powdered doughnuts. They made home-made noodles, too.

"They're not *zoo* animals," Iris said.

"If they didn't want people to look, they wouldn't wear the funny hats."

"I should go, too," said Carlotta. "Time for this old lady's nap."

Katharine Rose patted Esther's hand. "You think about what we said, Esther. I'll call you tonight."

The three left, letting the door bang behind them, and Iris started washing their glasses.

"Oh, don't worry about that, honey," said Esther, waving her hand.

Iris shook her head, not even meeting her grandmother's eyes. Her shoulders were hunched.

"I'm sorry I yelled at you," Esther said quietly. "I am. But you don't understand how embarrassing it is to be in this situation."

Iris took a deep breath. "Grandma . . . this house—" She shook her head and put the glass down. She turned off the water and walked out to the porch, her arms crossed. Esther hobbled after her. Lord, she felt old. When did her walk turn into a hobble?

"You're crying," said Esther.

Iris had tears in her eyes. "I don't want you to lose this house," she said. "I've lived so much of my life at this house. And it isn't fair that it could be taken away. Especially because you did it trying to be nice. You're always so nice! And I can't believe someone would do something so horrible, and I can't believe you might not live here anymore, and I can't believe that one day my grandkids wouldn't be able to splash around down by the dock. This house is more than *your house,* you know? It's ours. Our family's house. And this small thing I could do to help, you don't want me to do."

Esther sighed and stared out over the lake. How many times had she sat in this exact cedar chair, staring out over this exact same quiet lake? Sharing lemon bars with her grandkids or smoking cigarettes with Katharine Rose before her daughters made her quit? Sitting side by side with Felix, listening to the Rosary on the radio? She wished Felix were here. Oh, Felix. He'd know what to do. He always did.

Of course, if Felix were there, she'd never have gotten into this situation in the first place. He didn't like computers very much. And she wouldn't have been so lonely.

What do I do, Felix? she asked. She wasn't the kind of person who believed saints whispered in her ear. No; that was only for popes and religious sisters, or people holy enough for the stigmata. But when you're married to someone for fifty years, you simply know the way their mind works. Felix would be horrified if she asked for money. *It's just a house,* he'd say. *We don't sell our pride for a pier.*

But again—Felix wasn't here. Iris was. Her granddaughter, who would one day carry her great-grandchildren. She wanted them to be able to come to this house, to spend their summer days lying on the deck and eating sour-cream-and-onion chips. Maybe they'd have cooking in their genes.

THAT NIGHT, LONG after Iris had gone home, Esther sat out back on the porch and thought again of her husband. He would have been furious with her for this entire thing. Well, she was used to that. Felix was often a furious man. Kind and gentle and strong and playful, but furious? Yes, she'd use that word to describe him. Certainly.

Combat fatigue—Felix had never used those words. And that damn VA couldn't have given less of a care, not that Felix would have given them the time of day if they had. It was all so normal. The word *trauma*; what the hell did that mean? They'd all seen horrible things. Poverty and violence were just the background noise of their lives. Esther had plenty of friends whose husbands were the exact same way, she was pretty sure. Although Katharine Rose's Ed hadn't even been in Vietnam, because his father had needed his help on the farm. Esther had understood, because of her own father's 4-F, but Felix had never respected that.

Anyway, they didn't have Zoloft back then. They had Miller Lite and long boat rides.

So Felix drank. Well, who wouldn't? Everyone did, around here. Maybe Felix drank a bit *too* much, but the things he'd seen. He didn't like to talk about it much. Sometimes in the middle of the night, Felix would sit up so suddenly, it was as if he'd heard an intruder. Esther would reach out and touch him, but he'd yank his hand away. He hit her once, but only once, on accident. He had been asleep. He'd screamed, and she could see it in his eyes, as if they were windows. Tangled messes of blood and limbs and United States Army–issued khaki. His hand had flung up and struck her in the mouth. He'd never forgiven himself.

Once, a couple of his army friends had been in town. God only knew why. Big, burly men with tattoos and jittery eyes. Esther had made her special spaghetti sauce, the kind that had to simmer for ten hours, and one of them had had the audacity to ask if it was Prego. Fran hadn't liked the way they talked so loudly, so the two of them had gone to spend the night at Katharine Rose's while Felix and his friends got so sloshed, one of them threw up in her rosebushes.

Felix. Oh, Felix. The days when he would wake up, his eyes laughing. He'd offer to make pancakes and kiss her senseless. He'd throw the grandkids in the air and sing them songs, praising God for his family, the blessings at his feet, the life he lived. He'd stop his truck to move turtles to the side of the road.

And the days when he would wake up with his eyes cloudy. Every movement a little more intentionally angry. A slammed refrigerator door, a coffee cup shoved into the sink. He would turn on Esther and snap at her for the smallest things. The *smallest*—it hurt to think about this. Her Felix. Her sweet man.

Once they'd been in the grocery store looking for ice cream. Fran and Aaron and the girls were coming over for dinner that night; Olivia and Iris must have been in high school then. This wasn't long before he died. These teenage boys had come down the aisle, whipping around in motorized carts. Idiots! Laughing their heads off. They almost ran into Esther. Felix got angry—those carts were for people with disabilities. That's what he muttered to her, first. *Those carts are for people with disabilities.* I know, she'd said back. So disrespectful.

They came back down the aisle again, going even faster, and Esther had willed them to go away. *Don't do this, boys. Don't ruin my day. Please.* She'd said a Hail Mary in her head, quick as a rabbit.

"Hey!" Felix had shouted. "Those aren't toys. They're for people with disabilities." Felix cared so much about things like that.

The boys had looked at Felix, then at each other, and they had *laughed.* That was the worst thing they could have done.

Felix's face got bright red and his fists clenched. Esther felt her heart beating faster. She could save this situation. She could salvage it.

"Felix," she said. "Felix, let's just—"

"You think this is *funny*?" he said angrily. He was too loud for quiet, echoey Zephyr's. One boy stopped laughing, but the other snickered again. Esther's face got hot. She hated those boys. She would've set them on fire, if she could. Not for being obnoxious little twits, but for setting Felix off, for derailing a perfectly nice afternoon, for leaving her to clean up the smoldering ashes of one of his—moods. Breakdowns. Attacks. Whatever you wanted to call them. It was always Esther, afterward, alone. Other people might've gotten burned in the moment, but it was always Esther left sweeping up the goddamn mess.

And that, that right there, was why she'd responded to Hazel's pleas. Because Esther knew what it was like. That desperation. That feeling of being all alone in the universe, holding your problems and wishing someone else would swoop in and bear the burden with you.

"This isn't some kind of joke," Felix had snapped. "You punks are being disrespectful. You're—you're—"

"Chill out, Gramps," the one who'd stopped laughing had muttered.

And that was it. Felix was surprisingly strong, for an old man. He still cared about his fitness. Esther and Felix walked a few laps around the track at Waukegan High at least twice a month. Every night after dinner, they'd take a stroll, as long as the mosquitos weren't too bad. And he could still bring the dock in every fall, with a bit of help from Aaron.

So when he grabbed the boy by the collar and threw him to the floor, his head hit the ground loud enough to make a *crack*.

The manager was very nice about it. They weren't on a first-name basis by any means, but he'd seen Esther and Felix coming to Zephyr's for years. And of course, he agreed with Felix—those boys were being rude. But he still had to ask them to leave. He would convince the boy's mother not to press any charges.

Esther had had to drive, which she never did. The whole way home, Felix took shaky breaths. He sat in the front seat with the palms of his hands pushed against his eyes. When they finally pulled up their long driveway, they had just sat there for a minute, eyes forward, staring at their big, beautiful home.

"Felix," she'd said carefully, because you always had to be careful about these things, "I'm wondering if . . ."

"You can go on in. I'll run to Coontail's for the ice cream," he said.

"Maybe there's someone you could talk to."

"About what?" he asked. He didn't wait for her answer. He got out of the car, slamming the door extra hard behind him, and walked around to the driver's side. From Coontail's, he brought home not just ice cream, but supplies for sundaes, and that night he made massive, dripping desserts with hot fudge and Oreos and caramel sauce, just like Esther liked.

Fifteen

Help me.

He is running, and there she is, blood—

Help me.

Pop-pop-pop-

The air smells like smoke. Her hair smells like death.

"Where's Dad?"

Cooper jumped about a foot in the air. "Geez, Cricket! You scared me."

"Settle down." His sister yawned and reached for the coffeepot. "I need caffeine because somebody's pacing kept me up all night."

He winced. "Sorry."

"Don't you sleep?"

"Once in a while," he muttered. He was scrolling through his inbox, ignoring the three messages from his boss asking if he could let him know the exact date he'd be back to work.

"So . . . where's Dad?" Cricket repeated.

"He had to run into town, I guess. Why?" Cooper said.

"For what?" asked Cricket.

"Shit, Cricket, I don't know." He'd probably just gotten stir-crazy. It wasn't like Ellerie had much in common with Los Angeles. Ivan had been disappearing for mornings at a time. He didn't volunteer where he went, and Cooper didn't ask.

"Okay, okay!"

He and Ivan had kind of gotten into it the night before, anyway. They weren't made to live together. Iris had been over, sitting on the dock, in tears about her grandmother's house, Cooper begging her to let him just ask Ivan to share about the cookbook on social media. Maybe even contribute a recipe? *No,* she'd insisted, shaking her head. Esther wouldn't let her. The pride of that woman—it kind of bugged Cooper. Or impressed him. Somewhere in between.

Nobody up here wanted to be seen as a mooch. It was like a cardinal sin, worse than murder or grand larceny. Maybe even worse than the *being difficult* thing. But Ivan spent so much money on the most pointless crap—wineglasses made by Japanese samurai. Fancy imported cheeses. A carpet hand-sewn by a king in Bolivia. He could do a little to give back to his son's girlfriend's grandma.

Sort-of-girlfriend. Whatever. Yeah, yeah, labels were lame, but . . . shit. Iris! He'd never felt this way before. He thought about her at the weirdest, most random times. He saw a cheeseburger, he thought about how they'd gone to McDonald's in Waukegan at one in the morning and made out in the parking lot like sixteen-year-olds. All the hormones of a teenage boy, but also something in her that made him want to be a gentleman. He'd opened her car door.

Part of him wanted to just ask Ivan for a check. And Ivan would probably give it. But something stopped him.

The way this small, weird town in the woods was helping this woman keep her house—it seemed more powerful, somehow, than a check from a celebrity. Cooper wanted the cookbook to be made. If it didn't pull in enough, well, he could always ask Ivan then.

Besides, Ivan's favors came with strings. He acted like they didn't, but they did. Blank checks galore, but ask Cooper which he would have rather had: a dad who came to his high school graduation or a dad who bought him a Tesla.

He hated that stupid car. Although it did usually impress girls.

Not Iris. She'd asked why on earth someone would need a computer in their car.

The night before, Ivan had asked what was the matter, and Cooper had shrugged him off. None of his business; if Iris didn't want to tell Ivan, Cooper wouldn't tell him, either.

"Young love," Ivan had said with a sigh, and Cooper had snorted, which had pissed Ivan off. But God. Did Ivan just *forget* that Cooper had been there? He'd witnessed the Valentine's Day that Ivan had sworn he'd be home and instead taken off to Seattle for some restaurant opening, leaving Annabelle in that fancy dress eating Kraft mac 'n' cheese with him and Cricket for dinner. Or those pictures that came out, of him and the food writer . . . screw Ivan. What did he know about young love? Nothing. As if he and Annabelle had posed for Christmas card photos together and spent weekends on the lake. They hadn't been married, *really* married, for years. That other actress he was photographed with in Sicily, that one from the eight millionth *Law & Order* spin-off, had had the audacity to send flowers when Annabelle died. Cooper had thrown them in the garbage. Ivan had *never* felt for anyone the way Cooper felt for Iris.

Annabelle was more Cooper's and Cricket's than Ivan's. He hated that Ivan was acting like some poor grieving husband. He'd been going to bed early, and his typical eight-mile morning runs had been replaced with sipping coffee on the deck. Whenever Cooper asked him when he was going back to work, he'd just shrug. He saw the missed calls on Ivan's phone—*Gabi (3), Carmen (5), Matthew (7)*. Producers, scriptwriters, assistants. Everyone was wanting to know when Ivan Welsh would get back to filming. He was on vacation, but acting like it was some kind of grief retreat, and it made Cooper sick. It wasn't fair to skip out on work and act all devastated when you hadn't even appreciated the person in real life. Annabelle would have appreciated the sentiment, probably. But Cooper didn't, on her behalf.

Cooper had his own missed calls. The guardian ad litem from court wanted to know if he'd found Cricket a therapist back in Milwaukee yet. His own therapist, Dr. Hoss, had been calling, too.

He knew what would happen if he spoke with Dr. Hoss. He'd want to talk about the way Cooper hadn't been sleeping, and the way the noises had gotten worse. Something barely had to be that loud anymore. The closing of a cabinet could sound like a gun to him. The flashbacks played over and over in his mind like a movie that he couldn't turn off. This wasn't good. It gave him a jolt of desperation—he'd been trying. He'd seen the shrink, taken the sleeping pills, and still felt that girl's blood running through his hands. Was this just how life was going to be forever? That made his heart speed up, his eyes flicker around. No—he couldn't do that. Couldn't live like that. *We're not aiming for perfection,* Dr. Hoss had said, tapping his fingers on his knee. *We're aiming for coping right now.*

But he had ways to turn it off. Iris, for one. He thought of her, and all the images of The Girl were pushed aside. Iris was like a tether, keeping him pulled back to earth when his brain threatened to grow wings and fly away. Iris felt real when nothing else did. *Coping mechanisms*—were they allowed to be people?

He almost felt guilty. He hadn't exactly been the world's best legal guardian, and Cricket had enough absent parental figures in her life. But she preferred to spend all her time reading on the dock, or FaceTiming her friends, or scrolling TikTok. Whenever he tried to talk to her, she seemed vaguely annoyed.

And—well. Another guilt, too. The guilt of happiness, when you've seen such unhappy things. Someone should remember The Girl in her last moments. Someone should know what her eyes had looked like as she died.

Help me.

No. He squeezed his eyes shut. *Go away,* he begged her. *Please just leave me alone.*

Pop-pop-pop-

"Cooper? Are you okay?" asked Cricket.

"Yeah," he said, running a hand through his hair. "Headache, and I'm super tired."

"You look like you're going to throw up . . ."

"I'm fine. Sorry. I think I need to lie down, maybe," he said. "What are you doing today? Want to go swimming later? We can try to make it out to the island." There was a small piece of land a few hundred yards off the rental house's dock. They kept talking about seeing if they could swim out there without having heart attacks. He needed to actually make it happen one of these days.

"That sounds good."

"Love you, bug."

"Love you, dumbass."

Cooper went back into his room and turned the lights off. He pulled the blackout shades shut tight and cranked the fan as high as it would go, then curled up into a ball on the bed.

Stop, he begged his brain. *Please.*

But it wouldn't. There he is, in the ambulance with Eddie. There it is, the crowd, the bodies on the ground.

Stop—

A Christmas parade. Little girls in tutus, with glitter smeared on their cheeks. High school marching bands. A man dressed up as Santa with a clip-on beard that went down to his waist.

It will get better, Dr. Hoss had said.

But it wasn't getting better. It was getting worse.

This wasn't working. He got out of bed, picked up his phone, and called the person he loved.

"Online school," said Iris. "Huh."

Cooper shrugged. "She begged. I don't know."

Iris stood up and stretched her hands behind her head. They were sitting on Esther's dock. It felt weird, knowing that Esther was up there in the kitchen, shelling peas and watching daytime

TV. But Iris had said that Esther had the best dock in Ellerie, and she wasn't wrong. It went far enough into the water that you could dive, but not so far that it was out in the open. There weren't any neighbors visible on either edge, and it felt like the two of them were the only people in the entire world besides Esther. The soft *bump, bump, bump* of the boat against the dock and the frothy lap of the waves and here, in front of him: a beautiful girl. Shit, Cooper was a lucky man.

August was trickling away, turning the corner from midsummer to late summer. Cooper had signed the form that said Cricket could take all her classes online. She'd pleaded. She wasn't ready to leave. Her mom's grave was here, she kept saying. Annabelle's whole life was here. *A couple of weeks* was turning into *a couple of months*.

"Don't you think she'll miss stuff, though? High school experiences?" said Iris.

"I'm the wrong person to ask. I didn't do much of that stuff," Cooper admitted. He dunked a chip into the dip Iris had made, some kind of cheesy bacon-and-green-onion situation that she called cowboy crack.

"Why? Famous dad problems?"

"Nah, it was LA. A famous dad wasn't rare. It was just . . . I don't know. Not my scene."

"Weren't you *prom king*?"

He rolled his eyes. "Don't rub it in."

Iris chuckled, then dove into the water. Someone should *paint* her, she was so beautiful. She bobbed back up and wiped her hair away from her face. "I mean, you're telling me growing up with a celebrity in the family didn't have *any* perks? You never got to meet Lady Gaga?"

Cooper laughed. "Lady Gaga? No. He did judge the Great Chili Showdown with Trisha Yearwood, though."

"Oh my gosh. My mom would love that."

"I didn't meet her," said Cooper. "I wasn't really in his sphere.

When my mom took off, I was always with the nanny. Then he married Annabelle and I lived with her and Cricket until college."

She swam up to the dock and grabbed the edge. His feet dangled down beside her. She just smiled at him, a big goofy grin, and he grinned back. He missed Annabelle. He'd do anything to have Annabelle back. But something about meeting Iris felt . . . guided by her, somehow. Like she knew when she asked to have her funeral in Ellerie that it would change all their lives. That sounded like a big, crazy declaration. But when he looked at Iris Kelleher, he felt like making big, crazy declarations.

"What's the best thing Ivan ever cooked for you?" Iris asked.

"What is this, CNN?" he joked. "Why do you care? You writing his biography?"

"I want to know about *you*," she said. "I want to know everything."

He felt the same way. He wanted to know where she learned to dive, and when she started putting mayonnaise on her fries, and who her favorite person to go to the movies with was. He wanted to know where she'd bought her purple swimsuit. The most played song on her iPhone. Everything. Every single thing.

"Honestly?" He leaned back and looked up at the sky, blocking the sun from his eyes with his hand. "Pancakes."

"What?" She laughed. "*Pancakes?*"

"You don't like pancakes?"

"I love pancakes. Who doesn't? But . . . I mean, you can make pancakes with a box of mix and some water. Not too complicated. I thought it would be something fancy and foreign."

He shook his head. "No. Pancakes."

There was a memory hidden there, buried under piles of unanswered phone calls and missed milestones. It was a Sunday morning. After church, back when they all went, shortly after Ivan and Annabelle had gotten married. Annabelle, pregnant, was lying on the couch, singing along to Bob Dylan. Cooper was fourteen.

"This is the secret to pancakes," Ivan was telling him, carefully removing strips of bacon from a pan. "The bacon grease."

"The bacon grease?"

"Yup. Here, you pour the batter."

He did, slowly but surely.

Ivan pointed out when the edges started to bubble. "Don't let it burn," he warned. "Burned pancakes are disgusting."

"Totally," said Cooper. He'd never had a burned pancake in his life.

Ivan put his hand over Cooper's and helped him carefully flip the pancake over. They made a gigantic pile and loaded some up on a plate for Annabelle. They opened the fridge and got out the real maple syrup, the cherry jam, the Polish butter from the deli. The sun came dappling through the kitchen windows, and Bob Dylan sang about being lonesome when you go. Cooper took a bite.

"Teach me to make them," Iris said. "The way he did. We'll open a pancake restaurant and become millionaires."

"Not a bad idea," said Cooper.

Iris hoisted herself out of the water and lay next to Cooper. He shivered as cold lake water dripped across his abdomen. It was a little cold for a lake dive, but Iris had said they'd have to bring the dock in in a couple of weeks.

"If our family loses this dock, I don't know what I'll do," she said. "And I don't know what Grandma will do."

"Don't worry. She won't." There it was, that weird urge to be a gentleman. He wanted to slay a dragon or two or seven for her. He wanted to work late-night shifts to make sure she got to keep her family's house. Who *was* he?

"I can't believe we let this happen, you know?"

"Is that your Catholic guilt showing?" asked Cooper with a half grin.

"Shut up," said Iris. The Catholic thing—Cooper wasn't quite on board with it, but whatever. If Iris wanted to go sit in a church and talk to ghosts, it wasn't like it bothered him. Although the rosary hanging off her rearview mirror did keep him from reaching a hand up her shirt while they made out. Maybe that was the point.

It reminded him of Annabelle, in a way. Her drawers of rosaries and statues of saints tucked onto bookshelves. Annabelle loved God in church, but she loved him in other places, too. Sometimes they'd be out on a walk and Annabelle would just stare up at the sky and smile. The Jesus gene had skipped Cricket, though. She said if an all-powerful being created the universe but also allowed homelessness and war to exist, she didn't really want anything to do with him. Cooper had to agree.

He wished Annabelle were there. She would have loved Iris. He wanted to sit next to her and tell her about his dreams, and the cold. She'd reach out and push his hair off his forehead, the way she'd done since he was thirteen. *Everything will always be okay in the end,* she'd say. She always knew what to say.

After North Harbor, Cooper had quit his job and gone to Chicago for a while. He wanted to wait out the news cameras and the talking heads; he knew that soon enough, someone would shoot up something else and they'd all leave, following the scent of fresh blood. But until then, he hid. Annabelle, who could never cook, ordered them takeout every night and they binge-watched shows that were guaranteed not to have blood—the one about a small town parks department, and the one about a community college. Annabelle never asked any questions, but she was always just *there,* a hand on his shoulder, passing him the soy sauce. He told her he didn't want to talk about it, and they didn't.

Some days, though, he did. Some days he wanted to tell someone else about the look in The Girl's eyes, because if he didn't, it was like a parasite that would eat him alive.

He eventually headed back to Milwaukee. Back to his apartment, back to his friends. When he saw The Girl at night, he swallowed it down. Annabelle had enough to worry about.

Crack.

Cooper jumped, smacking his shin on the dock. "What the—"

Crack.

Iris glanced at him. "It's just the neighbors, probably. Sounds like someone's chopping wood."

"The neighbors are far away . . ."

"You ever heard someone chop wood, city boy? It's loud."

Crack.

Pop-pop-pop—

No.

Cooper squeezed his eyes shut. Not here.

Crack.

The things he pictured—it was always so weird. The details that stayed with him. The bumper sticker on the black pickup truck in front of him: *My Scholar Goes to St. Joe's Academy.* The empty can of Diet Coke rolling near the gutter. The bright pink mittens of the grandmother in the folding chair, over by the side of the road. How early did she have to get there to get a seat right up front? Or had someone saved it for her?

Crack.

Pop—pop—pop—

His heart is beating so fast he can feel it in his fingertips, his calves, his shoulder blades. The edges of his vision are blurring.

There she is, always. The Girl, with her blond curls, her scared eyes, her hands reaching, and there is Cooper, trained to save, ready for this moment, ready for anything. He can see his reflection in her silver jacket.

There are the blue and white flashes of the police cars. There is the body on the ground.

There is the ripping of life, into *before* and *after.*

People are running. People are screaming. No, there's one person screaming, and they're screaming his name.

"Cooper! Cooper! Wake up!"

And now someone slapping him, hard. God, that lady could hit!

He opened his eyes. Esther, gripping his shoulders, staring him in the face.

"You're all right," she said. "You're all right."

"Oh my God," he says. "Oh my God. I'm sorry. I just—"

Crack.

"Iris," snapped Esther, "go next door and tell Thomas to shut the hell up with that."

Iris didn't move. She just looked between Cooper and Esther, then back to Cooper.

"I've got him," said Esther, softer. "Go, honey." And then she did. Off like a rocket, up the stairs to the house.

"You're okay," Esther told him. "You just had a fright."

He took a shaky breath and ran a hand through his hair. "I'm sorry. I'm sorry. I—I'm sorry. I was out of it for a minute. I'm not feeling well. Maybe I'm hungover." He'd rather have her think he was a drunk than crazy, to be honest.

"No," said Esther simply, as if there was no room for argument.

He just looked at her, and she looked back. She wasn't going to buy any of his shitty excuses, so he stopped making them.

"You have someone you can call?" she asked. "A doctor, maybe?"

"I'm—I'm really okay," he said. "Sometimes, with the noises . . . it's a weird thing." He should call Dr. Hoss when he got home. He would. He needed that familiar voice.

"My husband was the same way," Esther said. "Couldn't handle loud things for years after the war. Sorry I smacked you, but that was the only way I could wake Felix up, sometimes. And Iris was going to have a goddamn heart attack. Here, I was bringing you down some drinks. Take a sip." She handed him a cold Miller Lite and he took a long gulp. The beer sailed down to his stomach, cold and fresh.

"Thanks," he said. "That helps. I'll talk to Iris. I didn't mean to freak her out."

"I have to go to Mass," Esther said. "Are you going to be okay down here?"

"Yes. I'm totally fine. I'm really sorry." He still felt like he was going to throw up. He had to go home.

"You call that doctor."

"I'm—I'm fine. I appreciate the beer. Oh man. That was embarrassing."

Esther stood and wiped the condensation from the beer off on her linen pants. She looked strangely calm, as if she'd done this a thousand times. "Don't worry about it. Help a little old lady back up these stairs, would you?"

Sixteen

There were two tricks to chocolate chip cookies. The first was to use butter that wasn't quite room temperature—Esther only left hers out for about an hour beforehand—so that the small chunks of butter could make fluffier cookies. The second was to ignore the recipe's suggested amount of chocolate chips. She poured in the whole bag, every time. Why skimp? If you wanted a chocolate chip cookie, you might as well go all the way.

The only reason Esther had been cooking or baking anything lately had been for the cookbook. She'd almost forgotten the reason she was in this mess in the first place. In fact, she hadn't even checked to see if she had new messages from Hazel in a week. She found that she liked the creation of the cookbook. Even if it made a grand total of ten cents and she was living on the street by the end of the year, she liked reading the recipes her friends had submitted and gathering them together. And although there were days when she wished she'd never told the funeral ladies about her problem, there were also days when she found herself excited about tweaking the ingredient lists and looking over Iris's layouts. When she lined up Linda's Jell-O torte and Barbara's lemon fluff pie and Katharine Rose's poppy seed tart, it looked like a real collection of recipes. Something to be proud of. It felt like a time capsule, in a way. Olivia had never wanted to learn to cook. Did she even know how to brown chicken? But how was she going to feed her family? Her community? Olivia was going to be a mother, for goodness' sake. You couldn't give a child Cheerios for dinner. And Iris, who'd always shown more of an interest in the kitchen, seemed more excited by the cookbook's layout and advertisers than the proportions of chili powder to black pepper in her chicken marinade.

Esther hadn't had a funeral in a few weeks, either. No heart attacks or strokes or car crashes to speak of. Apparently Ellerie County was going to just chug along and keep on living.

But the cookbook was coming along nicely. They were hoping to send it off to the printer as soon as possible, and planning to place an order for the number of copies they needed—one thousand. She couldn't even picture one thousand books. She still refused to let anybody tell why they were selling the book, even though Iris kept reminding her that her story could get her on the *Today* show. She didn't even watch anymore, ever since that handsome Matt Lauer had turned out to be a creep. Who could you trust?

No, these chocolate chip cookies held a different purpose. They were a bribe.

She stuck a finger into the dough and licked it clean. Eighty-two years old, and she still found herself licking the bowl.

The front door opened.

"Grandma? It's me." Iris.

"Hi, honey," Esther called out. "I'm making your favorite."

"Chocolate chip cookies?" Iris said, her eyes surprised. "Sweet. What's the occasion?"

"No occasion. Just love for my granddaughter. Help me roll these up, will you?" She hated to admit the arthritis was getting to her hands, but it was.

"Sure. By the way, grabbed your mail." She held up a handful of envelopes. Mostly junk addressed to Felix, probably, but she saw the familiar green envelope from the bank there as well.

"Thanks. Can you put it by the phone?" Esther hadn't had a

landline in years, same as everyone else, but that crowded countertop above her junk drawer would always be referred to as *by
the phone,* and Iris dropped the stack right where the clunky black
desk phone used to sit.

As they rolled the dough into balls, Iris chattered on about listing the Airbnb and which girl from high school had just had twins.
She talked and talked in a way Esther never would have dreamed
of talking with her grandmother. She was happy that they had that
kind of bond. In fact, she was banking on it, today.

Esther's grandmother had been a hard woman. She'd had to be,
hadn't she? Coming from Germany with nothing but a suitcase and
a prayer. They only ever called her Grandmother, and in the one
photograph that existed of her, she was glaring at the camera. Esther
remembered being terrified of her house, especially her porcelain
doll collection. The way those things stared! It was creepy.

Esther's own mother had been much better. She'd adored Fran,
her only grandchild. She still wasn't as warm and cozy as Esther
tried to be, but she baked her a three-tier on her birthday and always
sent checks on the anniversary of her baptism.

Iris slid the cookies into the oven and Esther sat down on one of
her barstools. "Iris, girl, we need to talk."

Iris glanced at her. "About what?"

"What happened the other day. Down on the dock." The scent
of chocolate chip cookie dough baking filled the kitchen. Good. It
was hard to yell at your grandmother when you smelled cookies.

"Yeah," said Iris, sighing. "That was freaky. I'm sorry you had
to see it."

Esther set her mouth in a thin line. She'd put on her favorite
pearl earrings today for an extra boost of confidence, the same way
she had before junior prom, when Richard Pike had chosen her of
all the girls at Catholic Memorial High.

"I don't need an apology."

Iris sat down and pulled her hair into a ponytail. These girls and their ponytails. It was like they'd never seen a blow-dryer before.

"I mean, when you think about what he saw at that parade . . . I just think it really messes with him sometimes," Iris said. "Which makes sense. Of course it does."

"Of course," Esther repeated flatly.

"So," said Iris, with a shrug, "sometimes he just . . . kind of freaks out."

"He's done this with you before?" Esther asked.

"*Done* it before?" That sharp tone tiptoed in. She got that from her mother. How many times had Fran used that I-know-best voice? A thousand, at least. They got it from their Larson side. Little female versions of Felix. "It's not something he *does*, Grandma. It just comes over him."

"How?" Esther asked gently.

"He just . . ." She waved a hand. "You know. Small things. He hates loud noises. So, like, if we hear a car backfire, he might zone out for a minute. And he doesn't get a lot of sleep, so that affects it, too."

Felix at the grocery store. Felix, taking her hand and dancing with her across their empty new house, the lake stretching out miles before them, a splash of possibility.

"He gets angry?" Esther asked.

"Not at *me*," said Iris. "I mean, he gets irritable. Annoyed at things . . . only when he's in a bad mood. I told you, he doesn't get a lot of sleep. And don't forget, he just lost his mom, and his dad is here and they don't really get along. Plus, he's Cricket's guardian now. It's a lot."

"Too much, maybe," said Esther.

Iris crossed her arms. "Is this an intervention?"

"Would it work if it was?"

"Grandma, you *like* Cooper."

"I barely know Cooper," she said, pointing a finger at Iris. "And neither do you. You've been together, what, a month? Five weeks? He's your renter. And then he's going to Milwaukee."

"I know enough," said Iris. "He's so nice, Grandma. Nice like you wouldn't believe. He asks me about myself, and he opens doors for me. Like it's the fifties or something! He's so smart, and well-read. And the way he takes care of his sister—that's always a good sign. Boys who are nice to their sisters."

Esther shook her head. "I know. I just want you to be happy."

"*I* know."

"It worried me," said Esther. "Seeing him like that. A person you could marry."

"Whoa. Who said 'marry'? You just said I've only been with him for a summer. Not even a whole summer!"

"Iris . . . you just be careful. You need to have an *awareness*. That's all I'm asking. You have to understand when people aren't all there, even if they're standing right in front of you."

"Like Joe?"

"Joe? Who's *Joe*?" asked Esther. "I'm talking about—"

"Joe, Grumpy Delilah's Joe. She told me he had . . ." She tapped her head dramatically. "Cooper's not *crazy*."

Joe—that poor guy. Esther remembered now. He'd had some difficulty out east, and when he came back, it wasn't so good. It wasn't the loud noises that did him in, but the quiet. Felix and him had spent many a night at Vernon's. But they went to daily Mass together, too.

"She said Grandpa helped him," said Iris. "Maybe Cooper just needs someone like that. Someone who understands. Maybe—"

"Someone like what?" snapped Esther. "Your grandpa didn't understand anything, anything at all." It was harsher than she meant it. But what the hell was Delilah doing, talking about Felix's private business?

Iris sighed. "I should go. I'm sorry. I have work to do. A new logo package for a client."

"The cookies aren't done. And Olivia and Kurt are coming by tonight for spaghetti. Stay, honey. I'm sorry."

"I'm not upset," said Iris, shaking her head. Ha. That liar. She kissed Esther on the head and went. Probably to go meet up with Cooper.

Iris: her brave, brilliant, beautiful granddaughter. So in love. Esther could see it in her, the way people who've been in love can see it. That's why she brought up marriage. She'd seen enough heartbreak from her daughter and granddaughters to know the real thing when she saw it.

But Iris had no idea! She didn't know what it was like, to be married to a person who was so wounded. Whose feelings were hurt so easily. It hadn't been just that one time, she *knew* it hadn't. It wouldn't be, either. They could call it depression or battle fatigue or PTSD, whatever they wanted, but the wives? They bore a burden, too. A heavy one. The men saw horror and the women made it go away. Esther's full-time job had been to keep Felix happy, to keep Felix from remembering, to keep Felix from getting too upset so his mood wouldn't become a cloud that covered the entire house and scared their daughter. Being Felix's wife was like being the wife of a diabetic—some people had to avoid sugar and provide insulin; Esther had to avoid Democrats and movies that showed blood.

But wasn't that what a wife was? Someone who supported unconditionally? The way Katharine Rose could look at a bird and know exactly what species it was, Esther could walk into a room and know exactly what type of mood Felix was in. That was what you got, after fifty years of marriage.

The worst, she knew, was not managing his feelings. That part was easy. So much could be soothed with time and a whispered apology, a cocktail passed from her hands to his. It was the slow,

soft beat of your heart reminding you that you were losing yourself. With every *sorry* you don't mean, with every argument you
forfeit. The pieces of yourself you hand over, the same way she
had used cookies to bribe Fran. *I'm sorry I slammed the cabinet
too hard. I'm sorry I mentioned Nixon.* The History Channel had
mentioned Nixon, not her, but she'd turned it on, hadn't she? To
lie beside a man and completely loathe your weakness—that was
the part that had been so unbearably hard to live with, day in and
day out. Esther had always thought she was the type of person
who wasn't afraid of anyone. But she was afraid of Felix. Not of
his hands, but of his mood—his *words,* the way they could cut into
her like the knife he always carried. The way he'd wake up screaming and it was somehow her fault for not keeping him safe enough.

She couldn't tell this to Iris, as badly as she wanted to. Iris loved
her grandfather so much. Her image of him: It was so crisp and
perfect, her beloved doting grandpa who picked the splinters out of
her heels and made her giant ice cream sundaes. How could Esther
shatter that? How could she share this horrendous truth?

No. It was her cross to bear, that's all. She didn't wish it on Iris,
or Olivia, or Hazel, or anyone. Marriage to a person who had seen
horror—you needed a certain constitution for it. She could handle
it. She wasn't so sure her granddaughters could. She *was* sure, however, that she didn't want them to have to.

She saw the love in Iris. But she saw something else in Cooper.
She saw the sadness. The kind that couldn't leave or settle in your
bones; instead, it just floated through your bloodstream, like stars,
or ghosts.

EVER SINCE SHE was a little girl, Esther had had a hard time paying attention during the consecration of the Eucharist. Those old
words she'd heard time and time again—she could have said them
in her sleep. So her mind wandered, dancing lightly around grocery
lists and upcoming birthdays.

She liked the new priest. Father Sam—he was a kind man. But she felt bad for him, in a way. It couldn't have been his dream position, a tiny Northwoods parish. With a face like his, he should have been one of those priests with a YouTube channel.

Esther glanced down the pew at her family as they knelt. She hadn't knelt for the consecration in years; her knees just couldn't take it anymore. Barbara always knelt with a loud guffaw, wheezing and looking around to make sure everyone saw just how much she loved the Lord.

Fran and Aaron were there, looking tired. They both worked too hard. Kurt was there, too, but Olivia wasn't feeling well, so Esther planned on swinging by with some peppermints later. The poor girl looked so swollen, she was ready to pop.

And there, at the end of the pew, was her Iris. Iris seemed to have been upset with her ever since she brought up what had happened on the pier. It was exhausting, trying to convince all these people that sometimes love didn't look like a pat on the back. That sometimes it looked like telling hard truths you didn't want to hear.

Esther closed her eyes and thought about all the things she should do. Start planning out her Thanksgiving menu. Go and see Bea, who'd been hit with the flu and hadn't been able to make the past two cookbook meetings. COVID had ruined her lungs; she was sick so often now. Bake another pie for Ivan. Dust her credenza. Water the mums on Felix's grave. On and on and on; if she didn't keep moving, didn't keep giving, what would become of her? Who would notice if she simply slipped away?

"Mom," whispered Fran, elbowing her. Esther's eyes snapped open. Damn it. The line for communion was already forming, and that drama queen of a martyr Barbara had seen her snoozing.

Seventeen

I'm just saying," said Olivia, wincing as she bent over to pick up a laundry hamper. "You seem pretty serious."

"Will you stop? I said I'd get that," said Iris. She was sitting on Olivia's bed, propped up against her eight million pillows. She sometimes felt a little weird sitting on the bed Olivia and Kurt slept in, but whatever. She wasn't under the covers.

"I can fold my own laundry," Olivia said testily. "And don't squish my pregnancy pillow."

"Is that what this is? I thought it was for one of the dogs."

"You're avoiding my question."

"It wasn't a question, it was a comment."

"Iris!"

Iris laughed. "What do you want me to say? We are serious. It's seriously serious." *Cooper, Cooper, Cooper*—see? She was smiling, even now, thinking about him.

"This quick?" asked Olivia, sounding somewhat skeptical.

"Grandma and Grandpa dated for, like, ten seconds before getting married."

"Don't let Grandma hear you talking marriage. You'll never hear the end of it. Weren't you planning on making some money and getting out of Ellerie?"

"Um, that was *you*," said Iris. "I was planning on being the self-less daughter and granddaughter who watches over the family."

"Well, he's definitely cute. And you wouldn't have to worry about paying for your kids to go to college, ha."

"Olivia. God."

"I'm *joking*. I think it's great. Better than meeting some rando on Tinder."

"I'm not on Tinder! I was on *Hinge,* and only for like, a week. Is that how you always fold your towels? That's not how you fold a towel."

Olivia threw a fluffy blue towel at her. "Then you do it."

Iris calmly started folding the massive pile of laundry. She actually enjoyed folding laundry, to be honest. She liked the feeling of looking at a gigantic plastic bin of tangled fabric and ending with neat, orderly piles. She could envision her future, as a mom of a whole howling troop of children, folding their soccer jerseys and flannel footies, Cooper's Marquette T-shirts that he always wore, too—there she went again.

Olivia flopped down on her bed and fanned herself. "Get this child out of me. I swear."

Iris had swung by to drop off a sweater she'd borrowed, but like always, she'd somehow ended up staying for a reheated mug of coffee and helping Olivia do random things around the house. She had to admit that she loved Olivia and Kurt's place—it wasn't as nice as her parents', and definitely not as nice as her grandma's. *A starter home,* Kurt kept calling it. But it had real hardwood floors and a creepy attic where Iris imagined piles of secret documents were hidden, even though Olivia insisted it was just insulation. There were bookshelves on every wall, disorganized and chaotic and overflowing. And while it didn't have lake access, it was close enough that you could read in the shady hammock in the backyard and listen to the waves. It was cozy.

"You reading that?" asked Iris, nodding to the massive *What to Expect When You're Expecting* sitting on Olivia's bedside table.

Her sister rolled her eyes. "They could sum it up in three pages. 'Here's everything your kid could die from, and by the way, you're going to have heartburn like a motherfucker.'"

"But how are you going to know what to do?" asked Iris.

"I live five minutes away from Mom and ten minutes away from Grandma. I'll be all right," said Olivia.

That was her sister: always coolly confident, so sure that if she took the right steps, she'd land where she was meant to. Everything had always come so easy for Olivia. There was a small part of Iris that whispered *because she isn't the one trying to clean up other people's messes,* and maybe that was true. Olivia wasn't selfish. But she wasn't *selfless,* either, not in the way Iris wished she could be. Iris at least *wanted* to be the selfless sort—that's what she was raised to be. All "no thank you" and "I've got it." But she couldn't help it. She wanted things she didn't yet have. At least Olivia admitted these things out loud.

And besides, Olivia wasn't wrong. They'd had a gloriously idyllic childhood, the kind they make Hallmark movies out of. Their parents were still married; both girls still went to church. Olivia had found a kind man who worked online as a book reviewer. Iris had a successful business, even though she wasn't sure her parents quite understood what a freelance graphic designer did. They visited their grandmother and washed their sheets and one of them even knew how to properly fold a towel.

So Olivia's daughter would be okay. She came from generations of Larsons, people who worked hard and cared about other people. What more could she ask for? What more could a child need?

Iris's eyes caught on a framed photo of Olivia and her husband on her dresser—the two of them, kissing, the lake in the background. It was right next to one of her, Olivia, their mother, and their grandmother, arms thrown around each other, Olivia in her lace wedding dress, bought at the fancy bridal store in Waukegan.

"How did you know about Kurt?" Iris asked suddenly.

Olivia didn't even have to ask what she meant. She just cocked her head thoughtfully. "I didn't," she said. "I decided on Kurt."

As if love were a decision you could make, or not make. As if feelings like the ones she was having now could be ignored with some soundproof headphones and heavy sunglasses.

"But what made you decide?"

Olivia shrugged. "Remember how when you forgot your valentines that year, and Dad left a meeting to drive them to you?"

Iris nodded. She'd burst into tears, opening her backpack and not seeing the paper bag she'd so painstakingly decorated. She'd been looking forward to the second-grade Valentine's Day party for weeks. That feeling of relief, of seeing her dad walk in triumphantly holding up the Disney Princess cards she'd picked out . . . it stuck in her mind like a flag.

"Kurt would do that," Olivia said. "You wouldn't even have to ask twice."

Would Cooper? *Of course,* Iris thought. But the follow-up thought—that he would if he was *there,* if he wasn't living in his own history, if he wasn't seeing a rifle behind his eyelids and denying it—haunted her. And that haunting she couldn't quite ignore.

"Come on," sang Cooper, his voice sounding fuzzy over the phone. "I'm outside."

Iris grinned. Of course she was hanging out with Cooper tonight; she did every night. Sometimes they went over to her parents' for beer or ice cream, but she loved spending nights just the two of them, on an adventure. *Everything* with Cooper felt like an adventure.

They didn't make plans. He'd just pull that Tesla into her driveway and call her, and out she'd run. August was September now, all golden leaves and fruit tarts. He'd been over that very morning, helping her peel a giant bowl of apples, measuring out the cinnamon and kissing it off her fingers.

She spritzed on one final spray of the Chanel perfume her dad's fancy sister had sent her from Boston two years ago that she never wore. She felt giddy. It had just been so *long,* so long since she'd felt this excited about anything.

She got in the car and slammed the door, and as she leaned over to kiss Cooper, who smelled like toothpaste, she had a flash of her earlier conversation with Olivia. She'd been so stupid. Of *course* Cooper would bring those valentines. Look at him! He was right here in front of her.

"Where are we going?" she asked.

Cooper grinned at her. "A new place. You like surprises?"

"Who doesn't?" she said. Which was funny, because—well, *she* didn't really like surprises. Sophomore year of high school, her mom had thrown her a surprise birthday party, and she'd walked into the bowling alley with her greasy hair pulled back in a ponytail. She'd thought she was being forced there for a family fun night, and she spent the entire party wishing she'd put on some mascara.

They drove the long, curvy road out of Ellerie and toward Waukegan. She rolled down the window and leaned back, sticking her feet out into the night air. "Don't forget to watch for deer."

"I want to see an albino one," he said. The famous albino deer of Ellerie, on every postcard.

"You will," Iris said. "Before you leave."

"I'm never leaving," he replied, wrapping her finger in his. She willed herself to believe it was true. "I'll stay for Halloween, then Christmas, then New Year's . . ."

"Musky Days," she laughed. "Our Northwoods holiday."

"What?"

"Festival celebrating a giant fish. Don't ask. You'll see next weekend. It's a sight to behold."

"I want to behold *all* the sights. I like the sight I'm beholding right now," he said. That cheesy grin! What a line. He should have written for Netflix. Iris adored it.

Cooper couldn't stay. Well, he *shouldn't* stay. He practically had a daughter now. Sometimes Iris felt bad for poor Cricket, up here in the woods with nobody but her brother and her father. Every time Iris saw her, she had her nose in a book. Online school—well, Iris wasn't sure about that.

But how could she let him leave? That drive to Milwaukee wasn't impossible, but it was far. What if he found some other girl to peel apples with? The thought made her stomach drop. She could pretend a little while longer. Maybe pretending would make it real, somehow. Her grandmother believed in miracles. Why shouldn't Iris?

As if he were reading her mind, he told her he'd gotten into a fight about Cricket with Ivan that day.

"Which, whatever. I'm always in a fight with Ivan. Ivan is a fight personified. But he was so mad about Cricket doing online school, and . . ." He shook his head.

"What?" said Iris.

"He doesn't think it's a good idea. He must have taken a parenting class when I wasn't looking, ha. He thinks she needs her friends and stuff."

"I mean, I get that. It's a big decision. I get why he wouldn't be—"

"He doesn't get an opinion, Iris," Cooper bit out. "He's such a mess, he can't even take *care* of her. That's why *I* have to do it. You don't get to miss the first thirteen years and then show up with some big ideas about the right thing to do, okay? Ivan's not exactly a good decision-maker."

She nodded, carefully. "Okay. Yeah." Not okay. Not yeah. But what else was she supposed to say? It wasn't like he was wrong. And besides, she didn't want to ruin this night. *Don't let him get worked up,* she begged God or the universe or the loons. She hoped someone was listening.

And it was over, just a small flash. He turned and smiled. "I'm sorry," he said. "I'm sorry, he just—I got this, okay? Cricket's my responsibility, and I've got it."

They drove through the night, passing the brutally dense forests on County Road M. Iris turned up the radio and sang along. Cooper kept looking over at her and grinning, and she laughed, shrieking at him to watch the road.

When they finally got where they were going, Iris's jaw dropped.

"Do you know where we are?" she asked Cooper.

Cooper grinned at her. "Do *you*?"

Of course she knew. The Golden Mast was the kind of restaurant you didn't forget.

"My grandma and grandpa—"

"—had their wedding reception here," Cooper finished for her. "I know. Esther's the one who suggested it."

Esther, her grandmother, who had opened a thousand and one juice boxes for her and hosted birthday parties for her down on her dock almost her entire life. She was trying, even with her worries.

She saw it, the way her grandmother worried. Iris wished Cooper hadn't gotten lost that day on the dock a few weeks back, but she had a handle on it just fine. She hadn't told Esther about the other times, the times it was longer than a minute. The times when he'd been drinking and everything felt a whole lot heavier and a whole lot louder. The times when he seemed angry at *her*. It was pretty simple, really—the noises thing. She'd nailed the outhouse door shut.

Besides, Esther had her own worries. The cookbook was off to the printer. A thousand copies . . . they were all holding their breath. Well, Iris was. If the funeral ladies held their breath, they'd pass out. They had aging lungs.

The Golden Mast had low lighting and model ships tastefully hung from the ceiling. The ancient oak bar was a thing of beauty, carved with mermaids and seashells and Our Lady, Star of the Sea. But it was hard to ignore the main attraction—the giant floor-to-ceiling windows looking out onto Trout Lake. The Golden Mast was the type of restaurant you'd have a wedding reception in in 1964: all dark wood and discounts for Knights of Columbus. Her grandpa had taken her there for a special lunch just after eighth-grade graduation and split a huge plate of crab legs with her.

"Happy surprise?" Cooper said, grinning.

"The happiest," she said.

When Cooper was in moods like this, and when she had chardonnay, Iris could forget about his other moods, forget even about the uncomfortable moment the day before when they saw a news report about a shooting at a summer camp and he made her watch the whole thing. *That kid,* he said, his voice sounding far away, underwater, as they showed the mug shot. *He looks like a kid.* He didn't, at all. He looked like a grown man.

The music felt loud, all of a sudden, and when she sang along to a line of it she realized she was a little drunk. It was one of those old Louis Armstrong songs where everyone knows the words but nobody knows the name of the song. Cooper laughed, ordered another bottle of wine, more appetizers.

"Your dad has an episode about shrimp toast," she said, nodding toward the plate. "He says he hates it."

"Of course he does. Ivan Welsh hates everything. Ivan Welsh hates joy." Cooper's words were slurring. They needed to slow down on the wine. They still had to drive home. The roads were dangerous at night.

"He does not," laughed Iris. "Let's—"

"Look," said Cooper, nodding toward the half-full bottle. "We need more."

"Cooper, we just ordered that."

"Where's that waiter?"

She shouldn't have brought up Ivan. "How's Cricket? Besides the school thing, I mean."

He smiled. It actually reached his eyes. "She's good. I love that kid. We should bring her here sometime. She'd love the view."

"Everyone does. You can swim off the dock, too," Iris told him.

Cooper hummed along to the music and flagged down the waiter.

"You folks ready to order?" He was younger than them, but his hairline was already receding. He was probably used to young couples in tipsy love. Generations of hearts and alcohol and seasoned french fries.

"We'll have one more bottle first," said Cooper, coughing.

"No," said Iris quickly. "Cooper, let's order. I'm starving."

"Fine! Order your food. But bring the bottle, too."

"Aren't you eating?" she asked.

The waiter looked back and forth between them. "You folks need more time to decide?"

"Chardonnay, Jeeves," said Cooper, pointing at the waiter.

"Cooper," said Iris, her cheeks flushing with embarrassment at his rudeness. "Don't be—"

"Don't be what?" said Cooper loudly.

"We'll both take the puttanesca," she said quickly. "Thank you."

The waiter, now annoyed, walked away, not even writing down their order.

"Well, *he* was kind of a dick," mused Cooper. He picked up the bottle of wine and tried to pour himself the last few sips, but knocked his glass over. It hit his bread plate and shattered.

"*Shit!*" he yelled loudly. Iris felt her heart start to race. This was the Northwoods. People here drank. A lot. But there were places where drunkenness was fine: Vernon's. The Silver Dollar. Your very own dock, with a can of Hamm's and the lake under your feet. But not a place like the Golden Mast. Here it looked trashy.

A man wearing a tie walked over. A manager, maybe. "Don't worry about that, folks. We'll get it cleaned up. Everything okay?"

"What the *fuck*," said Cooper, flinging his hand. It seemed like he was trying to shake the spilled wine off his fingers, but his hand grazed the manager's arm. The man put his arm on Cooper's shoulder. "Sir, I'm going to have to ask you to—"

"Don't *touch* me," said Cooper, and he stood up hard and fast, his chair falling behind him. Iris clapped a hand over her mouth. She felt completely frozen, as if someone was holding all her muscles and bones and organs in place. One wrong move, and she would shatter, just like the wineglass.

"You need to exit the premises," the manager said. "*Now.*"

The eyes of everyone, staring at them as they hurried out the door, whispers of *Fran's girl* and *Ivan Welsh*, the waiter cheerfully wishing them a good night and holding the door open for them, not yet realizing his tip wasn't waiting at the table. Iris, shaking with embarrassment, blinking hard. The host grabbed her elbow, murmuring—*You folks driving a car home, or a boat?* Because of course nobody cared if you drove a boat drunk. That never made any sense to Iris.

"I'll drive," she snapped at the poor host, who just didn't want her to die in a fiery car crash.

She dragged Cooper out to the car, opening the door to the passenger seat and throwing him in it. He seemed half asleep. She went around to the driver's seat and flopped down. He didn't even flinch when she slammed the door as hard as she could.

She didn't want her memories of the Golden Mast to be like this. She wanted her grandpa. Suddenly, she wanted him so, so badly, his gentle eyes, his arms around her tight. Even his cigarette breath.

Grandpa always knew what to do. He'd fixed Joe. He could fix Cooper.

She put the car in drive, but there was just no way. She could barely get the key in the ignition after three glasses of wine. Humiliated, she pulled out her phone.

What could she do? They could call an Uber and leave the Tesla there. But when she opened the app, it informed her it was experiencing longer-than-normal wait times. Damn it! How many times had she said the Northwoods needed more Uber drivers? She could try her sister, maybe, but no—she couldn't ask a nine-months-pregnant person to come pick her up this late. Her mother? No, Fran was the last person she wanted to see Cooper like this. Iris's family was endlessly forgiving, especially about alcohol incidents. *Drunk* was a Band-Aid. *Oops, someone drank too much—we've all been there.* But this was worse than drunk. She would never look at Cooper the same way.

Who'd *already* seen Cooper that way?

Oh no. But she had to. What else could she do? She dialed the number; she knew it by heart.

While they waited for their ride, Iris turned to look at Cooper. "Are you even going to apologize?"

And suddenly—like a shotgun—he was crying. *Sobbing,* shoulders shaking, deep, heaving, never-ending sobs.

"Cooper," said Iris, her voice full of panic. "I was—it's okay—I—"

"You don't get it," he said, his voice broken. "You can't get it."

She pulled him close to her, as if she were his mother, and rubbed his hair with her hand. "Shh," she said. "It's okay." What the *hell*?

"You don't get it," he repeated. "You will never fucking get it."

"I know," she said, feeling like she was going to cry herself. "I know. You're right. I don't. I won't."

His sobs gradually slowed to a trickle of a cry.

"Cooper," she whispered. "It's okay." What was happening? The terrifying part was that none of his triggers had even *been* there. There hadn't even been a loud noise at the bar. Nobody had brought up guns! It was like his mind was completely out of control, with no rules she could play by. It was an unwinnable game.

And then he was sleeping, drooling on the black-and-white shirt she'd painstakingly picked for dinner.

When she saw Esther's headlights pull into the parking lot, she finally started crying a little. There she was: a person who knew and loved her. Seeing Esther felt like finding your phone when you're sure you've lost it. A sweeping, immense *relief* poured over her.

Esther helped Iris get Cooper into the back seat, lying down, and Iris got into the front, buckling up and staring out the window. She couldn't even bring herself to thank her grandmother, who'd probably been crocheting or reading one of those paperbacks with a woman staring out a window on the cover. Esther drove them home in her ancient Corolla, taking the turns slow, squinting to see in the dark.

Suddenly, she slammed on the brakes.

"Look," she said. "Iris. Look."

She looked. It was an albino deer, glistening in the moonlight. The deer just blinked at them, as if waiting for them to take her picture.

Cooper missed the whole thing.

That night, Iris didn't want to be alone. She slept in her favorite old bedroom at her grandma's, under a thick weighted blanket.

When she woke up in the morning, she heard the summer sounds of Mr. Murphy mowing the lawn next door and birds chirping, fighting over worms. Esther had an entire spread waiting for her— French toast with strawberries, and bacon so crisp it was almost burnt, just like Iris liked it.

"I'm so sorry about last night," Iris said. "You know how it goes. You're drinking, you're laughing . . ."

Esther said nothing.

"Grandma. Please. I'm sorry."

She glanced at her granddaughter. "You're not the one who should be apologizing. I told that boy that restaurant. That place— it's special to me."

"I know."

"Not good, my dear. I'm concerned."

"Don't be, Grandma. I swear. He's just . . . having a hard time." Those sobs. She'd never seen that layer. Neither had Esther, and Iris intended to keep it that way, honestly. He'd seen things she and Esther would never understand.

Esther sighed. "I've got to get cooking. Funeral today. Mary Jo Carver, remember her? She used to give you Skittles after church."

Iris dragged an ancient bike out of the garage and rode it home, praying her mother or father or sister wouldn't suddenly drive by. When she got to her house, Cooper was sitting there on her front step.

"Well, well, well," she said. "Look what the hungover cat dragged in."

"Iris," he said, "I'm . . . I mean, I feel ridiculous. I'm such a dick. I'm so sorry."

"How'd you get your car back?"

"I had to ask Ivan to drive me this morning. It was a low moment, believe me."

"As low as getting driven home by your girlfriend's grandmother?"

"I'm buying her flowers. Today. Or some of that whiskey she likes. Oh my God, I can't even mention alcohol. I'm going to be sick." He pressed the heels of his hands into his eyes.

She had to laugh. He looked like a college kid, sitting there in the sunlight. Her Cooper.

The heart can play tricks on you. *He's fine, drama queen,* it told her. All those country songs about following your heart. A Bible verse floated up in her memory, reminding her not to lean on her own understanding, something about the human heart being deceitful. Her brain slapped her upside the head. *Fa-la-la-la,* her heart said, covering its eyes.

"Come on," she said. "I'll make you some coffee."

Eighteen

Hi, you've reached the confidential voice mail of Dr. Anders Hoss.
If this is an emergency, please hang up and dial 911. Otherwise,
please leave your name, number, and a brief message, and I'll
return your call within two business days. Thank you.

Cooper hung up the phone.

He could have left a voice mail. Should have. Would have, but for what? He wasn't going to Zoom his shrink with his dad one room over.

He hated being in the same house as Ivan, but the leaves had changed color and he still had no idea when they would leave. *Avoidance,* Dr. Hoss would probably say. But Cricket seemed like she was doing fine. Better than Cooper, even. She spent most of her days reading—thick stacks of Harry Potter books, tote bags of mysteries brought home from the library, books for teenagers with witches and magicians on their covers. She'd take giant bags of fruit out to the dock and sit there in a thick hoodie, eating peach after peach, reading an entire series. Cooper had no idea if this was normal. He'd missed Parenting a Grief-Stricken Teenager 101. She said she liked online school, and he believed her.

His own grief over Annabelle felt tangled up in everything else. It felt like something he had to escape from. And it was easy to do here. Even though Annabelle had been from Ellerie, they'd never visited as a family. That meant there weren't small signs of her everywhere like there would be in Chicago. The few restaurants held no memories of her; the sound of a boat didn't bring to mind her face. In fact, the main thing that made him think of Annabelle was the church. And seeing her face in Cricket's—they had the exact same shade of green eyes.

He knew they couldn't stay in Ellerie forever, no matter what story he spun for Iris. Eventually, he'd have to get a new job, and Cricket would have to rejoin the world. Life had to keep moving, even if it felt impossible without Annabelle. He couldn't picture leaving, though. He honestly couldn't visualize driving down the driveway, away from Iris, waving goodbye, going back to frying breakfast sausage and flipping pancakes. The real-world heaviness of long-term parenting would be there—dentist appointments and soccer games, driving Cricket to sleepovers and finding a way forward. It all had to happen, yet it felt so far away. He couldn't open his eyes and look at it just yet. He would, he knew. But—not yet.

But God, if Ivan would just *leave*. He was there and then not there. One night he'd make an entire pasta dinner for Cooper and Cricket from scratch; the next day he'd be gone for seven hours. He'd be yelling at his assistant, Gabi, on the phone while chopping onions for an egg scramble. Cooper had seen him a handful of times just walking among the thick pine trees between the deck and Lake Ellerie, reaching out and letting his fingers scrape against the tree bark. He didn't bother trying to talk to Cricket about her mother, or asking Cooper how long they were planning on staying. It was like he was content to live forever, half frozen, in the Northwoods.

And Ivan hated the online-school thing. Insisted it was a bad idea. Cooper caught him teaching Cricket how to make Monte Cristo sandwiches the other day, and Cooper had wanted to throw the custard at him. It was too late for daddy-daughter cooking dates, and too late for any of Ivan's opinions on Cricket's education to be worth anything to Cooper. Cooper could have done online school and Ivan wouldn't have batted an eye. He probably wouldn't even have *noticed*.

Cooper was the one making sure she got a shrink, making sure she was talking to her friends, making sure she was doing her homework. Well, kind of. He *intended* to make sure she did all those things. These were the things Ivan should be worried about, not whether Cricket knew how to panfry a Monte Cristo. Cooper shouldn't even have had to become a father yet. Add it to the long list of Ivan's failures and fuckups. It felt never-ending.

Cricket was down on the dock, eating a giant container of raspberries and reading. "Hey, bug."

"Hi," she muttered, not looking up.

"How's your book?"

She ignored him.

"Hey." He reached down and splashed some freezing lake water on her, making her shriek.

"This is a library book!" She held it high in the air, away from the water.

"That water's freezing." He looked across the lake and saw a boat or two, but also plenty of people in waders, taking their docks apart board by board. The surest sign of autumn on the lake.

"You realize it's October?" Cooper asked. "We can stay here a while longer. You can do the online school thing. But we're still finding a shrink. And maybe you should—I don't know, join a club or something."

"A club," she said flatly.

"Yeah. You need to interact with real-world people. Not just Zoom classmates. Don't you miss your friends?"

"No," she said with a shrug.

"What about Sophie?" Sophie's mom had actually called him to check in. Her voice had sounded tight. *I'd love if we could come visit*

Cricket, or she could come here for a weekend. Sophie misses her quite a bit. I can pick her up, she'd said. But Cricket had shrugged it off.

"She's pretty busy. It's soccer season."

"Well, think about it. Playing a sport or something. Dance class. Chess club—hell, I don't care. Just something. I think it would be a good idea."

Cricket rolled her eyes, and Cooper almost smiled. Here it was: the first taste of raising a teenager. Cooper and Cricket had always been close. All those sibling fights seemed kind of stupid when one of you was fifteen years older. She'd been less of an annoying little sister and more of a cute baby the girls at school had fawned over. And it's not like Cricket had had a dad to look up to. That had always been Cooper—at Cricket's First Communion and her soccer games and the one piano recital Annabelle had forced her to perform in before letting her quit. And besides, Cricket had been so mature her entire life. Responsible. A straight-A student, according to Annabelle's proud bumper sticker. But that *please stop talking to me, parental figure* eye roll seemed ingrained in the blood of thirteen-year-olds.

"I don't need a shrink," she said. "I'm not the one who doesn't sleep."

He gave her a look. "Hi, kid. Meet adult."

"You can't simultaneously tell me how badly I need therapy and then not go yourself when you're . . ." She waved a hand in the air.

"I'm what?" he asked hotly.

"You know. Wound up."

He wasn't *wound up,* necessarily. Just on edge. He was disappearing more often. That's what he and Iris called it. When his mind would bring him back to North Harbor. The smell of blood would fill his nose and he'd just zone out, only for a minute, and forget where he was. And sure, the whole not-sleeping thing was getting old. The loud-noises thing was embarrassing.

Okay, the drinking—that, too. The Golden Mast. His stomach turned. He hadn't seen Esther since, thank God. He'd sent the waiter a check for the tip, 200 percent of what their bill had been. But it wasn't his fault. Dr. Hoss had said it was supposed to get better, but with every new day, The Girl was in his brain a little longer, asking him for help, humming along to "Santa Baby."

"I have a shrink," he bit out. "And you will, too. We both have Fucked-Up Absent Father Problems, remember?"

"Speaking of dear old Dad, did Ivan go into town?" asked Cricket, finally giving up on her book and dog-earing the page.

"Are you dog-earing a library book? Learn some respect. And yeah, I think so."

Just then, as if they'd summoned him, they heard a voice. "Hey."

They both jumped and looked up at the deck. There was Ivan, leaning over the rail. He looked like shit. He had dark circles under his eyes, and it almost seemed like he was balding. The suave celebrity chef who'd been on the cover of *People* numerous times looked like he needed a nap more than anything.

Cooper shielded his eyes from the sun. "You okay?"

Ivan shrugged and reached up to slap a mosquito on his shoulder. "Hungry. You guys want dinner?"

"I could eat," said Cricket.

Cooper started to shrug—he wanted to call Iris and see if she had time to grab a bite. She'd just taken on a new client. Cooper could bring her onion rings. He loved to sit and watch her work—the way her tongue would just poke out of her mouth and she'd furrow her brow, occasionally stopping to crack her knuckles. He loved that girl. He *loved* that girl, even though he knew it was a bad idea.

But then he glanced back at Cricket. He felt like she needed him right then. He didn't want to stick her with Ivan alone.

Besides, Iris was kind of pissed at him. She wouldn't say that, but she was. He'd gotten mad at her the day before, for something that was 100 percent not her fault. But that outhouse door—it had come open again. It was killing him. He'd gone down himself and practically ripped the thing off the hinges, and Iris had asked him what he was doing, and he'd completely lost his temper at her. He felt terrible. He'd even ordered her flowers from Daisy Mae's in town. But something about that noise turned him into an animal.

"Whatever," he called up. "Sure."

The three of them hopped into Cooper's Tesla and drove into town, passing an entire family of deer. Ivan was quiet, just staring out the window while an Ed Sheeran song played.

"What the . . . ," muttered Cooper as they turned onto Main Street.

"Is that a giant *fish*?" asked Cricket.

There was an enormous papier-mâché musky in the middle of Main Street.

"It's so crowded," said Cricket. She was right—crowds of people were streaming out of buildings, carrying funnel cakes and red Solo cups, laughing. There was a huge banner reading *Musky the Fish of 10,000 Casts*.

"Musky Days," said Cooper suddenly.

"What?"

"Musky Days. It's a big fishing festival . . . thing. I don't know, Iris told me about it. I didn't realize . . ."

"That the entire population of Ellerie County would quadruple?" asked Cricket.

"There's no way we're going to be able to find anywhere to eat. Damn." That, and tons of people would want autographs and photos of Ivan. Cooper didn't feel like dealing with that, and by the look of him, neither did Ivan. "We could go to the grocery store, I guess." Cooper drove toward County Road E. Ivan still didn't say a word.

"Dad?" asked Cricket. "What do you want to do? Go buy food and make something, or . . ."

"Whatever's fine," said Ivan. "Actually—well, I'm a little tired." From all the not-working he'd been doing?

"We could just do, like, McDonald's," said Cricket, as they passed a sign advertising the Golden Arches.

Ivan wrinkled his nose, and that settled it, in Cooper's mind. Yes. They were going to take the James Beard Award–nominated dickhead to Mickey D's, and he was going to sit there and enjoy himself.

"I DON'T EVEN know what you're saying," said Cricket flatly.

Ivan glanced at the illuminated menu. "I've never been to Mc-Donald's."

Cooper rolled his eyes. "Crick, of course he hasn't."

"Excuse me," said Ivan, "I've eaten meat from street vendors hundreds of times. I'm not a snob. I just enjoy good food."

"But . . ." Cricket shook her head. "It's an American institution."

"So is the DMV. That doesn't make it *good,*" Ivan countered.

The family of six in front of them gleefully walked away from the counter clutching Happy Meals. Cricket just sighed.

"Well, I usually get a cheeseburger with added Mac Sauce," said Cricket.

"Mac Sauce?" asked Ivan, as if the words felt foreign in his mouth.

"Like ketchup, but better," supplied Cooper.

"And," said Cricket, "a supersize fry."

"From the documentary where the man eats himself into diabetes?"

"Exactly," said Cricket proudly.

Ivan looked back at the menu. The bored, acne-ridden teenage cashier yawned.

"What's that?" said Ivan, pointing at the dessert menu.

Cricket covered her face with her hands. "He just asked what a McFlurry was, didn't he?"

Cooper grinned. "A McFlurry is chemicals and sugar whipped into fake–ice cream oblivion that tastes like heaven on a spoon. M&M, Oreo, or caramel brownie?"

"Three of us. Three flavors. God has spoken," Cricket said solemnly.

"Speaking of God," said Ivan, nodding forward. There was Iris's priest—well, not *Iris's,* though that was how Cooper thought of him. Father Sam, Iris's priest friend, walking away from the pickup area with a greasy paper bag.

"Busted," said Father Sam with a grin. "How are you folks doing?"

"Surprised you're not at Musky Days. Blessing the fish or something," said Cooper.

Father Sam laughed. "It's wild. They tried to cancel Mass for it. They needed the church parking lot. Are you kidding me? I was there for a bit, making an appearance, but . . . it got a little chaotic."

"Feel free to join us," said Ivan. "It's my inaugural McDonald's experience. Kind of like a baptism. Your specialty."

Father Sam chuckled. "I'll let you guys have some family time. I could use an early night in. Just me and some *Mandalorian* sounds kind of ideal."

"Why don't you two get us a table," said Ivan, nodding toward the booths. Cooper looked at him in surprise, but did as he said, steering Cricket away and letting Ivan have a moment to mutter something to the priest. He glanced back a moment later and saw Father Sam's face had gone serious. When you thought about it, being a priest had to be kind of similar to being Ivan. At any given moment, someone was going to want something from you, and you had to be prepared to give it. Although instead of representing a brand, you represented God.

Cooper wasn't envious of either of them. After the shooting, he'd been a minor celebrity for about a week. He deleted every single email he'd gotten from reporters, but North Harbor was such a small town. Everyone knew who he was. They wanted to stop him and shake his hand. Praise him for his bravery. He represented hope to them. He represented a hero.

And some people thrived on that. One of the police officers from the shooting had been the *Wisconsin State Journal*'s Person of the Year and gone on *The View* to advocate for more background checks on gun purchases. *Like that would stop anything,* Cooper had thought. A crazy person wants a gun, they're going to get their hands on a gun. Pulling positivity out of death wasn't what Cooper wanted to do. He didn't want to make it *mean* anything. The thought of having to tell the story over and over, and repeat his own part in it, made him want to throw up.

Thirty minutes later, he sat with Ivan and Cricket at the Formica table, surrounded by greasy plastic bags and three large McFlurries. "Stairway to Heaven" was playing over the speakers, which seemed like a weird choice for a McDonald's.

"You know," mused Ivan, "it's not bad."

"Not bad? McFlurries are small clouds of heaven," said Cricket giddily.

"I like this caramel one," said Ivan. He scraped the plastic spoon along the bottom to get every last bite. Okay, Cooper had never seen him do *that.*

"Esther makes caramel with condensed milk," said Cooper. "I was over there for dinner a couple of weeks ago with Iris and she had this whole ice cream bar. I've never seen anyone make it that way."

"It's good," said Ivan. "I mean, I usually just do it with sugar, but the condensed milk way is kind of classic. One time Annabelle tried to do it . . . oh my gosh." He laughed.

Cooper cracked a grin. "Annabelle, cooking?"

"Hey! She made one hell of a frozen pizza," joked Cricket.

"Cheesy potatoes, too," Cooper remembered. "I would eat bowls of those when I came to visit from Marquette, remember?"

"I told her to boil the milk," said Ivan. "I meant *in the can,* hello. She poured it all out. It stuck to the pot and ruined it. The smoke alarm went off. It was . . ." He laughed again, covering his face with his hands. "I thought I was going to keel over, laughing so hard. She was so mad, and then she started laughing, too, and then we couldn't figure out how to get the smoke alarm to stop so we just unscrewed it and put it in the garage. It was a million years ago. She was pregnant with you, Crick. Her sweet tooth was wild for nine months."

Cricket smiled, and Cooper saw the sadness in her eyes. "She loved McFlurries, too."

"We should make ice cream," said Ivan. "I can order us an ice cream maker. They've got some cool flavors up here. Hey, that could go in Iris's cookbook."

"That would be fun," said Cricket. She sounded kind of excited, and Cooper felt the urge to remind her of all of Ivan's unkept promises. The we-shoulds that had colored their entire childhoods. But he didn't.

"Best dessert you've ever had," said Cooper. "Go."

"A frozen hot chocolate from Serendipity Three," said Cricket. "Mom and I went to New York with you when you were on the *Today* show, remember?"

Ivan nodded. "I was promoting the burger cookbook."

"That thing was so good," said Cricket. "What's yours, Cooper?"

"Harold's Doughnuts," said Cooper.

"Doughnuts are breakfast, not dessert."

"Not when they're eaten at two A.M." Cooper's favorite twenty-four-hour bakery in Milwaukee made the best yeast doughnuts he'd ever had. His particular favorite was the maple bacon, scarfed down after one too many tequila shots at Murphy's.

But a dessert was about more than the taste, too. Ivan always talked about that on *Ivan Eats*. When Cooper was growing up and missed his dad, he'd watch Ivan's show, as lame as that sounded. Ivan wasn't there, one bedroom over, but he was in Thailand or the Congo, eating breakfast and talking about culture. Food told you things, about the people who made it and the people who ate it.

So, his other favorite desserts: Sour gummy worms, eaten in the movie theater with his old nanny while they watched the latest Marvel movie. A chocolate shake, drunk while studying in the

Marquette library and watching the sun set over the lake. Pillsbury cinnamon rolls out of a can, eaten while visiting Annabelle and Cricket. A smoothie, in Maui, the one time his mom had asked him to come visit and they'd gone out fishing for sharks. Esther's cherry pie, the day he met Iris.

"What about yours, Dad?" Cricket asked Ivan.

He glanced around the fluorescent-lit McDonald's. It was late. The only other people there were a group of teenagers in the corner, blowing wrappers off their straws at each other, and the cashier, who was scrolling TikTok on his phone and randomly chuckling.

"This one," said Ivan. "This one right here."

And although Cooper could have pushed back, reminded him of the macarons of Paris and the granita of Sicily, although he could have called Ivan's bluff and reminded him that he hadn't actually been present for hardly any of their desserts, although he could have rolled his eyes and pushed back from the table, throwing the cups in the garbage and announcing it was time to go, he decided not to. He decided to believe it. Just this once.

Nineteen

*E*sther had seen on one of those home improvement shows—there were so many these days—a new sink that turned on when you put your hands under the faucet. She didn't spend much time thinking about home improvements, but she did wish she had one of those. She was always getting meatball gunk, or flour, or, in today's case, spaghetti sauce on the faucet handle.

Spaghetti sauce was one of her favorite things to cook. It was labor-intensive—she had to drive all the way to Zephyr's for the fancy Italian sausage, and it had to simmer on the stove for hours. But every single time she fed it to someone, their eyes lit up, and they gave a quiet *mmm*. That's what food should do to people. Make them feel at home.

Well, Olivia and Kurt needed some of that feeling. Nine months pregnant—Esther remembered that.

And those early days with a baby—she remembered those, too. Mary Frances had come into the world screaming and never stopped. The nurse kept asking, *What's her name? What's her name?* right after she was born, and Esther couldn't even hear the question. Her daughter refused to be put down for the first two years of her life. They had her tested for everything under the sun, but she didn't have any medical problems. Just an opinion, at such a young age.

The girls didn't realize how different things were now than when Esther had children. Felix had been as doting a father as you'd see back then, but she couldn't fathom Fran asking him to take her to the bathroom, or even him being the one to take her out of Mass while she cried. Now men were expected to be equal partners. Olivia's husband, Kurt, was even reading some book—*Dude, You're a Dad.* Esther had had to hold back laughter when she saw it. As if a book could prepare you for such a thing. No, parenthood wasn't something you learned from books. It was something you experienced, day in, day out. Esther had been a mother for fifty-one years, and she was still learning new things every day.

Olivia would be a good mother. Fran and Iris teased her about her lack of cooking skills and her aggressive nature, but Esther knew better. Olivia had grit—that was the most essential ingredient. Anyone can learn how to swaddle a baby, but not everyone can keep their cool when a child is crying at three in the morning for the sixth time that night. And she'd done the right thing, having her baby near her sister and mother and grandmother. Olivia had an army of support surrounding her, arms that would carry the baby and mouths that would sing to her. Esther had had Katharine Rose to forge through the muck of mothering with. But she hadn't had her *own* mother, down in Plain, smoking her cigarettes and getting diabetes. A girl needed her mother when she became one herself. That's just all there was to it.

"Esther?" Katharine Rose, banging on the front door.

"Hey there," she said, putting the top back on her slow cooker. "You're early." They had a meeting of the cookbook committee planned. The book was finally done, and she couldn't believe how real it looked when Iris showed it to her on the computer. Full-page advertisements from local businesses, real sections, and a table of contents. It was a cookbook, plain and simple. But they still had to sign off on the cover Iris had mocked up.

"Did you see the email from Father Sam? Funeral on Saturday. Thirty to forty people expected."

"Who?"

Katharine Rose plunked herself down at the kitchen counter, breathing a bit too heavily for Esther's liking. "Julie Mayfield."

Esther pressed her hand to her heart. "Oh." Julie had been going to St. Anne's for years and years, almost as long as Esther and Felix. She couldn't fry a chicken to save her life, but she cleaned the church sometimes; she'd run the St. Veronica's society before her knees gave out.

"Pneumonia did a number on her a few years back," said Katharine Rose. "I think she never fully recovered. Anyway. I'm going to do the shrimp bake."

"I can get on sides," said Esther. "Maybe some cheesy potatoes, and a couple of garden salads . . . I could do those English muffins with the olives."

Katharine Rose sighed. "It always feels a little sadder when it's one of our own."

"I know. I just know it."

Later on, when the rest of the cookbook committee was there, poring over the book, arguing about the size of their names across the bottom, Esther found herself thinking about Julie Mayfield. Soon enough, that would be Esther. She'd be another funeral to plan.

Was it really worth it, all this work, all these recipes? For what? A house? An old house at that, yes, but one with a beautiful view and piles of memories, a house where she'd brought home her daughter and watched her grandchildren cannonball off the dock. A house where she'd lived with the love of her life. But still—a house.

These were, ironically, the exact types of things she wished she could tell Hazel. She found herself missing Hazel at the strangest times. Her entire Twitter profile had been deleted, and even though Esther was ready to accept that Hazel wasn't a young mother after all, but a thief, she still missed their conversations. She hoped

Hazel was doing okay, wherever she was. Olivia and Aaron had helped her file a police report, but she'd been told not to get her hopes up. The internet made it easy to disappear.

Iris had come, too, even though her work on the cookbook was all but done. She seemed to be coming over more lately, just popping in and sitting on the dock. Her poor granddaughter, whose mind seemed a million miles away.

"You okay, honey?" Esther asked her quietly.

"Me?" Iris replied, snapping out of it. "Of course."

"Would you mind dropping that spaghetti sauce off at Olivia's for me? I should really clean out the oven a bit." That wasn't quite a lie, but the truth was, carrying that old Crock-Pot around was hard on Esther's back.

"Sure thing. And, Grandma, I've told you a million times, your oven has a self-clean option."

Esther wrinkled her nose. "And I've told *you* a million times, I don't trust those things. Whoever heard of an oven that cleans itself?"

"Ignore her, Iris, dear," said Katharine Rose. "If she wants to be stuck in the forties, let her."

"I read an article that said if you use those oven self-cleaners, the chemicals from your oven can leak into your home," said Bea.

"Where'd you find that? OldLadiesAreGullible.com?" said Katharine Rose. "Did Esther send you the link?"

Esther slammed the laptop shut. "That's enough."

"Grandma!" said Iris, surprised. "Careful with the Mac. Geez."

But Esther had had it. Had it with this world that thought someone who wanted to do things the old way was decrepit. So what if she wanted to put in a little extra elbow grease to clean her own oven? Why was that such a federal crime? It wasn't, was the answer. You know what was? Hazel, stealing her money, abandoning her with nobody who understood, leaving her feeling alone in a room full of people.

"I was only joking, Esther. I'm sorry," said Katharine Rose quietly. Well, wasn't that something? Katharine Rose hadn't apologized, ever, in their entire fifty-year friendship. Esther didn't know she knew how.

"I'm tired," said Esther. "*I'm* sorry. I need—I need to lie down for a bit."

Iris looked anxious. Esther knew her granddaughter wanted to ask if she was feeling okay, but that was the last thing she wanted, so instead, she walked into her bedroom and closed the door, leaving her three best friends and her granddaughter sitting in the kitchen, surprised.

AS ESTHER SLEPT, she dreamed of Felix. Of the way he smiled: tight-lipped when the Knights of Columbus were asking for more donations, and far and wide when one of his granddaughters burst through the door. Her Felix; she needed to drive over to his grave soon, pull up the flowers. It was that time of year. The sun was beginning to creep down during dinnertime and the tourists had all gone home, leaving everyone else to shake out the rugs and dust off the tabletops. The Huckleberry Gift Shoppe in town had closed up, and the mosquitos had left, too, as if they'd enjoyed their summer stay but had to get back to the office in Illinois, same as everyone else.

There were always things to do around the house, too. Especially in autumn. The dock had to get brought in and the Jet Skis had to be put away. One of these nights the temperature would dip below the frost line, and she would wish she'd poured the antifreeze in her pipes. The rosebushes, too, had to be covered.

And that was all just the practicals. *The end of the year,* the bank had said, but they were still sending angry letters. This time next year, the house probably wouldn't be hers. Someone else would be covering up the roses.

But quite honestly, the house was the least of her concerns. She knew she should be worried about it. Everyone else was—Aaron, with those deep forehead lines, Olivia and Fran, hushing each other when she walked in the room. Iris's own desperate insistence of the importance of the place, that they couldn't lose it, they absolutely couldn't.

But it was just a house. She'd burn it to the ground if she had to. Everyone around her was used to it, because it was what they'd grown up with. They should have grown up with nothing, like Esther had. She'd had to walk around the neighborhood selling eggs from their farm chickens in order to keep the light bill paid. So pardon her for not getting all up in arms about her fancy lakefront property being taken away. They'd had to take out those second mortgages; how else could they have put Fran through college? And Felix, well, he'd been a hard worker, no doubt about that. But the nightmares—they'd get to him, sometimes. It made keeping a job difficult, even though he was a Vietnam vet. Not that many people cared about veterans these days. It wasn't like when she was a schoolgirl—if someone who'd served walked by back then, you'd thank them for their service. Some of Felix's army friends had had their homes vandalized, eggs tossed at their garages. All for serving their country! It was despicable.

Although—so was war, certainly. Esther had asked Felix if he'd ever thought of going to medical school. He'd been a medic, after all; he knew all about arteries and wounds. But he always told her he'd spent enough time playing doctor, seen enough injuries to last him a lifetime.

Now, though, she had to get up and get started on the casseroles for the day's funeral. She got to work, opening cans of soup, chopping onions, searing chicken. The familiar sounds of her kitchen. That was one thing she'd miss about the house—so much counter space. Although maybe she'd downsize into one of those condos in Waukegan; that could be nice, too.

Maybe she wouldn't lose the house. Maybe the book would sell thousands of copies; maybe she'd walk into the bank and hand them a big fat check and a plate of cookies besides. She could swing wildly from it feeling like a reality to it feeling like a pipe dream. Esther had been raised to expect the worst and be pleasantly surprised if it didn't happen; farm girls weren't taught to be dreamers. But the skip in Iris's step, the pump in Katharine Rose's fist—well. It was hard to know what to think.

There was a knock at the door, which surprised her. Everyone who came to see her was the type to walk right in.

"Come on in," she yelled.

She was surprised—beyond surprised, absolutely gobsmacked— to see who it was.

Ivan Welsh walked into her kitchen, slowly, his hands in his pockets. "Hi there."

"Why, Mr. Welsh!"

"Ivan."

"Ivan, then. How are you? Can I get you a beer?"

He chuckled. "I love the Northwoods. Did you know in some areas of the country, offering someone a beer at eleven in the morning would be a little . . . out-there?"

She cracked a smile. "Have to stay warm somehow."

"I'll take one. Sure. What the hell."

She grabbed one from the fridge and tossed it to him. "Pardon the mess. I've got to make three different sides for today's funeral. Plus, I've got to make a few more things for Olivia before she finally gets that baby out."

He nodded, cracking open his beer and taking a long swig. "You sure stay busy."

"Not busier than anyone else," she demurred. "Not superstar busy."

"I'm not going to be a superstar much longer," he said easily. "I've played hooky all summer. They're going to cancel my show."

"They are?" Esther was all for grief. Letting people grieve—that was a part of life. But she had to admit, the way Ivan and Cooper and Cricket were still here? It was a little odd, was all. Nobody was working. Larsons were hard workers. Laziness was something she'd never tolerated. One of her and Felix's favorite rants to go off on together was about why high schoolers thought they were too good to flip burgers and scoop ice cream anymore. Although—she shouldn't be so judgmental. The poor man's wife had died, and besides, he obviously had enough money to relax a bit.

"I suppose," he replied. He sounded so nonchalant about it. It almost reminded Esther of her attitude about the house. Let everyone else lose their minds, if they wanted. She could respect that sense of calm.

"I wanted to ask about the cookbook," he said. "How it's all coming together."

"It's finished," said Esther. "We're going to sell it at the Christmas Walk next month."

Ivan glanced down at his feet. Back at her. Back at his feet. The awkwardness of someone who had something to say, but didn't know how to say it.

"I don't want to overstep," he said. "But I actually . . . well. Cooper mentioned. Something about this house."

Cooper Welsh—damn it, she could wring his neck, and not just for this, either. How dare he? Esther's face flamed with shame. She didn't want some viral website. She couldn't admit what she'd done, or where she'd gone wrong. And now Ivan knew.

"I just wanted to let you know," he said quietly, "that if I can do something . . . I will. I have—I mean, money's not really an issue for me, you know?"

Esther started scrubbing potatoes. She needed to feel hot water on her shaking, humiliated hands. "I don't need your money," she said flatly.

"I'm sorry. I'm not trying to—I don't know how to do this," he said, suddenly sounding frustrated.

Esther cleared her throat. "I don't mean to be rude. I appreciate it, Mr. Welsh, I do. That's extremely generous of you. But I'm going to be just fine. I apologize that you even got roped into this whole thing. It's really not a big issue. Iris and Cooper shouldn't have . . . well, never mind that now. So, thank you. But I'll be just fine."

They sat in silence for a minute, with nothing but the sound of those potatoes being washed within an inch of their lives.

"Annabelle loved this place," Ivan said suddenly. "Ellerie. She talked about it constantly. But I wouldn't really—I wouldn't really know that, as of late. We weren't exactly together. Married, but not . . . I'm not a very good person, Esther. I'm not like you. I don't have a family around me, a *community*, making casseroles for each other. My kids can't stand me."

"I'm sure that isn't true," Esther said quickly, although she'd gotten the impression it was. What did kids know? Surely, Ivan had missed some important moments. But he was making a living. Putting Cooper through school. Making sure Cricket had what she needed. That was what fathers were for, really. Not bedtime snuggles. No, that was a mother's job, and it always had been. Her own father probably couldn't have named a single book she'd read, but he'd put dinner on the table every single evening, even when they'd had next to nothing. Esther had had a roof over her head, always.

Although—hadn't Felix been more than that? Aaron certainly was. Kurt probably would be, too.

"Oh, it is," said Ivan, not in a way that was sad or upset, but in a simple, matter-of-fact tone. "I have a lot of regrets. But I'm trying—I'm trying to do things a little differently now. I can see how much I've missed out on. And, look, this is going to sound crude as hell. I know it's not how you talk in Wisconsin, but it *is* how we talk in California. I have money. A lot of it, obviously. And I don't want the love of my son's life to be devastated because her grandmother got kicked out of her beloved family home. I . . . owe Cooper. More than this house is worth, ten times over. So just— just keep me posted. On cookbook sales. Okay? That's all I ask. It doesn't have to be, like, I hand you a check. I could buy a bunch of the cookbooks for . . . I don't know. Charities. Something. We'll figure it out."

Esther looked out the back door over the lake.

A few years ago, Janie Jorgenson from church had lost her husband to the COVID, and not a month later, their only son had been killed in a snowmobiling accident. Just looking at her made you wince. She hadn't handled it very gracefully, either; Esther didn't blame her. But there were lots of nights at Vernon's, that sort of thing. She picked the cigarettes back up. More than that, if you believed Bea. And now whenever something bad happened to Esther, she would think, *At least I'm not Janie.*

Roses didn't bloom that spring or tomato plants got eaten by deer? *At least I'm not Janie.*

Hips that hurt with extra oomph when the rain comes? *At least I'm not Janie.*

Can't go on a walk down by Turtle Pond anymore without having to sit and breathe awhile? *At least I'm not Janie.*

And it wasn't just her, either; she'd heard the funeral ladies say the same thing half a dozen times. Everyone was grateful to not be Janie Jorgenson. It was as if Janie's purpose in life was to make you feel better about your own.

She was determined—absolutely determined—not to become *at least I'm not Esther.*

"Mr. Welsh, that's very kind of you," she said. "And you're right, that's not how we talk around here, but it *is* the truth. And if I may give you some of my own—"

She glanced back at Ivan Welsh. A celebrity, who had more than Esther ever did or would. But so much less than her, too. Had nothing, compared to her riches.

When Iris had called that night from the Golden Mast, Esther had gotten into her car immediately, even though she hated driving in the dark. She'd done it because she'd recognized that voice. The shaky *Grandma?* A tight voice that was trying to hold it all together, but was finally starting to see something quite desperate about the situation.

That voice was her own.

"Your boy isn't well," she said.

Ivan looked down again. "I know."

"He needs to get that taken care of," she said. "I'm worried about my granddaughter. Iris's tough, but she's in love. That can do things to a person."

Ivan cracked a smile. "Love can do all kinds of things to a person. It does all kinds of things, all the time."

He had a point there.

"Here," she said, handing him a knife. "Chop an onion or two. You may have made veal for the Princess of Wales, but we'll see if you've got what it takes to cook for a St. Anne's funeral."

"Esther Larson," he said, "it would be an honor."

Twenty

Cooper loved watching Iris cook.

She insisted that she didn't do it very often, but she'd been doing it more and more the past couple of months, inviting him over and setting out the plates. Sometimes her parents came over, or Olivia and Kurt, or Esther. The other night Father Sam had joined them, and he and Iris had cracked up telling stories from high school. Cooper loved the way Iris thumbed through her cookbooks, *hmm*-ing to herself, pulling down herbs and spices. He loved the way she used a giant metal bowl as her garbage can, throwing in chicken fat and potato peels. He loved the way she turned on Ben Rector and sang along. He loved the way she didn't measure anything, just used dashes and shakes, dipping a finger into the sauce to taste it before making a *hmm, this will work* face.

He'd liked watching Ivan cook at first, too. When he was little, and his mom was there, and Ivan wasn't a famous chef but just a guy with a restaurant. In the afternoon, when Ivan headed to Papu, Cooper would sometimes hang out in the back, watching Ivan chop the heads off fish and yell at sous chefs to keep things clean, before he got scolded and sent away.

But Ivan always paid so much attention to detail. From the proper way to julienne a vegetable to the plating, it was as if he was being judged on every single element of the restaurant. He liked to say that he pretended every single customer was a food critic for the *New York Times*. And when the *New York Times* food critic finally did appear, Ivan had earned a glowing thumbs-up from one of the biggest names in food writing. His book deal came shortly after that. After *Confessions of a Cook,* Ivan spent more time as a celebrity than a chef.

When he came home, though—first to Cooper and his mother, then Cooper and his nanny, then Cooper and Annabelle and Cricket, then hardly at all—he would cook. He didn't cook the same way Iris did, with dashes and stirs, opening the oven eight times to see if something was done cooking. Ivan was all about precision.

Cooper was somewhere in between them. Exact measurements were important in baking, so at the diner, he had to take care. But when he was a line cook, things were more slapdash.

"Don't look," said Iris.

"What?" he asked, grinning.

"I said don't look. You're going to judge me."

"You and your Midwest complex! I'm not going to judge you!"

She held up a chunk of Velveeta. "My secret ingredient to broccoli cheddar chicken soup."

"I love Velveeta. Who doesn't love Velveeta?"

"I can guarantee your father's never had Velveeta," said Iris.

"Now, *this,*" he said, reaching behind her back to grab the canned cream of celery, "is more damning."

Mid-October in Wisconsin, and they could smell winter coming. It came on the lake, where the turtles hopped off their log and disappeared, and it came in the woods, where the deer would trot across the sharp crackle of leaves. Cooper had had to go into town and buy a bunch of Ellerie County sweatshirts for himself and Cricket. Ivan said he ran hot.

Soup and bread weather, Iris had said, showing up at his door with a Crock-Pot and a bag of frozen broccoli and a loaf of sourdough from the bakery in town under her arm. Her mother had taught her how to make it.

"Bread's the only thing Esther doesn't make," Iris explained, dipping her spoon into the thick green broth. "She says you can't tame bread dough."

"Ivan, either, actually," said Cooper. "He doesn't bake in general, but he especially doesn't bake bread." Ivan was off at another meeting in town, God only knew what for, and Cricket was sequestered in her bedroom, doing homework. Cooper had gotten an email from the virtual school that she hadn't turned in a single assignment so far, and had they gotten the homework portal set up correctly? That lying little punk.

He probably should have been more upset. He should have— what, grounded her? Something like that. But honestly, school was such a waste of time sometimes, wasn't it? He didn't have the energy to argue with her, even though he knew he probably should.

"Their loss. Our gain. I'd be a million and a half pounds if my grandmother was baking me sourdough every day."

"You'd be beautiful," said Cooper. "But also, I can't imagine her apple pie is that much healthier than sourdough bread. She makes it with lard."

Iris threw a piece of shredded Velveeta at him. "Lard makes things taste good. And so does Velveeta."

Cooper laughed. It felt good, to have a good day with the woman he loved.

"Can I see the mock-up of the cookbook?" he asked.

Iris logged into her Google Docs on Cooper's laptop, pulling up the cookbook project. She had to admit, it looked pretty great all laid out. The cover had a vintage Northwoods feel, and the recipes were organized and categorized.

"This," said Cooper, scrolling through, "is incredible. Definitely better than any of Ivan's."

Iris laughed. "I wouldn't go that far."

"I would. Because it's all real food that real people can make. The type of food people actually eat for dinner. I love it, Iris. I'm going to buy a copy. Five copies."

She grinned. "You and nine hundred friends, hopefully."

"So, what are you going to do next?" Cooper asked, shutting the laptop and putting it back on the counter.

"What do you mean?" She got a dishcloth and ran it under the sink to wipe up the soup drippings.

"I mean, now that your big project is over. You picking up more freelance clients? Or buying another cabin? Because we're staying forever and ever and ever, remember?"

Iris shot him a look. "Don't torment me. I don't like to think about you leaving."

He smiled. "I mean it. What are you thinking, like . . . long term?" It wasn't really fair of him to ask. It wasn't like Cooper had big long-term goals. He couldn't see past leaving Redstone. He didn't have a job anymore, he'd been informed in a curt email a month earlier. Oops. "You just seemed like you loved making the cookbook."

Iris glanced at him as she wiped the counter. "Honestly? Haven't really thought about it. I guess just . . . keep doing what I've been doing. Pushing pixels and running Redstone." She didn't sound thrilled with those prospects.

The door opened, and in walked Ivan, a full two hours earlier than expected.

"Sorry to interrupt," said Ivan. "Oh wow—something smells *good*."

Iris winced. "Broccoli cheddar chicken soup. But I have to warn you, a can opener was an integral part of the process."

Ivan leaned over and smelled the pot. "Smells like Wisconsin. Cheese and cream."

"At least we bought artisan bread," said Iris, wiggling the bakery package at him.

Ivan chuckled. "Artisan—that word's everywhere these days, isn't it? I saw a sign talking about 'artisanal cheese curds' the other day." Cooper felt himself getting mad, wanting to jump in and defend Iris from Ivan's snobbery, but she just laughed.

"Right?" she said. "It's fried cheese. C'mon, people."

"I'll get out of your hair," said Ivan. "I'd offer to go out and get a burger or something, but I'm a little under the weather. I'll Uber Eats something and hang out in my room, if you need me."

And Cooper could have nodded, *okay, bye*—his dad, trying to give him space with Iris. But something stopped him.

Esther would never have allowed someone to just hang out in their room and eat takeout while a meal was being made.

Something about Iris's family's constant . . . *togetherness* made him squirm sometimes. They called each other multiple times a day, for literally no reason at all. *Just touching base. Just checking in.* Olivia would text Iris that some random girl from high school they hadn't talked to in ten years was pregnant, and Iris would send her dad a picture of an eagle in the tree outside Esther's, and Esther was always making everyone food. They walked into each other's houses without ringing the doorbell, just kicking off their shoes and opening each other's refrigerators. It felt so foreign.

But after a couple of months, they'd started doing the same to Cooper. Kurt had his number and would send him headlines about the Brewers. Fran didn't shoo him away when he cleared the table after dinner at her house, but handed him a dish towel instead so he could help dry. It went from feeling familiar to feeling welcoming, as if someone had handed him a thick afghan after he'd been out in the cold.

He could hand one to Ivan, too. Even though he didn't want to. It was right there, and he was cold.

"You can stay," said Cooper. "And eat with us."

Ivan was surprised, but Iris seemed calm and cool.

"Absolutely," she said. "Cricket was going to anyway."

Ivan just glanced at Cooper, as if trying to tell if he meant it. And although every bone in his body wanted to resist it, Cooper thought of Esther, always flinging open her front door and handing him a beer.

"Stay," Cooper said. "Stay."

"So THEN YOU shake the pan."

"The whole time?" Iris started cautiously moving her cast iron back and forth.

"Well, a few minutes," said Ivan. "You want to start to see some caramelization."

"The honey's a nice touch," said Cooper. "Shit, that smells good."

Ivan couldn't sit while other people cooked for him. So he was demonstrating roasted sweet potatoes.

"My arm's going to fall off," said Iris. "This thing's heavy. Do you add the thyme now, or just before serving?"

"Before serving. Nobody wants a crispy herb, you know? If I'm doing it in a dressing, I might add that earlier," said Ivan.

"Add the cheese and stir the soup, will you?" said Iris. Cooper grabbed the ladle and ran it through the thick, bubbling pot, tossing in chunks of Velveeta. The steam that came off smelled like all his favorite things—salt and pepper and olive oil and cheddar. He wanted to swim in it.

"I asked a kid at the grocery store yesterday where the apricots were. I've got to stop doing that. He said, and I quote, 'What's an apricot?'" Ivan smacked his forehead with his hand. Cooper wanted to kill him, but still, Iris was laughing. She pointed at Ivan.

"Hey now," she said. "We aren't fancy food people. We aren't *Mr. California*."

Ivan, to Cooper's shock, didn't even seem bothered. He *laughed*. This whole conversation—they were just laughing at themselves. As if nothing the other said bothered either of them in the slightest. Just choosing to be silly and enjoy each other's company.

"It's an apricot, not elderflower," Ivan said. "Let me try another one . . . apples?"

"Round? Red? I may have seen a picture once," joked Iris.

"Dad? What are you doing here? You're interrupting their romantic evening." And there was Cricket, walking downstairs and hiding a yawn.

"Hey. You get your crap done?" said Cooper, pointing the ladle at her and letting a drip of soup slop onto the floor.

"Some of it. It smells so good in here," said Cricket. Ivan walked Iris through not overcrowding the potatoes, and Cricket just looked at Cooper, using her psychic sibling powers. *You're cooking with Dad?* her face said. *It's not a big deal,* his face responded.

"Set the table, bug," Cooper told her.

She did, and lit some candles, too. "Ambiance," she said. "Always important."

"Always," agreed Iris. "Candles and artisanal bread. Might as well be at the Ritz."

"I love the Ritz. *Love.* Did you know that Ernest Hemingway sat at the bar and drank fifty-one martinis after the Nazis left?" said Ivan. "Talk about a hangover."

Iris glanced at Cooper. Okay, yes, he was a little hungover. Most days. Sue him. Everyone up here drank like fishes, as the saying went.

They sat for dinner, glasses clinking, bread being passed, soup being spooned into bowls. The dark autumn night seemed so far away from their candlelit table, from Cricket with her ripped jeans and Iris with one foot tucked under her opposite thigh. Ivan was asking her how much salt she put in the soup, and she was asking him if there was enough thyme on the sweet potatoes.

"You know where I learned to make these potatoes?" said Ivan. "Julia Child."

"Julia who?" asked Cricket. "That one of your friends?"

"She didn't," said Iris, her face horrified.

Cooper rolled his eyes. "She did. World-famous chef, bug. Crazy old lady."

"Stop! My grandma and her friends are absolutely obsessed with her," said Iris. "You *knew* her?"

"I wish," said Ivan, clutching his heart. "I saw her on TV, though. My mom would watch her when I was growing up. There was nobody who did it like her. All that butter—Paula acts like she invented butter."

Cooper tried to pretend Ivan hadn't just name-dropped the Southern chef with the racist potty mouth, but Iris jumped up. "Let's show Cricket."

Ivan pointed at Cricket. "Now *that's* a good idea."

"She needs to go finish her homework," said Cooper.

"This is the education of life, Cooper," said Iris. "She can write her college entrance essay on 'What Julia Child Taught Me.'"

"Sounds like a slam dunk," Cricket agreed.

"I hate when you three gang up," grumbled Cooper.

But there they were, turning on the TV, going to YouTube. And there she was, the six-foot-tall American with the singing, roller-coaster voice, reminding them to *never apologize.*

"She seems drunk," said Cricket. "Why is she breathing so hard?"

"This is before they had a crew of a thousand doing every single thing. They did this in one take. Do you have any idea how impressive that is?" said Ivan. "I mean, Julia completely changed the game for food-based television."

"And made some damn good roasted sweet potatoes," agreed Iris.

And there they sat, letting their soup get cold, watching someone else cook.

Iris's phone went off. She looked at it and shrieked, grabbing her coat. Olivia was in labor.

The next night, they went to the beach.

Not Iris. She was busy with her family. But she texted Cooper photo after photo of her niece. Emma Esther. Esther must have been over the moon.

The tide was high, so they were wading, Ivan and Cricket and Cooper. Ivan had his jeans rolled to his knees, and Cricket wore athletic shorts even though the air was cold and the water was frosty. There was nobody on the beach, and it seemed to stretch for miles; you could barely see the dotted pines on the other side of the lake. The water roared, lapping back and forth across the sand, and the last few birds squawked as they headed south overhead. A loon called somewhere, probably wondering where the hell everybody went. The sky was a deep prism of sparkling pink and gem-like navy, making everything golden, making everything feel new.

Cooper could feel the wind biting his ears and the damp sand between his toes, but something else, too—it wasn't as cold as North Harbor. In fact, it was a redeeming cold. Gentler than the knife-sting freeze of that Christmas parade.

They talked about food, because that's what they knew. They talked about Esther's pie. Cricket described her school lunches, gross movie theater fare like chicken tenders and frozen cookie dough, and Cooper reminded Ivan of the bacon-grease pancakes.

And then, Annabelle. They talked about Annabelle, and the way their hearts missed her, the way she had made everything around her light and lovely.

Cricket told a story about the time she and her mother had decorated the entire house for Saint Ivan's Day, an autumn Saturday in October. They'd taped up balloons everywhere to welcome Ivan home from a trip to Prague—*It was Paris,* Ivan said, remembering—and then Annabelle's stupid cat, Meyer, had popped them all with his claws.

Ivan threw Cricket over his shoulder, suddenly, with superhuman strength. She shrieked, pounding his back with her fists, laughing, and Cooper kicked water up at them both, getting them wet from the frosty waves. The lake beckoned and called, and Ivan spun Cricket in a circle, Cooper looking on and laughing, listening to the sounds of his family.

A NEW SOUND: coughing. Coughing that was different from anything Cooper had heard before. A type of hack that came from the pit of someone's body, a *not-right* cough that wasn't going to be solved by a throat lozenge.

He ran downstairs, and Cricket was there, too, on the stairs. They threw open the door to Ivan's room and saw him vomiting blood into a bowl.

Cooper couldn't breathe. His hands shook as he dialed 911 and Cricket cried, giving directions. They had to come all the way from Waukegan; it would be a few minutes. The paramedics were there, the ambulance—North Harbor, a gun, a dying girl, Ivan being put on a stretcher. It all swirled around in Cooper's head, until he sat and put his head between his knees.

"Call Dr. Ramirez, in LA," Ivan said between coughs. "I'm okay. Dr. Ramirez." He reached for his wallet and pulled out a faded business card.

DR. PEDRO RAMIREZ
Director of Hepatobiliary and Pancreatic Surgery

"Surprise," Ivan said, as the redheaded paramedic spoke into his walkie-talkie and wheeled him out the door. "I'm dying."

Twenty-One

*I*ris stared down at the small pair of eyes blinking back up at her.

"She's perfect," said Fran, for the eighty-fifth time. "The world's most perfect baby."

Emma Esther. Seven pounds, seven ounces. They were smitten. Blue eyes, like Olivia's, and Fran's, and Esther's.

"I'll quit my job and be your nanny if you want," said Iris. "Do you offer health insurance?"

"No, but I can make one hell of a gin and tonic." Olivia took a long sip of her drink. "God, this tastes good after nine months."

Fran waved her hand. "I had a cocktail or two with each of you in my stomach. And Mom drank like a fish when she was pregnant with me."

"They call everything alcoholism these days," said Esther, who was folding a massive mountain of baby clothes. "I mean, my God. A little DUI is a felony now. As if we haven't all driven home from Vernon's after a few brandy old-fashioneds."

"Grandma," said Olivia flatly, "you shouldn't admit that out loud."

Iris barely heard their banter. She couldn't stop staring at Emma, from her tiny seashell fingernails to her toes, the size of strawberry seeds. She snapped another photo for Cooper.

Kurt was sleeping upstairs while Fran bustled around the kitchen, emptying Olivia's dishwasher. It was like a coven of Kellehers and

Larsons had descended, the good fairies who would clean Olivia's house and snuggle Emma. Iris was still on the high of a good night with Cooper, a night where they didn't talk about guns and blood and his brain stayed put where it belonged.

"You know, in France, they stay in the hospital for, like, an entire week," said Olivia. "For free. Waukegan Memorial kicked me out after one night with nothing but a bottle of painkillers."

"Don't let your dad hear you," said Fran. "He'll think you've turned into one of those socialist healthcare people."

"Twenty-six weeks of maternity leave, too," murmured Iris.

"Larsons don't lay about for twenty-six weeks," said Fran.

"You let her lay as long as she wants," said Esther, pointing her finger at Fran. "I waited on you hand and foot after your babies were born, if I remember correctly. And I did it with a smile."

"Thanks, Grandma," Olivia said, and stuck her tongue out at her mother.

These women, Iris thought: her people. Teasing was their language, but the love in that room was so palpable, you could slice it with a bread knife. That little baby had no idea the matriarchy she was entering.

"The funeral ladies will be here over the next few days. You won't need to cook a thing," said Esther.

Olivia closed her eyes. "I hope Carlotta makes tortilla roll-ups."

COME OVER, ESTHER had said on the phone the next day. *Hurry!*

So Iris drove, her wet hair in a braid. She was going to meet Cooper for a burger that night, but she had time to swing by her grandmother's. She wanted to stop by Olivia's, too, to say good night to Emma.

She didn't really want to get dinner with Cooper, to be honest. She wanted to be with her family, her sister and mother and grandmother. She'd had breakfast with Cooper, and—well. First of all, he'd been hungover. He was always hungover lately. *Always.* And so when he'd reached for the vodka to make a screwdriver, she couldn't help rolling her eyes, and that had pissed him off a little bit, and the words *sue me* had been thrown out. She'd bitten back that it just didn't feel necessary to drink right that second, since he'd obviously had a late night, and—

He'd kicked a chair.

Kicked a chair! Like a child, having a tantrum. But also, not like a child. Like some angry person.

But he'd apologized, and meant it. And now he wanted to take her out to dinner, so she'd go. And she'd kiss his face off afterward, and probably forget the whole thing.

Until next time, that annoying good angel voice sang in her ear.

People fight, she reminded the voice.

He kicked a chair. People don't kick chairs in fights.

She turned her Ben Rector up louder.

But there would, of course, be a next time. Cooper, jumping at loud noises; Cooper, tears in his eyes. That fucking outhouse. She'd tried everything she could, but she was just going to have to remove the door for him, probably. Or hurry up and get the whole thing taken down. She'd figure it out tomorrow.

It wasn't fair. Iris's dad was the most easygoing person on the planet. Her entire life, she'd never seen him get angry enough to raise his voice. And Olivia had married Kurt, who volunteered at Vacation Bible School in the summers. She saw Olivia and Kurt all googly-eyed over Emma, and the small, worst part of her hated them for it. Easy love—it had to be nice. The kind of love that was just lazy mornings and holding hands, where your biggest argument was whether to order Chinese food for dinner. Why was she the one who'd fallen in love with an angry man? She hadn't told Olivia, either. Her sister could be judgmental as hell, as if she didn't realize not every single person around her had the privileged, perfect life of Olivia Marie Kelleher.

Well, whatever. Some people got that in life, to love someone who hadn't witnessed a horror. The love of Iris's life came with a lot of heavy baggage, and if her arms got tired, so what? Some people had horrible diseases, and she didn't. Some people had to live in concentration camps!

You just compared your relationship to a concentration camp, the voice said again, and she jammed Ben Rector up even further, till he was singing about white dresses so loudly, she thought it might blow out her speakers.

Iris was just about to pull her car around the bend leading to Esther's when a deer ran out in the middle of the road. She slammed on the brakes as hard as she could and yanked her steering wheel to the side, almost veering into a tree.

It was a doe with two small fawns. The babies ran off into the woods, but the mother stayed there a moment, just blinking at Iris.

I see you, she seemed to be saying. *What are you doing here?*

Iris carefully drove into Esther's driveway. There were already two cars there—Bea's Honda and Carlotta's pickup truck. Surely Katharine Rose was inside, too.

She hurried into the house, wincing at the cold. The four women were sitting around the kitchen island, toasting with red Solo cups.

"Iris!" squealed Katharine Rose. "Iris, Iris, Iris's here."

"New great-grandbaby and a new book, all in one week. Your grandmother's something!" crowed Bea. Her oxygen tank puffed loudly. She was looking thin.

Esther held the book out to Iris. Oh wow—there it was, with a cracked spine and the simple cover she'd whipped up.

The Funeral Ladies of Ellerie County Cookbook

Iris opened it and flipped through the pages, grinning. "You did it."

"*We* did it," said Esther. "This never could have happened without those sponsors. And it was your idea, remember?" Iris remembered. That day felt so long ago. How could it possibly have been only a couple of months?

"What do you think? *New York Times* bestseller?" asked Bea.

Chicken Casserole
Bea's Best-Ever Fudge Brownies
Italian Pasta Salad

She pulled the book to her chest and hugged it tightly.

THE AIR FELT taut. If she pressed too hard, it would snap, and hurt them both.

"I just think it might help, Cooper," she said quietly, not looking at him. "Talking to someone."

"I apologized for this morning. What do you want me to do?" She heard ice cubes rattling in his glass. Apologized, but still had a vodka tonic. Although, so did she—liquid courage and all. They had gotten takeout and were now sitting on the couch at Redstone, their feet all tangled together.

"Did you call that doctor back in Milwaukee?"

"Jesus, Iris. Now? Can't we just have a nice night?"

She'd prepared, even practiced in front of a mirror. But she was losing her resolve.

"I'm just kind of worried about you."

"I know. The chair—I feel like such an idiot. Hey, look at me." She did. Those gentle eyes. "I really am sorry. I'll call Dr. Hoss, if you want me to. Okay?"

"Tomorrow?"

He laughed. "You need a timeline? A calendar?"

She grinned. "It would help."

They ate their takeout, turned on a movie. But not just any movie. A movie that had a song by that one singer who had just done a huge rally on gun control.

"Gun control is so fucking stupid," Cooper muttered. Iris drew in a breath, sharply. No. No. She hated that singer! God, she'd murder him if she could.

"It's . . . yeah," she said. She didn't think it was stupid. Background checks—that made sense to her. Sure, that one politician in Texas thought *no guns ever,* but most people just wanted to stop things like the North Harbor shooting, didn't they? It wasn't so stupid, was it? It's not like anyone had a problem with her dad and his friends wearing thick orange jackets and shooting *deer.*

"It wouldn't do shit," said Cooper. "Wouldn't do a thing. They think they know everything, these Hollywood idiots. They're just like Ivan."

"How's Ivan doing, anyway?" asked Iris quickly, trying to change the subject. Cooper could go on and on about how much he hated his dad, but ever since the cancer diagnosis came to light, he'd been a bit softer. "Did you go meet that doctor with him in Washport?"

"Oh, he's fine. Ready to play Loving Doting Dad. He actually *likes* that dumbass's new album, can you believe it? He does the same thing they all do. They're all a bunch of idiots. They all—"

And on, and on, and on. The worst part wasn't the ranting; it was Iris, having to nod. Nodding along. *Yeah, yeah, you're right.* She wasn't a person with her own thoughts. She was just an audience.

"Fuck that guy," said Cooper, his voice so full of venom it scared her. "*Fuck. That. Guy.* Why'd you put this on, anyway?"

"Me?" she asked dully. She wasn't even surprised. Of course this was where it was going to go.

"Yeah. You know I hate that guy. You know, but you just don't care. Whatever. I don't need anyone to care. I'm not a child. You should have known, but you *can't* know. It's fine. Fine." He wasn't making any sense. He was gone again, gone to wherever he went. He was lost more often than he was with her, Iris realized with a thud.

She calmed him down—she was getting good at that. Apologized for putting on the movie. Told him she was exhausted and that she had to be up early the next morning to get some work done, which was total bullshit.

It wasn't until she was driving home that she realized he'd never actually said when he would call Dr. Hoss.

She didn't drive home. She turned left on M instead of right, pressed the gas pedal down as far as she could. She hoped Leah from church wasn't waiting in her patrol car. Iris had never been able to talk her way out of a ticket.

She pulled up in front of her parents' house and saw the glow of the TV—her dad watching the news. The light showed the silhouette of her parents, sitting on the couch, her mom's head on her dad's shoulder.

Iris stuck her fist in her mouth, trying to stifle her cries, but she couldn't. She just wanted to go in there so badly and tell them everything. Tell them about the way Cooper scared her when he yelled and the way he lost control. The horror show he saw behind his eyelids. She wanted her mom to rub her head and bring her water.

But she'd already ruined Cooper's night by letting him turn on that movie. She couldn't do the same to her parents. To Fran and Aaron, all cozy and warm, lit candles and library books, blissful in the knowledge of their new grandchild, and of their second daughter so happy in love. If Iris told her mother about this, whatever *this* even was—unthinkable. It would be like exposing a secret crack habit. She felt like an alcoholic, hiding bottles behind couch cushions. She'd never hidden something like this from her family. They were oversharers, not secret keepers. They were close, weren't they? But if they were, why couldn't she tell anybody about the man she loved and the way his eyes changed color when he got angry?

And there was this truth, too: Iris had nowhere else to go. She would wake up the next morning to an apology, to flowers, to a man who loved her so much. That was what people didn't understand. That *sorry* he'd give her wasn't a Band-Aid—it was *genuine*.

He didn't mean to lose control like that. But he didn't do anything to stop it, either. She would forgive him, and he would do it again, and the cycle would start over, and over, and over. This was a disaster, but it would continue to be one for years, and nobody was coming to save her from it.

So she sat outside her parents' house for just a minute. And she cried, and cried, and cried. For Cooper, and his sadness, but at the pit of her soul where everything started, she cried for herself.

Twenty-Two

*C*ooper's phone had been going off.

He glanced down. Three text messages, all from Iris.

> Hey! ☺ Are you running late?

> Where are you?

> Cooper call me. Getting worried.

Where are you? Where was he?

Two missed calls. Iris, Iris.

He was sitting on the back porch of the rental house, the bottoms of his feet just touching the wooden planks. They were dirty and splintered. Small, violent waves were whacking the pier, and that damn door to the outhouse was banging again. The temperature had plummeted, but he sat there in an old Marquette tank and swim trunks, because he didn't have any clean underwear. When he exhaled, his breath made cloudy puffs of air. The dark limbs of the trees surrounding the lake stretched up and tangled with tiny ice flecks of stars.

Where was he?

In North Harbor.

It's cold.

Bang, the door goes. *Pop,* the gun goes.

"Cooper?" It wasn't Iris, but Ivan. He stuck his head out onto the back porch. "I'm calling it a night. You're going to get Cricket, right?" His voice sounded like its was coming from underwater. He looked so small.

Cooper nodded. Cricket. His sister. She was in town, getting some homework done at Northern Latte's. *I need a break from this house,* she'd said. She was starting to get ready to go back to Milwaukee, maybe. But could they go now? Now, with those tiny orange pill bottles of Ivan's sitting on the bathroom counter. He shouldn't be alone, the doctor had said while the nurse handed them pamphlets for hospice. Ivan, diagnosed the day after North Harbor, hadn't known how to tell them—dying. Annabelle, the only mother he'd ever really had, the person who'd brought joy to weary corners of their family—dead. Cricket, his poor Cricket, floating through the world like a firefly, nothing touching her.

"Thought you were going out with Iris?"

"Not tonight," Cooper muttered. He should let her know that, probably.

Getting lost was what Iris called it. That Cooper *got lost* sometimes. When Cooper couldn't differentiate any longer between real life and The Girl stuck on repeat behind his eyelids. When his sanity was crushed under the weight of that fucking gun going off, and he had to stop talking and seeing and breathing lest he bring everyone else down with him. Dr. Hoss had said he was a hero, that he should have gotten a medal. He didn't have a medal or a trophy; he didn't even have a glorious tale to tell. Just the ghost of a girl who wouldn't leave him alone.

God, he was lost so often now.

Where was he supposed to be? Didn't he have somewhere to go? He should text Dr. Hoss. He should—

Bang, bang, bang, the outhouse door goes.

Help me.

Cooper needed a drink. He needed Iris, but he couldn't do this, couldn't scare her, couldn't upset her stupid saint of a grandmother. He stumbled into the kitchen and got a beer, just to feel something cold in his hand. He was so hot; he was sweating through his T-shirt. He pressed the beer to his forehead before opening it and downing it, like back when he used to shotgun PBRs in college.

It helped, a little, so he grabbed another one. He chugged that one, too, then dropped the can on the floor and lay down on the couch and felt the scratchy fabric rub against his cheek. He pretended it was Iris, rubbing his head. Or maybe Annabelle, checking his forehead for a temperature. Or his very own mom, singing him a lullaby. His eyes closed.

And then, he was there again.

In North Harbor. Eddie needs to shave. His eyes are tired. "Santa Baby" is playing—what a weird song for a family Christmas parade.

Pop.

"What the fuck was that?" asks Eddie.

Pop—

People are running and screaming. Cooper tries to move his legs, but he can't. His heart is beating so fast he can feel it in his fingertips, hear it in his ears.

"Cooper!" Eddie screams in his face. "Cooper—"

This is what it's like, to see a tragedy: it's seared into your brain like a brand. Cooper's brain needs a Band-Aid and a painkiller.

Because he sees her every time he closes his eyes, he hears that gun with every burst of Technicolor noise, he runs as far as he can, as far north as the compass will take him, into the woods, with the foxes and deer and loons, but he can't do this anymore and he needs to go home but he can't go home and how is he going to take care of Cricket and what is Cricket going to do without either of her parents but just her stupid fucking brother and everything is over and dark and gone and he will wake up every day for the rest of his life with the taste of metal in his mouth and the feel of blood on his fingers and this darkness will completely overtake him like a wave of the lake and he will drive away from Iris and press down on the gas as hard as he can until the spinning wheels of his car careen off the road and carry him away and he will hear that gun shoot and shoot and shoot and—

Bang.

But this wasn't a gun. It was the front door. Cooper sat up fast, and the entire world turned upside down. The couch was hanging from the ceiling. He was going to be sick.

"Cooper! What the hell?" Cricket stood there, and she looked pissed. "You *forgot* me."

Cricket. Who he'd let down again, and again, and again. Whose whole life had been one big disappointment and devastation after another. He couldn't even pick her up from the coffee shop when he was supposed to. He couldn't even—

Behind her was a person—who *was* that? The priest. Sam. *Father* Sam; he was younger than Cooper. He had his collar on. Did he have to wear that thing everywhere?

"I started walking," she said angrily. "Because apparently you *fell asleep.* I called you a hundred times."

Cooper just blinked.

"I saw her walking when I was driving back from the vigil Mass," said Father Sam slowly. "Are . . . you okay?"

Cooper could have gotten her. He just needed to wake up. Why had she started walking? Why was this priest always fucking *there*? Every time Cooper turned around, he felt like he saw him, wearing black and looking pretentious.

"Hey, man, you need to sit down," said Father Sam.

Another girl in danger. His sister, his Cricket, walking home alone, getting picked up by strange men in strange clothes driving strange cars, and now he's in their house. Cooper is a person who saves people, if not The Girl at the parade with the sparkling eyeshadow and blood leaking from her head, then his own sister—if nothing else, this, he can do. He can be there for Cricket. This man—who is he, again?

This is not a good man. Wearing black, looking nervous, hurting people.

And so Cooper pulls his fist back and punches the man in the jaw.

"Shit!" Father Sam yells, grabbing his face. Cooper pulls his fist back again: hits him, hard. His hand doesn't hurt. It's iron—it feels nothing but the sheer brute force of anger.

"Cooper!" screams Cricket.

He hits the priest again.

"Snap out of it!" yells Cricket. "Cooper, please!"

He *has* snapped; he's an animal. He sees black, the blue of a lake, the crimson of blood and Christmas decorations, of a girl begging for help, of Cricket needing him to save her.

"Cooper," Father Sam spits out, "wake up—wake *up*—"

His muscles are on fire as he hits the man a third time, and now the man isn't talking.

He hits him again—

And again—

And again—

"*Daddy!*" screams Cricket. "*Daddy, help!*"

And there he is.

There is Ivan.

There is Ivan, racing up the stairs—Ivan, who has been gone for so long, who wasn't there, wasn't there when Cooper graduated or won trophies or spelled words correctly, wasn't there at Boy Scout troop meetings, wasn't there unless it was televised, wasn't there for the bike rides and boo-boos. Oh, Cooper wishes—he wishes he were young again, when Band-Aids fixed anything, when hugs solved any issue, but he is not. And so Ivan—he wants Ivan *gone,* what is he *doing* here?

Ivan is not a big man. But he wraps his thin, sick arms around

Cooper. He pulls him back with a surprising, supernatural force. Cooper's fists flail, still trying to find Father Sam.

He flails, and flings, and his limbs are everywhere, and Ivan locks his hands together. He's a prison cell holding Cooper back. Cooper reaches for the priest, but Ivan holds him firmer. Cricket is sobbing.

"Now, you listen to me," Ivan says quietly in Cooper's ear, holding Cooper as he pushes against him, out of control, tasting metal, a feral thing, less than human. "I know you hate me. I know you wish I was dead. I know I've been a piece of shit your entire life, but I am not gonna let you go. Listen to me. I am *not going to let you go.*"

And finally, when the solar system has exploded from his fists and the earth seems to go black, when the taste of metal encases his tongue so firmly he can't breathe, when the power encloses his eyelids and presses in on his face with the weight of a thousand suns and sons, he falls to his knees, and sobs, and lets himself be held.

Twenty-Three

"You can say you told me so," Iris said.

Esther rubbed her granddaughter's head and squeezed her tighter. "I would never."

"But you did." Her voice cracked.

"Hush."

"I'm an idiot. You can say it."

"I gave thirty thousand dollars to a stranger on the internet, and you didn't call me an idiot once."

Nobody really knew what had happened to Father Sam, or why he looked as if he'd been hit by a truck. But when Cricket had called Iris, she'd been helping her grandmother snap green beans for a funeral brunch the next day.

And now, two days later, Iris lay on Esther's couch. Cooper was out of the hospital. Esther had made her a giant grilled cheese sandwich with three slices of cheddar and a tomato. She poured her tea from the flowered teapot they never used. There were circumstances that just seemed to require tea, and this was one of them.

Iris just cried. She couldn't stop crying. It felt like her eyes were a broken faucet, just leaking all over the place. Her jeans had fat, dark splotches all over them. That old saying about crying until your tears ran out wasn't real; she'd been crying for days, and still her tears were getting everywhere.

"My girl," said Esther softly.

"I don't want him to leave."

"I know."

"I love him."

"I know that, too."

Iris squeezed her eyes shut. She felt like a little girl.

"What does your mother say?" Esther asked.

Iris still hadn't told Fran, which was crazy. She told Fran *every-thing,* had for her entire life. But she didn't want to tell anybody about this side of Cooper. She only wanted them to know the way he opened the car door for her, and the way his eyes looked when he laughed. The way he gave money to every single person who ever asked for it. The way he cared about Cricket, making sure she was doing okay, checking in on her. The way he pressed his hand against Annabelle's gravestone as if he were praying over it. The way he listened, *really* listened, to everything Iris ever had to say. *He's so sweet,* Fran had whispered to her the first time Cooper came to their house for dinner with extra hot dog buns. All those things were true. They were just as much a part of Cooper as this.

She hated that Esther knew this secret.

"You know what you need to do," her grandmother said quietly.

"I can't."

"Iris Frances."

"I hate my middle name."

"That's your mother's name; show some respect."

"Grandma, I love him. I know you don't get that—"

"Don't get that?" Esther shook her head. "As if I wasn't in love for over fifty years. You sound like a child, Iris. A damn child."

Iris glared at her grandmother. She was being cruel. "He just needs help."

"He most certainly does need help. And until he gets it, he shouldn't be trying to take care of anyone else. A man who's seen violence, he carries that with him. Carries it in his *bones,* girl. Are you listening to me? I know. *Nobody* knows like I know."

"But Grandpa was okay," whispered Iris. "He was okay. He made it out of the war . . . he was okay."

"No, he was *alive,*" said Esther, and she stuck her finger in Iris's face, as if her granddaughter were a child at school getting berated by a nun. "That is not the same thing."

Iris covered her face with her hands, and they sat in silence for a minute.

Her grandmother pushed Iris's hair from her eyes, as gentle as a breeze. "You think I don't know this feeling? You think I don't recognize that voice you get, worrying about him, calling me? You think I didn't have days where I woke up wondering what I'd gotten myself into, how I was going to manage him? *Manage* him, like that was even possible. I lost months, *years* of my life to that feeling, Iris Frances. I would have jumped in front of a truck for that man and there were days I thought he might push me in front of one. I can't—I can't watch you do that. I *can't.* Please don't."

Iris stood to leave. "I have to go. I told him I'd bring him dinner. That hospital food probably sucked."

"Iris . . . I know you think I'm saying this because I don't like Cooper," she said. "But you're wrong. I *love* Cooper."

"I have to go, Grandma," she said, her voice breaking. "I have to go."

IRIS DROVE AS slowly as she could.

When she drove past St. Anne's, something made her pull over. That old gravel parking lot was hard on her tires, but she didn't care. She pulled her jacket around her tightly. It was the first day where you could see your breath. October—she hated October. Everything was dying.

The narthex needed a new carpet. It smelled stale in there, even though it was one of the liveliest places in town. But that day, there was a holy hush over everything. Nobody was there; not the St. Veronica's ladies, or old Barbara going over who the hospitality ministers would be that weekend. Every step she took felt loud.

She walked into the main chapel and sat down defiantly in a pew. She didn't genuflect. Fuck it. Why should she? God, the God of her childhood, Mr. Hot Shit. Big Man in the Sky. Always listening, always seeing. Never helping, never fixing.

She had to get out of there. Her heart was racing, pulsing with anger at someone she couldn't quite get to. She stood back up, hurrying out, feeling the eyes of ghosts on her.

And then she saw him—Father Sam, walking out of the bathroom. When his eyes landed on her, he stopped, his face almost apologetic. Oh God. His face was completely black-and-blue, with a scratch down the side. One of his eyes had practically swelled shut.

"Hey," he said nervously.

Iris put her hand to her mouth.

"It's not as bad as it looks," he said. "I'm a priest, though, so I can't use the 'chicks dig scars' argument. I just look like I got my ass kicked. Which I did."

Iris's eyes filled with tears.

"Iris." He sighed. "I'm okay. Really. It's . . . I'll be okay."

But that wasn't why she was crying. It was because you can't see the product of violence without thinking of the perpetrator. She couldn't see the battered man in front of her without knowing what she had to do next.

Cooper sat with his head in his hands.

"I love you," Iris said. "I hate that I'm contributing to your sadness. Because I know you're so, so sad."

He didn't look up.

"But you know I can't do this anymore. And you know why."

He nodded.

"Cooper," she whispered, "I want you to be okay. But that's . . . I can't sit here while you . . . disintegrate. I can't change your life." She would if she could. Would do anything, *anything*—she'd give away her grandma's house. She'd move. If any of it would help, she'd do it in an instant.

"I love you," she said again, her voice cracking. "Jesus, this is hard."

He just sat there, a boulder of silence.

"Please look at me."

He turned and looked. Iris was going to miss those eyes. She was going to miss the way he looked in that forest-green T-shirt. She was going to miss the way he looked in every T-shirt.

She handed him something, and he took it. There it was: the cookbook. He wordlessly put it down next to him without even opening it.

"What's your plan?" she asked.

He shrugged. "I can't take care of Cricket. Not right now. I need to figure that out. And then I'm gonna . . . drive."

"I'm worried about you."

He picked up a small handful of pebbles and started tossing a few into the garden. "Check in on Cricket. Her mom's gone and her brother's fucking crazy and her dad's dying."

"I will. I promise." Iris was practically whispering as she trod on holy, sacred ground. "I'll make sure she's okay. Are you going to come back?"

"If I do, will you be here?" he asked.

She slid her fingers into his.

THERE WAS A hard knock on the door, waking her up.

"Iris!" It was Olivia. "Where the hell did you put that spare key?"

Iris rolled over in bed, and her eyes fell on her laptop. Her inbox was full of clients asking where their projects were.

"Go away," she yelled back.

She heard the key being put in the lock and the door being opened. "Under the frog? Really? That's, like, the first place a burglar would look. It *smells* in here, holy shit."

Iris covered her eyes with her hand. She felt hungover. "Olivia, leave me alone."

"No. Oh wow, okay—I found the smell. When's the last time you took your garbage out?"

"I don't remember. Where's Emma?"

"With her very capable father." Olivia flopped down onto Iris's bed. "Scoot."

Iris hefted her body over and Olivia snuggled in. It reminded Iris of the time they'd rented *I Know What You Did Last Summer* as kids. Her mom had been away for work for a weekend and her dad had never heard of it. Olivia was so terrified that she'd slept in Iris's bed for months. Iris wasn't scared a bit.

"Grandma told Mom and me what happened," Olivia said quietly. "Don't be mad at her."

"I'm not."

"I told Kurt."

"He probably thinks I'm an idiot."

"Kurt loves you like you're his own sister. You should have told us this was going on."

Iris rolled away and faced the wall. "I didn't want to. I wanted you to like Cooper."

"I do like him, Iris. I *still* like him. I'm scared for him. So is Grandma. So is Mom."

Here the tears came—not in a sobbing fountain, but in a silent slip down her face. She remembered that first night, when they'd jumped into the lake at Vernon's. Well, she'd gotten her wish. Everyone would be talking.

"He left, huh?" her sister asked quietly.

Cooper, jumping into that lake after her, his head coming back above water and that hair so dark you couldn't see it against the sky.

"Okay, sister mine," Olivia said. "Up."

Iris shook her head.

"Iris, get up. Come on." Olivia stood up. "You have things to do. Garbage to take out and work to do, probably. Have you eaten? I brought you a lasagna Grandma made."

Iris pulled her thick blue quilt over her head. It used to be her grandpa's. She'd always loved it, and Esther had given it to her when Felix died. She could still kind of smell woodsmoke on it.

"Iris, damn it." Olivia pulled at the quilt.

"Olivia! I told you to leave me alone."

Her sister sighed, annoyed. She loved Olivia. She hated Olivia.

"Fine," Olivia snapped. "But where's your mop?"

"My what?"

"Your mop. Your floor is disgusting."

Iris glanced out from under her quilt. "You don't even know how to mop."

"I went to law school, dumbass. Where's your mop?"

"Front closet. But—"

Olivia walked out of the room, slamming the door behind her. Iris closed her eyes and went back to a half sleep, one where she kept forgetting about her broken heart and all it entailed.

A few hours later, she opened her eyes all the way. The sun was starting to set; a whole day had gone by. She pulled herself up, slowly; she didn't want to, but she had to pee. When she walked out of her bedroom, she saw her house, cleaner than it had ever been. The floor was sparkling; you could have eaten off it. The garbage had been taken out, and the counters wiped down. Even the bathroom smelled of Pine-Sol. Oh God, Olivia had cleaned her *toilet*? She'd never live that down.

On the kitchen table, there was a box of Thin Mints. Their favorite. Olivia bought forty or so boxes every spring and kept them in her freezer, but she was so ridiculously stingy with them. Not even Kurt could have one. Especially this past year, when she was pregnant.

Iris was so loved. Love coursed through her veins. It grew, and grew, like wildflowers you couldn't get rid of. She was surrounded by it. She breathed it in.

There was a hot pink sticky note haphazardly stuck on the box. *You were right. Had to call Mom to help with the mop.*

She didn't call Olivia that night at the Golden Mast, but she could have. Olivia would have brought her valentines to school if she forgot them, too.

That night, Iris got a phone call: Grace, from college. She was only two and a half months late.

"I heard your voice mail forever ago, sorry," she said breezily. "It was my filming season. Anyway. What's this about a community cookbook?"

Somehow, Iris mustered up the strength to tell her the whole story. She gave more background than she needed to, but she didn't care anymore. The idea of being embarrassed by a trickster online felt hilarious to her. Weren't they all tricked by people right in front of them, day in and day out?

"Huh," said Grace. She sounded disinterested, and Iris remembered when they were paired together for a group project and Grace's big contribution had been bringing Starbucks to every group meeting. "That's . . . cool. Don't really have any ideas of how we could collaborate, though. Unless you've got some influencers on board? Do you know anyone with a platform?"

Then, Iris *did* laugh, and who were people calling crazy again? Because she must have sounded unhinged. But to think that there were people in the world who would seriously rank Ivan's platform above Esther's: Right then, it felt like the funniest thing in the world. It felt absolutely absurd. She hung up without saying goodbye, grabbed a Thin Mint, and opened the curtains.

Twenty-Four

*Y*our entire life could change in the time it took someone to say "gun."

Your entire career could be over. Your life could be over. But more than that, too—your faith. Your confidence in the rightness of the world. Your ability to go to a gathering of people, or sit with your back to the door. The calm, serene confidence you placed in the utter goodness of the human being.

It could be taken from you.

Suddenly, and all at once.

He left Cricket and Ivan the Tesla, throwing down his credit card that connected to Ivan's account to rent a car. Although apparently Ivan was bleeding money—from oncology bills, and skipping out on *Ivan Eats*. He was being held in breach of contract by the Food Network. Nobody knew he had pancreatic cancer besides Gabi.

The long stretch from the Northwoods to Milwaukee made Cooper want to scream. Dying town after dying town, paper mills on life support and new Kwik Trips at every highway exit. A giant Target boasting that they were paying seventeen bucks an hour.

Finally, he got off the interstate and drove down Lake Drive. He loved the apartment he'd been renting in Milwaukee. It was right near the lake, with a brick exterior and a wood-burning stove. It stood there, empty, the pipes probably frozen to shit. Whatever; the landlord had been getting his checks. Inside, a room Cricket had never used, sitting empty and waiting for her.

He pulled into the driveway and sat there, staring at the front door.

He needed a drink. He needed Iris. Something, anything, to get him to that sweet spot. He picked up his phone—he could just call her, tell her he missed her.

Love is choices, Esther had said.

He'd gone to see her, right before he left. They'd sat out on her back porch.

"I'm not going to play that wise-old-lady card," Esther had said. "Old people aren't any wiser than young people. We've just seen more. You've got smart old people and idiotic old people who should just shut up and sit down."

Cooper had looked out over the lake. It had snowed the day before he took off. He'd never seen it snow before Halloween. The seasons all crashed together in Ellerie, overlapping and colliding. The snow was so thick on the ice that an entire family of deer was calmly trotting across it. A mom and her three fawns, following close behind.

He glanced back at Esther. Her breath was coming out in short puffs of smoke.

"Too cold out here for you," he said.

"I'm from Wisconsin, boy," she snapped. "Don't tell me what *cold* is."

He was surprised. She'd never talked to him like this; he'd never even seen her angry. Her eyes immediately adjusted, a look of regret passing over her face.

"Listen," she said. "I was married to my best friend for fifty years. I was married to a man who loved me and loved his daughter. But he was sick, and that sickness, it hurt us badly. You understand me? That sickness was a rot in the floorboards of our lives."

The mother deer paused, and her children paused behind her.

Her head flicked over. She'd spotted Esther and Cooper. *We're no danger to you,* he thought. She stayed frozen.

"I know you love that girl. I love her, too. But you need to take care of yourself before you can take care of anybody else. Not because of some fortune-cookie, rah-rah crap. But because you do not want to pass that pain on to a family. You be a man, and you get some help. It's time," Esther said. "Love is choices."

Cooper wanted to walk across that lake, and just keep walking, maybe lie down and take a nice nap in a bed of blindingly white snow. The cold felt good on his skin and bones and hair. And when Esther got up slowly, waving off his attempts at helping her, clutching the snowy handrail as she hobbled back up the stairs, the mother deer stayed staring, after Esther had made it inside, after Cooper had felt tears on his frozen cheeks, after the snow had stopped falling and everything lay still.

Love is choices.

The weight of a choice—heavier than the weight of a gun, sometimes.

Calling Iris would be a Band-Aid, one that he wanted so fucking badly, before he bled out.

Calling Iris would be a shot to her heart.

He unlocked his phone, dialed a number, and waited for someone to answer.

"Cooper Welsh," said Dr. Hoss. "Jesus Christ."

DR. HOSS'S OFFICE felt like an old comfort. The fake fireplace, the box of tissues—it all felt like nothing had changed at all. Of course, everything had.

Cooper sat in his old place, the corner of the blue couch, and Dr. Hoss sat in the gray armchair. Cooper waited for the therapist's signature session starter—*How have things been?*—but Dr. Hoss didn't say a word. He just stared at Cooper, calmly blinking.

Cooper waited, and waited, and waited, until the awkward

silence became annoying. Why was it on him to start this? He was the one who'd showed up. He was the one who had driven over there in the wintery slush. He was the one who was paying the bill! The one who'd left the only place that had ever felt like *home,* one of the only people who'd ever felt like *family,* after he'd buried his stepmother and tried to take care of his fucking sister, and now he had to sit here and start a conversation.

He opened his mouth to say something, but to his surprise, what came out instead was a sob.

And then another.

And there he was—that therapy stereotype he'd tried so hard to avoid, just bawling out his goddamn eyes on a couch. He cried, and cried, and heard gunshots, and felt that tide he could never see but always feel pulling him closer and closer to a place where he didn't have to feel like this anymore. A place with Annabelle, and the girl he'd just let *die.* A place where Ivan would be soon, too.

He cried for all those little kids who'd had to sit there and watch people get shot right in front of their eyes, all those little kids who would have to sit on this same couch.

He took big, gasping breaths, and before he knew it, he looked up and saw that twenty minutes had gone by.

"Cooper," said Dr. Hoss quietly, "I'm so glad you came in today. That was brave."

He was afraid if he opened his mouth again, he'd just be sobbing once more, so he clamped it shut.

"I want to propose something to you," said Dr. Hoss. "If you want to keep meeting with me, that's fine. I'm happy to do that. But I have a colleague in Madison who's been doing some real ground-breaking stuff around post-traumatic stress disorder. At UW. He's also Catholic, which I believe you said is your faith tradition. I think he may be able to help you in a way I haven't been able to."

Catholic—what did that word even mean? His intake form probably said he was Catholic. Annabelle burying saint statues and

Esther playing Gregorian chants while she cleaned. Can you get kicked out of a religion for beating the shit out of a priest?

"He recently had a paper published about the benefits of his work with veterans," said Dr. Hoss. "I would really encourage you to at least answer his phone call. Is it all right if I give him your number?"

Cooper nodded.

THAT NIGHT, COOPER stood in front of the fridge and stared at the six-pack he'd bought. He'd needed basic groceries; the smell of his fridge had sent him gagging. He'd spotted the Miller Lite and tossed it into the cart without thinking.

He wanted to open every single one and drink them one right after the other. He wanted—

He wanted—

He grabbed a bottle, cracked it open, and poured it down the sink.

Then the next, and the next, until he had nothing but the cardboard carrier.

He was starving, but for some reason, he didn't reach for the peanut butter he'd bought. He went to his suitcase, which he still hadn't unpacked, and pulled out the cookbook Iris had pushed into his hands before he left. *The Funeral Ladies of Ellerie County*, with its green-and-brown cover and pages of dinners.

He could have made anything, but he went with something simple, contributed by Katharine Rose. Something he'd seen Annabelle make a thousand times, one of her only regular recipes. He had frozen hash browns deep in the back of his freezer, and a chunk of cheddar he'd gotten that day at the store. He got to shredding. He didn't have garlic; garlic powder would have to do, never mind that he couldn't even remember when he bought the small purple shaker in his pantry. Salt, pepper, butter, oil. Mix it all together.

As the cheesy potatoes bubbled in his oven, he sat and watched them cook. He'd seen Iris do this over and over again, and it had always made him laugh. *A watched pot never boils,* he'd remind her, and she'd stick her tongue out. Watched cheese doesn't melt—same concept. His phone buzzed, and he glanced at it. A text. Father Sam.

> Good luck, Cooper Welsh. I'm praying for you. Text me if you ever make it back this way.

His stomach grumbled, and his oven dinged.

DR. BAUER DIDN'T look like some fancy scientist who was going to fix Cooper's broken brain.

Cooper had been picturing someone in a lab coat, or someone with a wise-old-man beard like Dr. Hoss. But Dr. Bauer was young—he couldn't have been that much older than Cooper. *Colleague,* Dr. Hoss had said, but there was no way they'd been in the same graduating class or anything. And he looked like he belonged in a show where all the hot young doctors had affairs with their nurses.

"Cooper. Pleased to meet you." He held out his hand, and Cooper shook it. "Before you ask, I'm Australian, not British."

"Noted."

"The accent—people mistake them. We put the royals on our money, but we aren't Brits. Anyway. Did Anders tell you much about what I do here?"

Cooper shrugged. "Virtual reality. Like a video game."

Dr. Bauer smiled, not unkindly. "Sort of."

"So . . . where's the Nintendo?"

The doctor laughed. "First, I need to know some things about you. This is an introductory meeting. I got the basics from Anders, but . . . I'd like to hear it from you. From your perspective."

"Why?" asked Cooper, scratching his face.

Dr. Bauer leaned back and crossed one foot over the opposite knee. "Are you familiar with the term 'exposure therapy'?"

"A little," Cooper lied.

"Exposure therapy is exactly what it sounds like. It *exposes* people to their phobias, their fears, their traumas. If you're afraid of spiders, you try to avoid them, right? Bring someone else in the kitchen to kill them. Don't go into the woods. Easy. But if your phobia is something you *have* to confront, that gets a lot harder. If you're afraid of driving, it's going to seriously impact your life."

"Noises," said Cooper, clearing his throat. "I—the sounds. Loud noises. That's what . . . gets me lost, sometimes."

Dr. Bauer nodded. "Very common. What we're trying to do is get away from *avoidance*. That's going to make life harder, make symptoms stick around longer . . . I'm going to guess you've had some struggles from being around loud noises."

That outhouse door.

Cooper shrugged. "Sometimes."

"What we want to do is retrain your brain, if that makes sense," said Dr. Bauer. "Expose it to the things it's trying to avoid. So . . . my office isn't exactly a *fun* place, you know? It's a place that might hurt, sometimes. And a lot of what we do here is still pretty experimental, even though exposure therapy is evidence-based medicine."

It might hurt. You know what else might hurt? A mom who leaves you, another mom who dies, a sister you let down, a father who was never there, the woman you love telling you she can't handle your alcohol-induced outbursts.

"It's an *option*," Dr. Bauer stressed. "Therapy isn't one size fits all. Neither is trauma."

Virtual reality. Returning to North Harbor. It sounded more like a movie than real life.

But what else had worked? Not talking to Dr. Hoss. Not the sleeping pills. Not the Miller Lite. Not even Iris, in the end.

But it wasn't Iris he pictured just then. It was Cricket. She was the one who'd seen everything, and she was the one he couldn't stand to let down one more time. He couldn't fix his stupid, broken self for his own future, and apparently, he couldn't do it for Iris.

But Cricket—that was who haunted him. Her face as he'd exploded. He had to try for his sister. He couldn't let this be her story. He had to change the ending.

"Can you tell me about what brought you to Dr. Hoss originally?"

Cooper looked out the window at Lake Mendota. It was so much larger than Musky Lake; it felt more like an ocean. It was a nice view, though. Dr. Bauer had a nice office. Maybe this was what Cooper should do. Fix broken brains. Listen to sob stories. Remind himself, every single day, of the shitty ways humanity can cut into our veins. Look at that ancient lake, which had borne witness to the evil things people had done to each other for generations.

"I was a paramedic," he said.

Twenty-Five

One month later

*E*sther had lived in Wisconsin for eighty-two years. She understood the power that weather held, and she understood it better than most. The snow could completely upend even the most carefully laid plans. And these days, you could plan almost everything to a T—you could decide what day you were going to have a baby, decide the exact temperature of your home, decide your name was Hazel and you desperately needed money for a stroller when you were probably a fifty-seven-year-old named Marcus.

You could not, however, control the weather.

The force of nature was powerful. It was responsible for more deaths than anything else in history, from droughts and famines and tsunamis. Wisconsin didn't have hurricanes and Esther had never felt an earthquake, but she knew the way a winter storm could waylay your plans. Black ice could send cars careening into lakes; low visibility in the snow had killed people as recently as last winter. Plummeting temperatures could freeze pipes. Heavy hail could break windows. Thick snowdrifts could cave in roofs.

And the weatherwoman on TV, the one who always wore pleated skirts, was predicting twelve to fourteen inches on the day after Thanksgiving, the day of the Ellerie County Christmas Walk.

"Why do I have to carry the booze backpack?" complained Iris.

Esther rolled her eyes at her granddaughter. "Because you're the spring chicken, honey. Comes with the territory. And don't call it that. It sounds tacky."

That was, of course, exactly what it was. They'd fit exactly two bottles of peppermint schnapps and two thermoses of Swiss Miss into Felix's old camping pack. Technically, alcohol wasn't allowed at the Ellerie County Christmas Walk, but everyone brought . . . well, a booze backpack.

"It'll lighten up after cocktail hour," said Katharine Rose, slowly pulling her jacket on. She'd been moving a bit slower lately. Esther had asked Aaron to go over and plow her driveway the past two snowfalls. Katharine Rose's own useless sons were down in Madison, visiting the lake house to show it off to their trophy wives, but not wanting to lift a finger to help their elderly mother.

That wasn't kind of her to think. They were probably busy.

"You do know the amount of alcohol we drink up here and consider 'cocktail hour' would be considered 'in-patient deserving alcoholism' anywhere else?" asked Olivia, pulling the little pink hat Bea had knitted for Emma tighter down over her daughter's ears.

Katharine Rose looked at Esther. "Kids these days."

Esther chuckled. She could never have imagined saying such a thing to her father, who put back a six-pack solo every night after a hard day's work on the farm.

The Ellerie County Christmas Walk was one of Esther's favorite days of the year. The Christmas tree lighting would be followed by all the shops on Main Street opening their doors, offering cookies and gift shopping and caroling. Vern brought his horses and hitched them up to an old-fashioned sleigh, giving rides to any families willing to wait in line. At the end of the night, Bea's husband, JP, would usually dress up as Santa Claus and pass out candy canes. The Boy Scouts sold hot dogs, and this year, the funeral ladies of Ellerie County would sell their cookbook.

But also this year, there was a problem.

Twelve to fourteen inches was a lot of snow—a *lot,* even for Ellerie County—to get all at once. Vernon had already said the horses wouldn't be able to make it this year, and about half the shops on Main Street weren't even opening up. *Don't bother,* they were saying. *Who will drive over here in a snowstorm?*

All that work. All those hours. All that casserole.

Should she have let Ivan Welsh promote the book? Maybe she should have. She'd heard, of course, about his sickness, what all those meetings in town were about. She rarely saw him anymore, but Iris had taken up a friendship with Cricket. She and Ivan were still in Redstone; Iris had completely missed the tourist season, but she insisted Ivan had been paying her plenty. Esther wasn't sure if she was just trying to stay close to Cooper or if she genuinely liked spending time with the girl, but apparently Iris had been teaching her to bake. And that was something everyone should learn how to do at some point in their lives.

And another problem, a bigger problem, that weighed on all their chests: Bea. A cough had turned into pneumonia had turned into something else, something they weren't sure of, that involved tests and breathing machines and steroids. She was all the way out in the Waukegan County hospital. Her unit didn't even allow visitors.

Jinger had let them set up their folding card table in Northern Latte's. Fran carefully unloaded copies of the book from the tote bags she'd brought, displaying them as if it were Barnes & Noble. Carlotta brought her silverware sorter from home to work as a cash register.

"Remember, Mom," said Fran, "even if this doesn't work, we have other options."

Esther nodded. But she already knew the truth.

She was going to lose the house. And if she did . . . well, she'd always said it was just a house. She had her friends, her community, her church. Her daughter and her grandchildren. Her great-granddaughter, as cute as a button. She had plenty. More than enough.

She, Katharine Rose, and Carlotta poured themselves some hot chocolate with schnapps and cheers'd their red plastic cups. Olivia and Kurt took Emma to go see the monkey that lived at the candle shop, and Fran went to go check out Grumpy Delilah's pottery store, promising she'd be back.

"Go with your mother, Iris," said Esther, waving a hand. "We'll be fine."

Iris cracked a smile. "And miss all the fun?"

"Looks like it's going to be a slow night, guys," Jinger called out from behind the coffee bar. "Anyone need a latte?"

"We're fine, sweetheart," called out Carlotta, wiggling her cup in the barista's direction.

"Well, I want to be your first customer," said Iris. She opened up her wallet and plunked down a twenty-dollar bill. "I want it autographed, too."

"Just call me Greta Garbo," sang Katharine Rose.

"Bea said she met Greta Garbo once," said Carlotta. "She had a cousin who lived in Janesville." A silence fell over them.

Oh, Bea; the way she'd cheat in euchre and sing hymns while she chopped carrots. Their Bea. None of this felt real without her. None of it felt like it mattered. A house—who cared?

Esther sipped her hot chocolate. She wasn't going to have her house—her beautiful, beautiful house, that Felix had built the roof on, that she had brought her babies home to. But in God's name, it was the richest she'd ever felt.

By 10 P.M., it was time to call it. Olivia and Kurt had taken the baby home ages ago, and Fran had gone as well, promising to send Aaron to pick them up. They shouldn't be driving in snow like this.

"Let's count how much we made," said Carlotta.

"Why?" laughed Esther. "We've counted every fifteen minutes. Two hundred smackaroos."

"We should go to Vegas," said Carlotta. "Play the slots!"

"Ten copies," said Iris, her voice cracking. She wasn't laughing. "Ten copies. How? Three of them were to our family members." And two to Father Sam, who insisted he was sending them to his own mother and grandmother. His face had healed nicely, but he still had a light scar on his temple from where he'd smacked his face on the coffee table. Iris's eyes flickered there every time she saw him. Esther noticed. It was too bad, too. He was a looker.

"You can't control Mother Nature, Iris, dear," said Katharine Rose gently. "Nobody was going to come out in a snowstorm like this. We'll sell the book after church next weekend."

But that wasn't going to do it. The population of the town was going to shrink tenfold, the only tourists being the ice fishermen and snowmobilers who came for fish fries and left by Saturday morning. That twenty thousand dollars—it was gone, gone with the wind, and it wasn't coming back.

So why was the sunny optimism still stubbornly clinging around? It was the power of the funeral ladies. When you'd seen what they'd seen, Esther knew—death after death after death, wars and divorces, oxygen tanks and new hips, burnt pasta bakes and fingers scalded by boiling water—you couldn't *not* hold a larger perspective.

Bea, that sickness: It had reminded them of something so precious. Of the fragility of life, and the cost it carried. A house? Who cared what a house cost? If you could measure something in dollars, you might as well push it into the lake.

"What the hell are we going to do with all of these cookbooks?" asked Esther. "The cardboard box I move into won't have much storage."

It was supposed to be a joke. She'd meant to be *funny*. But there was Iris, and she wasn't laughing. She was crying.

"Oh, sweetheart," said Esther.

"Maybe I can help," Iris said wildly. "I could sell Redstone."

"Iris. Honey." Katharine Rose put a hand on her arm.

"So much change," said Esther. "All so fast . . ." These lessons were hard to learn at eighty-two; they were surely harder to learn at twenty-six.

"I could get another job," Iris choked out. "We can't lose the house. We can't."

"It's a house, Iris Frances. Four walls and a roof," said Esther.

Carlotta walked over to the bar and rummaged around behind it.

"Are you allowed to be back there?" yelled out Katharine Rose. Jinger had gone home ages ago.

"Aha! I knew she had these." Carlotta pulled out a battery-operated candle and clicked it on as she waddled back over to the table. "We need a candle, yes?"

Iris put her face in her hands, and her shoulders shook. "I wish Grandpa was here. I keep thinking that."

"I do, too," said Esther. "Every single day." She'd go to his grave tomorrow and make sure the snow was cleared off it. She kept thinking that Felix would be upset that she'd lost the house, and perhaps he would. But she also thought he'd be so proud of her for the cookbook. He'd give her that smile, the same one he gave her when he ordered those hash browns so many years ago. The feeling of Felix's hand in hers as they walked across the parking lot at the movies—she could still remember it, after all this time.

"I wish . . . ," Iris said again, but stopped. Esther knew who else she wished for, but she kept her mouth shut.

Carlotta made the sign of the cross, and they all did the same. "May this prayer meeting of the funeral ladies of Ellerie County come to order. Lord in heaven, thank you for the gift of this night," she said. "Thank you for the gift of our recipes and our hands to make the food. Thank you for the roof over our heads, the warmth in our bones."

"Thank you for safety from storms," said Esther.

"For Esther's son-in-law, for driving us," said Carlotta.

"Your hands have blessed this project," said Esther. "We know your guiding hands will keep it safe."

"We pray for our dear, dear friend Bea. Her total healing and her perfect faith," whispered Carlotta.

"Lord, we pray for our baby girl Iris, whose heart is hurting so deeply," Katharine Rose chimed in.

Esther squeezed her eyes shut and prayed through every saint she knew. Mary, for a mothering spirit. Saint Joan of Arc, for courage. Saint Teresa of Ávila, for honesty.

"We pray for forgiveness for Hazel," said Esther, reaching as far as she could into the dusty basement of her heart.

"And we pray for the repose of the soul of Felix Larson," said Katharine Rose. "Felix Michael Larson, whom we have loved."

Felix, who had lived in that house they loved so dearly, that safe haven, those four walls. She would burn those walls to the ground for Carlotta, or Iris, or any of them. Esther sent her prayers to heaven. She exhaled, and let them fly.

THE NEXT DAY, Esther woke to the sound of her driveway being snow-blown. Aaron, she assumed, and kept her eyes closed. She was usually up before the sun, reading the Psalms and drinking her coffee, but today, she felt every inch of her eighty-two years.

But then, she heard a knock on the door.

She glanced down. She was in her old striped pajamas, and—her teeth. Her biggest vanity.

"One minute!" she called. Her own daughter didn't see her without her teeth in. Certainly not Aaron. "Come on in—I'll be right out."

But the door didn't open. Esther hurried to get her dentures in and splash some water on her face. She pulled on a sweater and went to the door.

Standing there was a boy with dark hair and snow on his eyelashes.

"Cooper Welsh," she said.

"Hi, Esther," he said. "Can I come in?"

HE SHOWED HER what he'd mocked up. An Instagram post, with Ivan talking about the cookbook.

"No mention of you at all," he said. "None. I can handle all of the shipping, all of that crap."

"I'm not going on the *Today* show."

"I don't think Ivan has Savannah's number."

"And no pictures of me. Unless it's the one from Olivia's wedding. I look all right in that one."

"Deal."

"Did Iris call?" asked Esther, handing him a cup of coffee with shaking hands. "I told her . . . it's a house. Just a house."

"Not to her," he said. "But no. She didn't. I knew the Christmas Walk was yesterday. I saw the weather. I . . . had a feeling. And . . . can I tell you something?"

Esther simply looked at him.

"I drove here by myself, and a car backfired outside Stevens Point," he said.

"And?"

"And?" He held up his hands. "I'm here, aren't I? Do I look like I'm freaking out?"

"You think you're all better, do you?" Esther set her mouth in a thin line.

"No," he admitted. "But I think we're all messed up, and some of us are working on it, and some of us aren't. And I'm working really, really hard."

Esther looked at him. The two of them had nothing in common, nothing at all. Poor little rich boy who'd grown up with an army of nannies, who had witnessed horrors in front of his eyes. Esther, the farm girl, who spent her days making food for the grieving. But they both knew the power of a damn good meal. And both of them loved Iris Frances Kelleher.

And for just a flash, it wasn't Cooper Welsh she was looking at, but her very own Felix, with his crooked smile and bright eyes. Felix, still working miracles, still mending hearts, even from up in eternity. *A medic never sleeps,* he'd said sometimes when asked about Vietnam. *You never really stop being one.*

You can say you don't believe in saints; that was fine by her. But she knew Felix was there in that room. She knew it like she knew how to make a piecrust, and she'd been making those for seventy years.

Twenty-Six

*C*ooper sat by the lake, waiting.

Being back in Ellerie after a month and a half felt like climbing into bed under the warmest blanket you could find, even though it was freezing.

Why Ellerie? he and Cricket had always asked Annabelle.

He knew why, now.

Cricket was the one who had asked him to come back. She kind of hated him now, which he understood. But Ivan didn't have a lot of time left, and he'd been asking for Cooper. Cooper hadn't gotten to say goodbye to Annabelle. None of them had.

He drove up the day of the Christmas Walk, and he prayed the entire time. He'd been doing that lately. Dr. Bauer wasn't one of those Jesus people who went door-to-door to save your soul, but he did talk about the connection between meditation and prayer, and Cooper found he actually kind of liked talking to the God he thought might be up there. He'd popped into churches and stared at the stained glass, wondering what Iris was looking at just then. He started reading poems about nature by this woman Esther had once told him about, because they reminded him of Ellerie, and he'd find himself making the sign of the cross after. He talked to Annabelle sometimes, too, and Felix, Esther's husband, whom he'd never met in his entire life. Right this minute, the snow was so thick, he asked anyone who was listening to help him get there okay. They didn't even plow the roads past Highway K.

He made it by going fifteen miles an hour, turn by turn, listening to the thick roar of his tires over the drifts of snow and the *squeak, squeak, squeak* of his wipers attempting to keep his windshield clean. When he drove down Main Street, he saw mostly closed shops—the bait and tackle was open, and the pottery store. And there, in Northern Latte's, were the funeral ladies.

They were by themselves with a giant pile of cookbooks. But they didn't look upset.

In fact, they looked like they were having a party. The coffee shop was glowing, and they were cracking up about something. Esther slapped the table with the palm of her hand. They all had plastic cups—no doubt filled with booze—and that one that always lied, Cooper forgot her name, was laughing so hard she had tears on her cheeks. Oh, Iris, with those three self-righteous grandmothers. One was missing. The one who told the tall tales. He hoped everyone was okay. But Iris, she'd gotten more beautiful. How was that even physically possible? What a cliché! Someone give him a Hallmark movie to be in. Whatever—it was true. Ivan was the writer, not him. Love, healthy love, love without the fog of ghosts, it made you see things clearer. She'd been beautiful before, but she was almost shining now.

It looked so cozy and picturesque, as if it were brimming with happiness.

That's what he wanted.

But he didn't stop. He drove all the way to Redstone, where Ivan and Cricket were still staying. He went inside to find Ivan asleep and Cricket looking more tired than a thirteen-year-old should be.

They'd made giant plates of spaghetti and she'd filled him in—about Ivan's medicine, and the doctor's prognosis, and her friend

Sophie's mom who kept calling and asking where Cooper was. He filled her in—about Dr. Bauer, and virtual reality, and being able to hear loud noises without flipping out and even sleep at night sometimes.

They didn't have any answers to all the questions ahead of them, but God, he was home, and that much he knew.

Footsteps suddenly crunched beside him, and he saw a puff of smoke as someone exhaled.

"Hey," he said, not turning to look.

"Hi," said Father Sam.

"Thanks for meeting me," he said. "I know . . . you didn't have to." He rubbed his hands on his arms, trying to warm up a bit. The early winter air was thick with cold and his own breath.

Father Sam stood next to him and shrugged, looking out over the lake. "Kind of a job requirement."

"Yeah."

"So, you're moving back?"

"I don't know," said Cooper honestly. "But Ivan isn't well, and Cricket needs my help. Once . . . once she needs to go somewhere else, I'm not sure what the plan is. I don't think I can take good care of her, at this point."

"You don't," said Father Sam flatly.

"I don't," Cooper responded quietly.

The two men stood there in a comfortable silence. Cooper shielded his eyes from the sun with his hand.

"Man, when that sun bounces off the snow, it's a killer," he said.

"Yeah. The light can really hurt if you're not used to it."

Cooper should apologize to this man he'd beaten the daylights out of. He knew that. But when he looked at Father Sam, he saw forgiveness in his eyes, even though Cooper hadn't said sorry.

Father Sam looked at him. "You deal with your shit?"

"Are you allowed to swear?" Cooper asked.

"You didn't answer the question."

Cooper leaned back and put his hands under his head, looking up at the sky. He'd forgotten how blue it was up here. He prayed for just a minute, barely above a whisper, and the words tasted sweet on his tongue, like Ellerie, like lake water and piecrust and Iris.

Twenty-Seven

*S*he heard he was back long before she saw him.

His name was a whisper in the town, a murmur that stopped when she walked into Coontail's. She could smell his body soap at Vernon's. She could smell pancakes made in bacon grease whenever she walked past Turtle Pond.

And she knew it was him who'd gotten Esther to say yes to Ivan's Instagram post. Soon the money was flowing in—a charming small-town cookbook that Ivan Welsh had enjoyed? With a limited printing? They sold out in three days. Their little cookbook was going to California, and Hawaii, and South Africa. People in France would be making cream of chicken casserole from a can. Her grandmother's apple pie. It had felt impossible a few months ago, and now it was a reality. What on earth had made her change her mind? Iris didn't know.

She and Fran were driving Esther to the bank to hand over the check. There it was: twenty thousand dollars. Even after buying massive bottles of Jameson and new throw pillows for Carlotta, Katharine Rose, and Bea, Esther had it—her house.

"Oh, Mom," said Fran. "I'm just so happy."

Esther smiled, looking out the window. "I am, too. I think people will enjoy the book."

"I meant about the house," Fran said.

Esther shrugged. "I told you girls from the beginning. It was always just a house."

But it wasn't. Iris wanted her babies, and her grandbabies, to swim off that dock, and wake up to a sunrise shining through those giant windows. She wanted Esther's and Felix's spirits to permeate its walls. And she didn't want some Twitter scammer to win.

"Did we ever try and see if we could figure out who Hazel was?" Iris said.

"There was nothing they could do," said Fran. "She'd shut down all of her accounts."

"She'll get an extra few years in hell for that one," muttered Iris.

"Iris," sighed Esther.

"Purgatory," her mom corrected her lightly. "She can get all cleaned up before going to heaven." That concept had never seemed particularly fair to Iris. Someone with the weight of mistakes that heavy shouldn't be able to just shower them off like a layer of dirt.

"How are you not angry, Grandma?" said Iris. "How do you not want to throttle her?"

Esther smiled back at her. "I'm driving to go pay money that I owe, that I earned from writing a real book. I'm with my daughter and granddaughter, and afterwards, they're going to treat me to Culver's. How is that not enough to be happy about?"

"We are?" said Fran.

"The flavor of the day is Moose Tracks. I love when they put those peanut butter cups in it. Drive, girl. I'm not getting any younger."

IRIS HAD TAKEN to spending time with Cricket. She spent a lot of afternoons sitting with her in Northern Latte's, finishing up a few client projects while Cricket took her classes. For some reason, now that she had nobody checking in on her, Cricket seemed more motivated. Iris turned down inquiries for new logos and website designs. She didn't want to do graphic design anymore. Her mother would—and did—cringe at turning down perfectly good income.

But the rate Iris had charged Ivan for the Airbnb was enough to live on in a place like Ellerie for a while, and she wanted to do something else. She didn't know what just yet. But she was okay with that, for now. The uncomfortable place was the honest one.

In the meantime, she'd seen an ad at the library looking for someone to teach internet usage to senior citizens part-time. She was working on her application.

"He called you yet?" Cricket asked, not glancing up from her math lecture. Iris just shook her head. She was starting to think he wasn't going to.

"He will," insisted Cricket. "He's been spending a lot of time with our dad."

"Good. That's good," Iris said. "This application is asking if I have experience with older generations. Should I just attach a PDF of the cookbook?"

"Send them your texts from Esther. Tell them you taught her how to send GIFs."

As much as Iris missed Cooper—and oh, she missed Cooper, she missed the way his hair smelled, she missed the way he tossed her into the lake, she missed him so much it made her lungs tighten—there were things she didn't miss, too. And without those around, without the worry and the panic that had clung to her that last month, she felt like she could breathe a little. Stretch her muscles and open her eyes. Stop worrying about someone else's ghosts.

CRICKET AND IRIS would also spend long afternoons cooking at Esther's, working their way through the funeral ladies' cookbook.

"It's super underdone," Cricket said, cutting into the pork chop she'd just taken out of the oven.

"How long did you brown the sides for?" Esther asked.

"I skipped that part," Cricket admitted. "I thought it was optional."

Esther shook her head. "No! The panfrying helps get the cooking started, and besides, it seals in the juices."

Iris glanced up from the garlic she was chopping. "How small do I have to make these? My hands are starting to get sore."

Esther smiled. "No cutting corners, either of you. These things take time. Whoever you're giving the food to deserves your very best."

"But we're the ones eating these today," said Cricket with an eye roll.

"Don't be silly," said Esther. "You deserve your very best, too."

IRIS WAS WALKING to the pond when she saw him.

That walk, down to Turtle Pond, was her favorite to make in the winter. There were no cars of tourists, no seasonal sleigh rides. Just miles and miles of thick, snowy pine trees, smelling like woodsmoke and snowblower gas, calling her home.

As she walked, she was thinking of what she was going to do. Cricket would probably go with Cooper back to Milwaukee; she'd have Redstone to run. She hadn't even listed it yet, but she was planning on a booked-out summer. She had her last few clients, and this food blog idea, bopping around in her head. She'd thought for a minute that she *should* leave Ellerie. Go to Madison—hell, go to Chicago. Minneapolis. New York! Los Angeles! She could go anywhere. But why go anywhere when you could live here? Leave her grandmother, her parents, her sister, Emma? Leave the way the sun looked peeking up over Musky Lake on a May morning?

No. The Northwoods was her home, for now. She could always change her mind one day. Who knew where the world would take her? Who knew anything at all?

As she turned the corner to Bobcat Road, she stopped. There was someone standing by the log at Turtle Pond, her favorite place. And she'd know that figure anywhere.

Cooper looked up and saw her. He smiled. A real, calm smile.

"You again," he said.

She kept walking, cautiously. "You again."

"I wondered if I'd see you here," he said.

"It's a small town."

"I know it," he said with a chuckle.

"Why didn't—" She cleared her throat. "Why didn't you call me?"

Cooper looked at her kindly. "I'm not . . . ready."

It was like someone had punched her in the gut, in the 8-degree weather. The sharpness of the cold bit her eyes, and she felt them start to water.

"Okay. Well, all right."

"No! That's not what I meant! Iris, I love you. I'm in love with you. I meant that I'm still working out some of my stuff. And I don't want to put you through that until I know that I'm as healthy as I can be."

She nodded. A tear threatened to slip out, but it was so cold that it froze to her face a little. "You're talking to someone?"

He laughed. "You wouldn't believe this thing they had me do. Virtual reality for a shooting."

"*What?*"

"It sounds crazy. It *was* crazy. But . . . it helped. It actually *helped,* the way nothing else has, and I'm feeling good. It's so good, to feel like I'm doing something. And it's working. But I want to go slow. *Because* I love you."

She just nodded. That made sense to her, in a backward sort of way. "You scared the shit out of me."

"I'm so sorry."

"I thought you were going to wind up fucking *dead* somewhere."

"I know," he said, his voice cracking.

The wind whipped around them, and he pulled his jacket tighter.

"Iris," he said quietly, "I could apologize every single day for the rest of our lives, and it would never be enough. I'm just . . . I am so sorry. Being with you now would make it even worse. I need to make sure I'm steady first. And then, if you'll let me, I swear to God, I will spend the rest of my life making it up to you."

They stood in a heavy silence for a moment. But Iris was learning not to hurry. The important things in life, the conversations you needed to have the most, took time. They couldn't be measured in minutes or hours.

"I joined the funeral ladies," she said abruptly.

Cooper laughed. That *laugh*. "You what?"

"Don't laugh."

"I'm not laughing. I am laughing. It's funny. It's awesome, though."

"They needed someone, with Bea . . . well. You heard about Bea."

"I heard about Bea," he said quietly. "Not so good, huh?"

"Not so good. And besides, they needed young blood. Carlotta said they need a hot girl to get young men to come back to church, but Esther said it's because once they all die, St. Anne's is going to have to pay for catering, and they won't be able to afford it."

"Those women," Cooper murmured, "could move heaven and earth. Anything they put their minds to."

"You can, too," said Iris. "You figure it out. You figure . . . it all out. I'll be here."

"You will be?"

"Where else would I go?" she said. "This is my home."

She turned to walk back home, and Cooper called after her one more time. "The turtles," he said. "When do they come back?"

"Lent," she replied, without turning around. "They're Catholics."

Cooper laughed. A loon called. And to a girl raised in the Northwoods, the song of a loon can sound a lot like hope.

Twenty-Eight

The week before Christmas, Cooper spent most nights on the scratchy blue pullout couch of Ivan's hospice room.

All things considered, it wasn't so bad. Maybe the family members of those about to die were given the comfortable couches. Ivan had been telling Cooper stories, stories and stories and stories of his life, things Cooper had never heard before. There wasn't much else to talk about. Ivan talked about the uncomfortable couch in the room the night Cooper was born. He'd almost thrown his back out, he kept saying. *The pain medicine makes him a bit forgetful,* a nurse murmured to Cooper. Cooper didn't mind. He liked hearing the story.

Cooper had tried to look up his mother, to tell her. There was her Instagram profile: Hayley Moss. TikTok videos of essential oils, selfies on a beach in a bikini. He didn't even have her number. Neither did Ivan. He sent her a DM, but she didn't respond. *Ivan Welsh's first wife, Hayley Moss,* the Wikipedia page said.

Hayley was not who he pictured when he thought of a mother. That would always be Annabelle.

Cricket came, too. Thank God she was so smart, or she'd have failed out of eighth grade. She spent nights at Esther's, in the guest bedroom. She was too afraid to sleep by herself. Cooper couldn't blame her. In January, when this was over and Ivan was a memory, she was supposed to go and live with Sophie's family. They'd driven up a couple of times, quite the hike from Chicago. Bea would have called them FIBs, *fucking Illinois bastards,* but she was only a hall-way away in the exact same hospice. The funeral ladies took turns sitting vigil, bringing her wrinkly husband coffee that was prob-ably spiked. Esther told him she'd been saying so many Rosaries her fingers were getting calloused.

Ivan told Cooper about all his travels, from Bangkok to Warsaw to Honduras. He told him about food, because after everything that had happened, that was still their common language. How to make fried chicken with Korean pepper paste. How to choose the best oxtail from the butcher. How to know when your pork is cooked perfectly.

There were so many things Cooper could have asked him, about why it took this long for him to get his shit together. If it was the cliché of a sickness or the horror of losing Annabelle or if it was simply that some people were bad at love, the way others were bad at cooking or driving. But he didn't. What was the point? You could learn, eventually. And then the people you extended it to could accept it or reject it. *Love is choices,* Esther had said. This was Cooper's. Love—he was getting better at it. Earlier in life than Ivan. Cooper had had a good teacher, hadn't he? He'd had Annabelle.

The anniversary of North Harbor came and went. Cooper told Cricket he needed a day to himself. He drove down to see Dr. Bauer, who sat with him for two hours and helped him breathe through a thick fog of grief, and then he drove back up in the same day and went to a daily Mass for the first time in his life. If Father Sam was surprised to see him, he didn't say so. They went out for beers afterward and argued about college football.

Father Sam had insisted on coming to the hospital on one of the last days, which had almost bugged Cooper, because Ivan's life had not been one of righteousness or virtue. Annabelle hadn't gotten the peace of a priest at her death, and she had deserved it. But then—what was deserved, really? Here, then, was the truth, as bitter as a bourbon old-fashioned: Nobody deserved anything. Everything anyone gave each other was a gift: a grace, something to behold.

Father Sam said some prayers and Ivan nodded along. The nurse who was in the room stopped and stood, silently, in the holy place. Cricket leaned into Cooper and shut her eyes.

Hospitals, Cooper learned, are full of numbers. Blood cells. Heart rates. Oxygen levels. Ivan was falling asleep more and more, taking long naps. The kind hospice nurse told him that eventually, he just wouldn't wake up. That's how it would happen.

When Ivan was awake, he talked to Cooper and Cricket, but in those final few days, he started to become disoriented. He called Cricket Gabi, or started speaking Spanish, which Cooper didn't even know he knew. He asked where the call sheet was and what time they had to start filming. He requested specific food: naan and South African pap and fresh mozzarella, even though he was barely keeping down broth. In his worst moments, he asked for Annabelle, and Cooper couldn't bring himself to tell him the truth, so he just kept saying she'd be right back.

Esther insisted that Cricket needed a break, and Cooper thought she was probably right, so he let Esther take her down the street for some McDonald's. Cooper knelt next to the bed and pushed his head against the thin blanket, feeling Ivan's arm on the other side.

"I saw that you tried," Cooper whispered. "I saw it, this summer, you trying to take care of Cricket. You being around. It wasn't too late. I saw it, okay? I promise I saw it."

Cricket came back with two caramel brownie McFlurries. Ivan wouldn't open his eyes. She screamed, and screamed, and Cooper held her as nurses came in and made phone calls and talked in murmurs.

"I'm not letting you go," he whispered in Cricket's ear as she finally collapsed against him. "I'm not letting you go."

IVAN'S FUNERAL WAS small, which was probably how he would have wanted it. Cooper, Cricket; Gabi, that idiot. The sun was out even though it was bitter cold; the high was negative twelve. Sophie and her parents drove up. In came Iris, and her sister, wearing her baby in one of those sling things. Esther, who had baked the pie for Bea's funeral the week before.

Iris sat behind Cooper. She didn't hug him or touch his shoulder or whisper any stupid platitudes. But he knew she was there. He could feel it.

After the funeral lunch, where Gabi asked Carlotta if the pasta salad was gluten-free, Sophie's mom and Cricket went into town for coffee. Cooper went over the list with Gabi of who had to be called. This would be headline news. Ivan's name was going to trend on Twitter. The great Ivan Welsh, James Beard Award winner, would be buried in Ellerie, Wisconsin. It would become a tourist stop, where die-hard fans would come lay flowers and sprinkle salt. And as tacky and strange as it sounded, it seemed right, too. He was next to Annabelle.

But that day, the day of the funeral, Sophie's mom came back from coffee with a serious look on her face. Mrs. Tatum; God, they should have built statues to that woman, who cared about a thirteen-year-old who wasn't related to her enough to ask all these questions and drive to the Northwoods. Cooper appreciated her so much. She sat down with Cooper and explained—Cricket wanted to stay with him, in Ellerie. Mrs. Tatum was concerned. Was he ready for that?

And, oh—how badly he wanted to say yes. But he knew how hard he was still battling those loud noises. He knew what Cricket deserved. *Deserve*—that word again, thick with meaning.

"I hate you," Cricket told him, zipping her suitcase closed. He didn't say anything.

"You're just like him," she said, choosing the words she thought would hurt the most. "You're exactly like Ivan. Leaving me like a piece of trash. You promised. You promised you'd never—"

"I promised to take care of you," he said in a low voice. Breathing slowly, the way Dr. Bauer had taught him. "That's what I'm doing."

She glared up at him, her eyes sharp with tears. Oh, Cricket. He remembered holding her the day she came home from the hospital. The heartbreak she'd endured felt unbearable, but it wasn't. People could bear a whole hell of a lot, he was learning.

"I will never, ever forgive you," she said.

He just nodded. He knew she meant it. But he knew something else. He knew that love did not always feel the way Cricket wanted it to feel, the way they *all* wanted it to feel. Warm like a summer day in Ellerie, with the sun shining down on the dock and the woods seeming endless. It could feel like that, sure. Of course it could. But sometimes it felt like this: like an icy winter, the kind where your knees shake and your knuckles crack. Like lying dormant. Like roots under the ground, pulsing and surviving down where nobody can see them. Until one day, something sprouts. And suddenly, you can.

But Cricket, Cooper knew, would have to learn that for herself.

"You'll come back," he told her. "You'll come back."

She stormed out of the house, getting into the minivan and slamming the door shut. Mrs. Tatum gave him a tight hug, whispered that he was doing the right thing, that she'd see him Saturday when he drove down. They drove away, and Cooper felt a small piece of his heart leaving Ellerie.

"You'll come back," he said again, out loud. A promise to Cricket. A promise to himself.

WINTER IN ELLERIE was long, endless gray days. You would look up and just see a strict wall of grayish white, from the snow to the ice-frozen lake to the pit of endless sky. Cooper didn't give a single interview about Ivan beyond the two-sentence family statement. He went to his and Annabelle's graves once a week. Sometimes he'd see Esther, visiting Felix and Bea. They'd nod to each other. He'd taken a chunk of his massive inheritance and bought a house that overlooked the lake, not too far from hers. It had a dock.

And of course, he'd see Iris. He'd see her at Northern Latte's, working on her writing, or outside Redstone, shoveling the driveway for snowmobiling tourists. He'd see her walking out of the library, stepping into the grocery store, filling her Camry at the gas station. He'd see her in his mind as he drove to Madison to see Dr. Bauer, or to Chicago to visit Cricket every other Saturday. He'd see her in the faces of all the people in the PTSD group therapy he went to in the church basement two towns over. He saw her at Mass, sitting with her family, holding her niece and resting her head on her mom's shoulder. He saw her in the front window of Bobcat Books, propped up front and center: *The Funeral Ladies of Ellerie County Cookbook.*

And when spring came, and the puddles on the street grew large, with the soundtrack of icicles dripping and mud squelching and cars driving with their windows down, he went to go see the turtles.

He knew when he woke up that morning that she'd be there, and there she was, looking out over the pond. When she heard the ice crack beneath his feet, she turned. They stood there, the weight of a thousand years between them, all the things human beings do to each other, the ways they seek out another person who understands the things they've seen, the ways they tear apart and come back together over and over and over again.

"You again," he said.

"You again," she said. "You never taught me how to make pancakes."

"Come on," he said. And she did.

Recipe

Esther's Piecrust

MAKES 2 SINGLE CRUSTS

2 cups all-purpose flour, plus more for dusting
1 teaspoon salt
2/3 cup plus 2 tablespoons shortening
7 tablespoons water

Measure the flour into a mixing bowl and mix the salt through it. Use your hands to work in the shortening until the shortening particles are the size of giant peas.

Sprinkle with water, 1 tablespoon at a time, mixing lightly with a fork until all the flour is moist. Gather the dough together with your fingers so it cleans the bowl. Press it firmly into two evenly divided balls. Then keep in waxed paper in the refrigerator or roll out for a pie.

Dust your counter with flour. Roll out your dough to not quite 1/8 inch thick. Roll lightly—don't add too much flour, or the crust will be tough. The dough should be rolled out to about 1 inch larger than the pie pan's circumference.

Acknowledgments

God's hands guided this project, and I'm grateful his twisty-turny road led it here.

Alex Slater, thank you for not being completely shocked when I sent you a novel about elderly women baking pies in the woods. You're the best advocate a girl could ask for in this crazy industry.

Tessa Woodward, it was an honor to have your expert hands guide this book. I'm still pinching myself. To the entire team who worked on the book, including Ivy McFadden, Stephanie Vallejo, Madelyn Blaney, Kerry Rubenstein, Diahann Sturge, and many others: You have my endless gratitude.

Thank you to the childcare team at Almost Home—you make everything I do possible. Further gratitude to the baristas at Roots Café and Whelan's Coffee in Oconomowoc, Wisconsin—thanks for the caffeine and Wi-Fi.

A thousand thank-yous to the Cigar Club: Tsh, Sarah, and Haley provided monthly encouragement and accountability, which was very much needed. Thanks for turning me from a fangirl into a friend.

To the many friends who have cheered me on throughout the years—I'm the luckiest girl on earth. My people show up at events, buy books, share about them, and are just the very best people to have in my corner. They won't let me have eighteen pages of acknowledgments so I'll just have to personally thank each of you over a taco next time I see you.

Emily Linn, you were there. There are no words, so you'll have to just take these: Thank you, thank you, thank you.

Thank you to the people who shared their stories of PTSD with me to help craft Cooper's life. You know who you are, and it was an honor to hear your story.

My siblings are as ride-or-die as the Kelleher girls, and for that I'm incredibly grateful. Sorry about that one time I ordered wine at Wittig's.

Mark and Grace Courchane are my most generous, loving supporters. My mom is the one who handed me the community cookbook that inspired this entire book and didn't get (that) mad when I stole it forever. Thank you for all of the tuna noodle casseroles, brats, Jell-O cakes, pasta salads, and bacon-wrapped dates. And for everything else.

Krzysztof: Thank you for being a really, really great dad to the best things that have ever happened to us.

All I want in my life is to make the world a little more beautiful for Benjamin, Teresa, and Bridget. I love you one hundred much times infinity.

About the Author

Claire Swinarski is the author of multiple books for both kids and adults. Her writing has been featured in the *Washington Post, Seventeen, Milwaukee Magazine,* and many other publications. She lives in small-town Wisconsin with her husband and three kids, where she writes books, wears babies, and wrangles bread dough.